Silver Quetzal

Lalaith Quetzalli Caresi

PUKIYARI PUBLISHERS
www.pukiyari.com

In a time when history has turned into legend and ancient traditions have almost become lost, she who once denied her heritage, shall not be able to deny her fate; as the one who has come to prepare the return of an ancient king and fulfill a promise believed lost, sealed with a <u>Silver Quetzal</u>.

For Veronica.

Index

Prologue

There was once, thousands of years ago, in a valley in the outskirts of the Toltec capital, a temple built of stone and wood surrounded by the most marvelous and beautiful garden, as well as the most amazing forest. This was the "Flower Temple".

In charge of said temple was Xochiquetzal, whom some called an enchantress, and whom the villagers were assured was descended from the very gods. Truth was that, goddess or not, the woman had the favor of the King and High Priest of the Toltecs: Ce Acatl Topiltzin Quetzalcoatl.

In the service of Xochiquetzal were the four priestesses and their respective guardians: the first was for the East, she was called Iris and her protector was the Atlante of the Wind; the second represented the South, was known as Carnation and her keeper was the Fire Atlante; the third was for the West, with the name of Acacia and her bodyguard was the Water Atlante; while the fourth and last was Lily and her guardian the Earth Atlante.

All who inhabited the Flower Temple were said to be different from the average villager. In possession of characters, attitudes, and ideals foreign to the time and place where they lived. But despite any possible eccentricity, no one forgot that Xochiquetzal had the support of Quetzalcoatl, which meant that she and all that followed her were completely untouchable.

One day, while the priestesses fulfilled their usual duties they could observe Xochiquetzal and Quetzalcoatl conversed under the shadow of a tree. Such meetings weren't exactly news, as they'd been taking place for years; for as long as most of those in the temple could remember they were, in fact, quite common. It was the belief of some that the interest the King had in the Enchantress went beyond a mere friendship. Those who were particularly romantic, would be assured that he looked at her with love and complete devotion in his eyes.

Precisely in that moment, beneath the discreet looks of the priestesses, enchantress and ruler conversed:

Xochiquetzal, dressed in her usual long tunic in white manta and knitted veil, knelt in between dozens of beautiful flowers; her eyes were on Quetzalcoatl, standing before her, wearing an attire very different from the one he wore in public, simpler, more discreet, though no less elegant.

In that moment the Toltec King pulled out an object he'd been carrying among the folds of his clothes, placing it in Xochiquetzal's hands.

"It's beautiful..." she whispered, looking at the object in admiration.

"It's for you," he informed her.

"For me?" The young woman seemed very surprised, suddenly. *"I'm not sure I deserve something of such great value."*

"You deserve that and so much more," he assured her, going down on one knee. *"No gift is too much for the 'most beautiful flower'."*

"Oh, my lord..."

"I've told you many times, Xochiquetzal, not to call me that."

"But that's exactly what you are sire, my lord, my king."

"I don't think you could be ignorant of the fact that my interest in you goes beyond that of a king and his adviser."

"I know," she sighed. *"Though I'm still not convinced that I may be worthy of your affections, or the post you offer me."*

"There's nothing you're not worthy of. Whether they be feelings, a crown or anything else. That's why I've brought you this gift, so it might serve as token of my promise."

"Promise?"

"You well know that as much as I might wish to announce right now what is in my heart, the current situation does not allow it."

"The closeness of that encampment of nomad warriors seems to have everyone in the village quite tense."

"But that shall not last forever. That's why I give you this gift now, with the promise that the day will come when I shall come for you; and you will enter Tula on my arm, as the queen you've always been in my heart and shall be for my people. That is, if you will have me."

"It would be my honor."

The young woman then took the gift and put it on, with the resolve never to take it off again, sealing the promise made on that day.

Days passed in the temple, one after the other, days full of hopes and dreams, the illusion of a woman in love, anxiously awaiting the opportunity to finally scream that love to the whole world.

Regretfully, that day would never come…

What seemed to be at first a morning like any other transformed drastically with the sound of an agony-filled female wail at the temple's entrance.

Priestesses and Atlantes, the ever-watchful guards, hurried, worried for the Enchantress's safety, fearing a possible attack on the temple. But their foreboding feelings seemed to be safely pushed aside when only finding two individuals at the temple's doors: one a messenger from the town, the other the enchantress herself.

"What's happening?" the Priestesses asked with concern.

And they had reason to be, with the Flower Enchantress kneeling on the ground, her dark tresses covering her face, hiding her expression; and even then, her sobs could be heard by all, as well as the fact that her body couldn't seem to stop shaking.

"What could have made her like that?" Carnation inquired, extremely worried.

"What did you say to her to make her like this?" Lily demanded information from the messenger immediately. *"What was it?"*

"*Calm down Lily,*" Acacia said serenely. "*It's not the messenger's fault if he brings unfortunate news.*"

"*What matters here is to find out what the news were,*" Iris pointed out, turning towards the messenger herself. "*So, what news have you brought our mistress?*"

"*I'm afraid the news is truly bad, not only for the Lady Xochiquetzal, but for us all,*" The messenger admitted. "*Lord Quetzalcoatl has vanished without a trace.*"

"*What?!*" All the women gasped, shocked to their very cores.

"*Missing?*" Acacia seemed to be the only one capable of keeping calm a midst the chaos. "*How is that possible?*"

"*Like you just heard,*" the messenger confirmed. "*He vanished.*"

"*No one disappears just because,*" Lily insisted, losing her patience. "*Not even the most powerful magic can manage that.*"

"*Indeed,*" the messenger conceded. "*It is said that a man arrived seeking him out two nights ago, claimed his name was Tezcatlipoca. Lord Quetzalcoatl agreed to walk with him, talk in private, neither of them has been seen since. There are rumors that perhaps our King might be dead.*"

"*No!!!*" The new choked cry that left the enchantress's lips seemed to squeeze at the hearts of everyone present.

"*My Lady!*" Priestesses and Guardians cried out in unison, alarmed.

"*He broke his promise...*" Xochiquetzal whispered in between sobs. "*He said he'd come to me once it was all over, that we'd be together; that he'd be my king and I his queen. But now that shall never be, he shall never come back. He's broken his promise!*"

And waiting not a moment longer she rose to her feet and left the place at a run, fleeing the temple through a side entrance; not quite noticing how the beautiful gift that her king and lover had given her had been left behind, laying on the stone floor.

"*My lady!*" All those present cried out again.

But it was too late, she was too far away to hear them calling anymore; and it was likely that even if she'd been closer, her mood would have made such a thing impossible.

"*Xochiquetzal...*" For some reason Lily was the only one who called her mistress by her name and not her title.

"*She forgot this.*" The Earth Atlante called the others' attention to the delicate object.

"*We shall keep it safe for now and await our mistress's return, so we might give it back to her.*" Iris decided easily enough.

What they didn't know was that Xochiquetzal would never be returning to the Flower Temple, it was as if she too had vanished into thin air.

Following the sudden disappearance of the Enchantress Xochiquetzal, things began getting progressively tougher. The four priestesses and their guardians had lost from one day to the next those important people who'd until then kept them protected from what the rest might think, say, or do to them; they'd been left alone. There really weren't that many people in the city who approved of the idea of women having power, whether that meant magic or influence whenever they tended to the sick or anyone else requiring their services.

The difficulties reached their breaking point when the magical alarm of the Flower Temple woke its inhabitants abruptly in the middle of the night. The crude reality made itself evident in few minutes, they were being invaded.

Those who'd infiltrated this place, seeking to eliminate what they saw as a threat to their lifestyles, even if it was simply because they were different; they almost expected to see their victims fleeing, and yet instead what they found was eight individuals willing to fight, to die for what they believed in.

The priestesses in their short tunics and skirts ensemble made of raw manta, with embroidery of their chosen blossoms, veils covering their hair and most of their necks and shoulders, leaving only their faces visible, feet bare and on the inside of their wrists, the symbol of their magic. The Atlantes in their leather clothes, elaborate armor pieces covering their chests, as well as part of their legs and arms, faces hidden behind stone masks; they had no need of weapons.

What no one knew was that, while the battle began at the front doors, a small figure slipped away through a hidden back door. It was a female figure, no more than a child, in a two-piece tunic made of raw manta and enveloped in a dark cloak; in her hands she carried a sack that seemed to be full of parchment rolls and a box of intricately carved wood.

The little girl ran as fast as her small legs allowed her, dodging fallen branches, risen roots and stones as much as possible with the aid of what little moonlight managed to slip past the trees in the forest; ignoring the bangs and screams caused by the battle happening behind her while the tears dampened the veil covering her face. She had a mission to fulfill and so much depended on it, on her, she could not fail.

The battle was long and violent. Blood and tears soaked a field of aconites, nettles, savin and tamarisk. And by the time the sun rose the following morning, not even one of the fighters had survived.

Nothing was ever known about the girl, an orphaned child taken in by the temple, no one had the slightest idea of where to even begin looking for her, nor had they much interest. Her load too was lost that night, a secret cargo, infinitely valuable, that would not see the light for a very, very long time…

In the following years rosemary, dondiegos and heleniums grew in what had once been a battlefield; and in between them all a single coltsfoot bloomed, announcing an inevitable future: one day there would be justice…

Chapter 1
Gloxinia

It was minutes before seven o'clock in the morning and the hallways of Mater University in Mexico City were filled with students hurrying to their respective classrooms.

Among them all a young woman stood out: of beautiful turquoise colored eyes, jet black hair in perfect tight curls to the middle of her back, approximately 5' 3" tall, slim figure and skin of a beautifully tanned, almost golden tone. She was wearing an elegant knee-length fitted black skirt, with a short-sleeved v-necked pink blouse, as well as tights and stilettos; her hands were manicured and there was delicate makeup on her face. Anyone would say that the girl looked more like a model than a student. But truth was that she was, indeed, a student, a twenty-three-year-old college student in the last year of the Exterior Relations major. Everyone knew her as:

"Fiore!"

The gal turned to her side, where she could see several girls around her age who had just stepped out of several cars and were walking in her direction; they all had light-colored eyes, their hair dyed either red or blonde, though the darker roots tended to be obvious. One could even see the things they had done to their hair and the ways those had damaged it.

The procession of popular girls was interrupted by another group; this one of young girls either the same age or a few years younger, with similar built and complexion, except most of them had darker eyes and hair, and their attire and makeup looked more natural than in those of the first group. They were students from a variety of majors, from Law all the way to Design. The leader of that group was a twenty-one-year-old gal with chocolate eyes and mostly straight light-brown hair, dressed in denim capris and a white sleeveless top; she was also in her last year of college despite her youth, her major: Publicity and her name: Veronica Resendiz Yolotl.

There was much speculation around campus regarding conflicts that supposedly existed between Fiore and Veronica, with them being the leaders of the two most popular groups in the University, though truth was that the two women hadn't spoken more than perhaps two words between them.

The day began as usual, the first class was "Intercultural Communication" and was taught by Professor Francisco Solis. He wasn't exactly the best teacher in the university, and some believed he wasn't even truly worth the title, but most didn't truly care in the end, his was one of the easiest classes to take, you needed only to agree with everything he said.

"Humanity is condemned to repeat history," the professor said that morning. "In the most basic level, those who have begun as inferior, regardless of how much they might try to deny it, they will never cease being so."

Most of the students weren't even truly paying attention to him, just nodding their heads every so often, pretending to listen, understand, and agree with everything the man said, even though most hadn't the slightest idea what that was, exactly.

"A very clear example is our country," the man continued, "Mexico has defeat in its blood. Can someone tell me why this is?" He looked around at his students before focusing at a girl, almost in the middle of one of the groups: "Miss Molina…"

Isabel Molina, with her hair dyed an almost orange red, straightened and a bit dry, her skin artificially tanned, wearing a red, maroon and black pleated skirt above her knees, a white blouse just transparent enough to show off the red bra she was wearing underneath and knee-high black-leather boots.

"Because throughout all of Mexico's history, for as long as it's been such, the country has been under the control of another." The girl answered with the air of one who cares not at all what she's saying. "Whether that be Spain, the United States, foreign companies, rich businessmen, it doesn't matter; Mexico is completely dominated by outsiders. That's how it's been through all its history, and how it shall always be, there's no way around it."

No one contradicted her, most simply nodded again. They all knew that Isabel was the daughter of Augusto Molina, a well-known, rich, businessman, from an important family. She was also part of Fiore's group, both of them being the most popular girls there, everyone wanted to be one of them, or date them. It was also well-known that they shared their professor's opinion regarding how bad their country was, that had been made clear from the start of the semester. The rest of the class would rather not think too hard about it. It was the best way to get through the class effortlessly…

At the end of the school-day Fiore walked to the parking-lot, where she went straight to the royal blue BMW, immediately climbing into the back.

"About time you got here Fi!" A girl called as she settled into the copilot's seat, a moment before she'd been all over the driver.

"That ridiculous French teacher went over his whole speech of how much Canadians alter the pronunciation of some words, again," Fiore replied in a neutral tone, though with a bit of heaviness to it.

"That professor is a jerk, I don't know how you stand him," the other gal replied.

"I have to," Fiore reminded her. "I need a good grade in that class if I want to go to France with you and Rick."

The guy, Rick, said nothing, simply shrugging, putting the car into drive and stepping on the accelerator hard as they got out of the parking lot.

"Well of course you must come to France with us, and if that idiot doesn't recommend you, all you need to do is ask your daddy for some money. Easy, right?" The other girl insisted in an almost shrill tone, as if it were nothing at all.

"I don't know Jess. You know my dad and I haven't really talked to each other since I decided to come to Mexico City; we had a fight and have yet to make up," Fiore stated in a bit of a somber tone.

"Well, I think you had every reason to fight with him," the other supported her. "I mean, wanting you to stay in a third-class village when you had the opportunity to be here in the capital, to enjoy the very best."

"That's true."

"I really don't understand your dad, with him being from such a first-class place like Italy, to want to force you to resign yourself to such an insignificant life. In a little town where the most you would ever be is wife and mother to god-knows-how-many brats; maybe a seamstress or something like that in your free time. But that's not for you, that's not for us; us daughters of the higher ranks of society are the best and we were born to have the best."

Fiore didn't reply to that, it was as if something in the words of her 'friend' had offended her somehow.

Jessica Maeve Favre Vale, young Mexican girl of French descent, with a businessman for a father and a socialite for a mother. High-class, she was used to the greatest luxuries and to things being exactly like she wanted them to be. With dark amber eyes and auburn brown hair, she liked to wear the most expensive clothes and would never allow herself to be seen wearing the same thing twice.

Fiore had been living in Jessica's penthouse since shortly after the two met; Jess had expressed a particular joy in being able to live with someone worthy to be her peer, or that was what she believed at least.

A wide and beautiful garden extended beneath her feet, while behind her stood an imposing structure made of white stone: a temple. The sun was slowly rising high on the sky, its rays slipping through the thick tree-branches that seemed to surround the estate completely, there were mountains in the distance.

<What is this place?> the young woman wondered as she looked around with a mix of confusion and curiosity. <Why do I feel like I've been here before, a long, long time ago?>

And then she noticed something else, in the same direction where the sun was rising, someone was coming: a young man dressed in strange clothes.

<Those clothes...> she thought.

Words failed her as she looked down, to discover that she too was wearing a different clothing style from what was usual, the same style as him. Clothes that looked like they belonged to a different place, or a different time, or perhaps both; and yet for some reason they looked familiar to her.

<Who is he?> she wondered, observing the man attentively, trying to commit every detail to memory. <Why is it that even without being able to see his face I feel like I know him already? My heart is beating so fast and even my breathing has become uneven, it's as if my body were awaiting something my mind cannot grasp, but what?>

He stopped but a few steps from her, so close and yet so far away... and she still couldn't make out the features on his face. Nothing was clear beyond his dark hair and tanned skin.

He extended a hand silently, as if intending to touch her and she mirrored the gesture; even then, a few inches separated them, and for some odd reason neither of them would move to try and get closer, it was as if the idea didn't even cross their minds. They just stood there, immobile, one before the other, almost touching.

It took several moments for her to break the silence spell that seemed to have fallen upon both, and she didn't seem to notice when the voice coming from her lips spoke in a different language and with a softness she had never used before.

"Who are you?"

Her question got no answer, not even a sigh, instead a different sound filled the place, one like that of glass breaking; it was enough to put her on alert.

For a moment she was sure she'd just seen a fine and delicate object appear in the space between their hands, but it was there and gone so fast she wasn't sure if it had been real and not just her imagination.

Just an instant later darkness swallowed it all.

In the morning, a new school-day and everything was pretty normal, though no one could have known that the normality wasn't going to last...

The teacher hadn't yet begun his class when they all could hear someone knocking on the door: it was the prefect, Ramon Gutiérrez who, after exchanging some brief words with their professor, turned towards the students.

"Ladies and gentlemen, our school has been honored with the opportunity to host a very distinguished guest," the Prefect announced.

That was all that was necessary for the whispering to begin, while they'd had guest-lecturers before, it was obvious that whoever the prefect was there to introduce, was more than just an orator, or a visiting professor. Also, the man was laying it on thick with that introduction, which made it obvious that the school wanted to make a good impression with whoever was visiting.

"He's a graduate from Oxford University," the prefect went on, "and is here in Mexico to do research work to finish his doctorate thesis."

The guest entered in that moment: tall, with an athletic build, at least seven years older than most in the class, with eyes so dark they almost seemed black, white skin with a slight tan, messy hair somewhere between black and brown and just long enough to brush the back of his neck, he had a goatee and right then was wearing black denim pants, black shoes, a forest-green button-up shirt with the top two buttons undone. He seemed to somehow mix an air of importance and authority, while at the same time carrying himself in a way that showed humility; something that when put together with his looks had at least half the student body sighing in no time at all.

"My name is Draco Yao Tamay," the man introduced himself in an easy tone, as if he were unaware of all the attention… or simply didn't care for it. "I just arrived in Mexico City, though I've spent the last few months traveling around the country. Before coming here, I used to live in London."

"Anyone have any questions?" the prefect inquired, after noticing that Yao had nothing more to say.

"Why come to Mexico when you used to live overseas?" Leon, a blonde guy sitting at the very back of the classroom, asked with evident curiosity.

"I always wanted to come to Mexico," Draco answered sincerely. "My mother's family was originally from here, though they left for the United Kingdom a long time ago. I haven't been here in a long time, since I was rather young. Always wanted to know more about where that side of my family came from."

Fiore heard the man speak and couldn't help but feel like she was picking up on a lot more than just the words he was saying right then.

"Do you live on your own?" another student wanted to know.

"Yes," Draco nodded. "Ever since I reached legal adulthood and left my foster home. My parents passed away in an accident when I was a teenager."

Fiore whimpered quietly, enough that no one heard her. She had felt something the moment he said that but couldn't understand it. She couldn't remember feeling like that before; it was as if something in his words pained her…

"Why do you travel so much?" one of the female students asked.

"Because… I'm looking for someone," he answered enigmatically.

That answer was perhaps the biggest surprise for everyone there, no one was expecting it that was for sure. A quiet murmur filled the classroom.

But in Fiore's case, there was something else she wasn't expecting: and it was that just for a second an image had crossed her mind, the same she'd seen in a dream…

<What's the meaning of this?> She asked herself in shock. *<This I'm feeling inside… this profound feeling… what is happening?>*

Chapter 2
Cyclamen

Fiore walked down a dirt-road, a wind-breaker on and a small suitcase over her shoulder. As she walked she remembered exactly what had brought her there:

It was almost the end of the school-day and Fiore got a surprise when the secretary called her to the office to tell her something important.

"What's going on?" the young woman asked as soon as she stepped in.

"We just received an urgent message, miss," the secretary explained softly. "Your grandmother has had a relapse and is currently in a delicate state. With you being her emergency contact your presence has been requested."

"My grandmother..." Fiore parroted, surprised.

"Yes," the secretary nodded, moving papers from one side to the other, notoriously nervous. "As you can probably imagine this is a somewhat unusual situation, but I've already spoken to your professors. You'll be excused from classes tomorrow and Friday, thus you'll have three days to make the trip and make sure your grandmother is alright."

Fiore didn't even get the chance to get a word in edgewise, it seemed that the decisions had already been made.

And that was the reason why she'd gotten out of bed earlier than usual, gotten on a second-class bus for a three-hour ride (it would have been less time, but the bus made frequent stops), to then get off in a high-way crossroad, there wasn't even a proper station, only a bus-stop; and from there taking a half-hour walk to the village as no bus actually went straight into town.

Fiore was filled with anxiety right at that moment. She hadn't set foot in the town since leaving, back when she was eighteen, to continue her education in Mexico City; not to mention the harsh argument the day before her departure… she didn't even want to imagine what her return would bring.

The town's inhabitants could see that young woman walking by, in elegant black dressing pants, a delicate red and white blouse and red high-heels. An ensemble so completely different from what the people there wore.

Fiore eventually got to the last house in the town. It was a bit bigger than the others, but still only one floor, made of wood and sun-dried bricks, no concrete, good blocks or any materials that she'd consider truly appropriate.

The moment she stepped into the house a woman approached her, she was shorter that Fiore, though that could have been because she was a bit stopped over, of advanced age, with skin darkened by the sun and wrinkled by age. Her hair was completely white, straight, and in a braid that almost reached her waist. The woman looked Fiore up and down and immediately wanted to know what she was doing there.

"I'm looking for Mrs. Azalea," Fiore responded softly.

"And why is the 'missus' looking for the Azalea?" the old woman asked in a somewhat nervous tone, and with an accent that made it seem like she had a hard time pronouncing the words. "We want no more city-people coming to bother the Azalea."

"I'm her granddaughter," Fiore announced simply.

The old woman was left speechless in her surprise and simply stepped aside to let the young one pass.

Fiore stepped into the bedroom then, where she saw an old lady with short white hair; her skin, just like that of the other woman was darkened and full of wrinkles; she was sleeping, in a nightgown made of embroidered manta. At the foot of the bed stood the closest thing they had to a village doctor.

"How is she, doctor?" Fiore asked quietly.

"I'm afraid that information can only be given to a direct relative," the doctor told her respectfully. "Like I already told the woman who was here before."

"I'm her relative," Fiore announced authoritatively. "I'm her granddaughter, Fiore Yolotl Nahui, just got here from the capital."

The doctor waited for her to show him an ID, before nodding.

"I see," he nodded calmly. "Her status is delicate. She came very close to a heart attack two days ago and hasn't fully recovered yet. Even though I'd usually recommend my patients spend some time out in the country, some r and r, fresh air, somewhere where they might be able to breathe more oxygen and less smog... I'm afraid that in her case that simply isn't enough. A town such as this does not have the quality in health care that she needs. If she wants to live longer, and especially with a good quality of life, the most advisable option would be for her to move to some city."

"You tell her that," Fiore muttered with a hint of tiredness that made it obvious it had been a point of contention before. "I tried to convince her of that when I left, five years ago, but it was pointless."

"I very much doubt that her life was this much at risk five years ago," the doctor stated, very seriously.

"I'll see what I can do," Fiore nodded with a sigh.

Truth was she didn't hold much hope, but at least she'd try.

It took a couple of hours, but eventually everyone left. Fiore decided to prepare something to drink. She didn't even seem to need to stop and think about it as she took the small pot and set some water to boil, then went to open a cupboard and pulled out a paper bag full of dried flowers, extracting a fistful of those and adding them to the water. Her actions were completely automatic making a familiarity with them and the place itself obvious.

Everything was so familiar to the young woman, she didn't need to focus to prepare the tea, so instead her mind began wandering, to an old memory from a little over fifteen years ago:

A seven-year-old Fiore, give or take, was over a chair, standing on her toes and stretching herself as much as she could as she tried to reach a paper bag on the highest kitchen shelf. It seemed like an impossible task, even with all the effort the little girl put into it, the cupboard was simply too high.

And then someone else came in, her grandma, with less years marking her skin and her steps. And she took the bag with the dried flowers, only to hand it over to the girl with a smile.

Both then proceeded to prepare the tea, together, their favorite activity…

The sound of water boiling was what finally pulled the gal from her memories.

Still acting automatically Fiore extended a hand to take a dish towel without any need to see it, she used it to take hold of the hot pot; using the other hand to handle a colander, pouring the water through it to rid it of the flowers before serving the tea in two cups. Then she placed those, along with a few homemade cookies, a little jar with honey and a couple of spoons in a tray, which she carried to her grandmother's room.

The older woman was finally awake, and she seemed to want to say something, something the girl noticed immediately.

"Don't speak," she said, softly but authoritatively while adding some honey to each cup, before placing one in the old woman's hands, waiting a moment to make sure those hands weren't shaking before letting go. "The doctor said you shouldn't talk right now. You have to rest."

The old woman began drinking the tea without saying a word, nodding in approval when confirming that the girl still knew how to prepare a good cup of flower tea.

They both drank their tea in comfortable silence, and the young woman took the empty cup once it became evident that the old woman couldn't move enough to put it back on the tray. A single word left the elder's lips before he fell asleep again, her eyes fixed straight on the girl's back as she left the room:

"Xochitl…"

The next morning two feminine voices could be heard arguing in two different languages inside the Azalea's house. No one knew how that particular verbal fight had begun exactly, and certainly hadn't heard anything like it since the young woman had left the village, five years prior.

"I just don't know what it is about me that upsets you so much!" Fiore cried out, running out of patience.

"*You, hiding the way you do,*" her grandmother replied, speaking in her own language and not English the way Fiore did.

"If I was hiding I wouldn't be here," the girl pointed out.

"*You are, but it's not really you,*" the old woman said in reproach. "*You don't show yourself as you are. With that thing you do to your hair, and the painting on your face, the clothes you wear and those things you put in your eyes.*"

"I've changed nana, we all change with time."

"*Not everything must change. The clematis bloom the same each year, and that doesn't make them any less beautiful.*"

"I'm not a flower."

"*Yes, you are. 'Flower', that's the name your parents gave you when you were born: Xochitl. Not that strange name you go by nowadays. Yet another mask you use to hide your truth.*"

"'My truth' like you call it, has done nothing except make a laughing stock out of me. I don't want to be an Indian girl!"

"*So 'an Indian girl', 'a laughing stock', that's what you think I am.*"

"That's not what I meant nana. You're content with this life, I'm not."

Azalea did not insist further, though it was obvious they still didn't agree on the matter, they probably never would.

"*But at least while you're here I will not allow you to hide who you are.*" The old woman said eventually.

"I know," the girl murmured quietly.

And certainly, in that moment her tanned skin looked natural, without the golden hue added by the fake-tan cream she tended to use; her hair wasn't in curls but completely straight, falling almost to the small of her back; and finally, the eyes, which had looked turquoise before, in that moment the true dark shade was revealed, a brown as dark as the seeds of the cocoa tree.

"You don't even speak Nahuatl the way you used to."

"Because there's no need nana. In these times we don't need to speak Nahuatl but English, and foreign languages. You're the one who keeps refusing to accept reality."

"The only thing I refuse to accept is that my granddaughter has changed so much that I don't even recognize her anymore. Where has my girl gone? My little flower…?"

"I've told you already I'm not a flower! Neither of us are. They call you the Azalea, but that's not your name, or at least it didn't use to be. You're more than this nana… We both are. We're human. If we don't change we get left behind, we don't progress."

"Is that what you think of those of us? Of this village? That we don't progress? Is that what you think of the children you used to play with when younger? Of all of those who helped us when you were a kid, when your parents… my son…"

Fiore, no, Xochitl inhaled abruptly but refused to allow the emotions those words provoked to dominate her. It had been many years since that tragedy, more than a decade… she wouldn't allow it to hold her back, no more.

"I'm not a little girl anymore," the gal said, finally. "And the doctor said you'd do better in the city, where you could have access to better health care."

"I don't trust those city doctors, all they do is make us sicker."

"They could heal you."

"I am healed by my herbs."

"When will you understand that we're no longer in an age when plants are enough? And even then, it wasn't always so. We have better things now."

"I'm not interested. I have my herbs, and if those don't heal me then it will have been the will of the gods."

"Wake up nana! We're not in the fourteenth century anymore! There are no more gods or ancient customs, that's the past."

"A past that shall return, so it's been written."

"That's nonsense."

"*It is a prophecy, a promise. You used to believe in it when you were a child.*"

"I used to believe in a lot of things when I was a child." A small sigh escaped the girl's lips. "And then I grew up, matured. Like I said before, a lot has changed."

"*The exterior might change, but the inside will always be the same. What has been said will be, shall be, and you cannot change it.*"

"All that shall be is what I've worked for, for years, not whatever some nutjob recited or wrote in some piece of paper thousands of years ago."

"*The prophecies shall come to pass; all promises will be fulfilled, and you will finally learn the reason of your existence...*"

The young woman did not reply anymore, she simple shook her head and left the house, slamming the front door hard.

The sun had set already when Azalea entered the room that for twelve years had belonged to her granddaughter... and right then she was occupying it again, even if it was only for a few days. One visit, that was all; the first since Xochitl had left to study in the capital.

The gal was sleeping in that moment, and as she watched her, the old woman couldn't help but remember the last time they'd both been in that house, before the bond between them snapped...

An eighteen-year-old girl was running down the dirt-streets of the village, all the way to the open door of the house at the end of the street, where her grandmother waited for her. She was wearing jeans and a short-sleeved blue top, both new, the same as the black shoes on her feet. Her black hair was in an elegant twist on the nape of her neck, with some curled bangs framing her face and there was a bit of makeup on her face, not too much, but just enough to make her look different than usual, especially the shadows on her eyes, colors chosen specifically to make them look a lighter color than they actually were.

"I did it!" the girl cried out with a bright smile, almost jumping with excitement. "I did it nana!"

"What have I said about that language?" was her grandma's answer.

"I'm sorry nana," she apologized immediately, switching to Nahuatl. *"It's just that in the capital they only speak English, so I've gotten used to it in the last few weeks. But the important part is that I passed. I aced the admission exam! I'm going to go to school in the capital!"*

There was no response from Azalea, which soon began worrying the girl.

"Nana?" she inquired, inclining her head to a side in a gesture of confusion.

"Who are you miss?" the old woman asked unexpectedly.

"What?" That only confused her further. *"What are you talking about nana? It's me, I'm Xochitl, your granddaughter."*

"No." Azalea shook her head. *"Those are not my granddaughter's eyes, nor is that her hair. Those aren't the clothes my Xochitl wears."*

"You don't like them?" She turned a little this way and that, so the other woman could get a better look at her. *"I bought them with the money from my part-time job. I also bought you a dress, and a pair of very nice shoes."*

"Don't you like the clothes I make for you anymore? I make them with all my love. Is that no longer enough for you?"

"That's not it nana. These are the clothes people wear in the city, that's why I bought them."

"And what about your hair and that paint on your face, on your eyes? Did you choose those because that's how things are in the city too?"

"You don't understand..."

"No, I don't. I don't understand what's brought you to reject your origins, to disavow yourself..."

"Nana..."

"You're not my granddaughter anymore."

Those were the toughest words Azalea had ever said in her whole life. Five years later they still pained her. Those were the words that had made Xochitl pull away from her, that made her leave the village at the end of the summer; that made her bury her past and become what she was today: Fiore...

"I think we both made a lot of mistakes that day," Azalea whispered to herself, tears falling down her face. *"And the worst of all is that we cannot turn back time, no one can. What we've lost, we'll never get back."*

Azalea placed a cup of hot tea she'd been carrying on her granddaughter's night-table then, before turning around and leaving for her own bedroom.

"No matter what happens I will always love you." The old woman murmured without looking back. *"My beloved granddaughter... my Xochitzin..."*

And without further ado, she left the room.

Kneeling before a window that overlooked the ample and beautiful back garden, full of so many different flowers that it'd be impossible for most to name them all, Azalea kept her eyes on the star-filled sky, praying to some supreme or divine being.

"Oh, my Lord..." she murmured with a hint of sadness. *"I am afraid. Not of what awaits me, for that I've known since my son's departure. I fear for my granddaughter, my Xochitl. I don't think she's ready for the fate that awaits her. She's spent so long denying her past, her own self, her name... it frightens me to think what might happen. Never have I doubted the wisdom of your decisions, my sire. I've always been your faithful servant, and I always shall be. I just humbly ask you to look after my Xochitl, don't let her fall into shadows. Please, don't allow the same mistake from a thousand years ago repeat..."*

The moon was already on its highest point in the sky when the twenty-three-year-old woman finally woke up. She didn't need to look for her watch to know dinner time had long since passed. Though that was of little importance, seeing as she wasn't hungry. What did call her attention was the cup of tea on her night-table. She tasted it, finding it as good as always, though cold. It'd been a while since it was left there.

It was as if the tea's coldness rushed through her whole body from one moment to the next. A foreboding feeling made her get off the bed in a hurry and without even stopping to put on some shoes, she ran to the room at the end of the hall, her grandmother's.

She stepped in and could see a candle about to burn out, barely the smallest of flames still fighting to keep going, giving off minimum light, barely enough to make out the figure laying on the bed.

"Nana..." the young woman called.

There was no answer.

"Nana answer me please." the girl insisted.

Still nothing.

"*Nana.*" Finally, almost as some sort of last resort, she switched to Nahuatl, hoping to get an answer then. "*Nana wake up.*"

But it was useless, and deep in her heart Xochitl knew it already. No matter what language she might speak, there was just no way her grandmother would be able to answer. She wouldn't be waking up, not ever... she was gone.

"*No...*" Xochitl moaned, barely noticing the moment her knees hit the ground. "*Don't die... don't leave me... Nana!!!*"

Chapter 3
Iris

Standing silently beneath the sun, in a simple white dress and knitted veil covering her black hair, Xochitl observed without moving the space before her. The hole in the ground where Azalea's body had been deposited, with no coffin, only wrapped in a long piece of raw manta with embroidery on the hem, covered by many different flowers.

Nearly the entire town had come together, dressed similarly to her in their simplest clothes, in either white or raw manta, most weren't even wearing any shoes on their feet. Some of the women, especially the eldest ones, wore veils over their heads, but they were few, and Xochitl was the youngest wearing one. They were all there to say their farewell to an elder who had been beloved by all. Though no one approached Xochitl, even after having heard of her connection to Azalea, they didn't know her, didn't remember her, she was a stranger to them.

Xochitl didn't seem to mind, finding herself alone, even surrounded by people; or perhaps she just hadn't noticed, distracted as she was with the memory of the last time she'd been in a funeral:

It was the middle of the day, but if it weren't for clocks it'd be impossible to tell, as a great deal of clouds kept even the lightest of sun-rays from reaching them. The day, cloudy and slightly rainy, seemed to fit well with the mood of everyone in the village. And it was that a multiple funeral was taking place that day. Two married couples had died in an atrocious highway accident in the southeast. One of the couples had been well-loved people in town:

she a teacher and gardener, he a metal-smith; the other couple were people who'd never lived in the town, they lived and worked overseas, but they were still on their way there.

It was said that the couples had been on their way to meet each other when the accident had taken place. It had been a fortunate coincidence that none of them had had their children with them at the time. And it was that the accident had left more than just four people dead, it had also left two orphans: a thirteen-year-old boy, and a six-year-old girl.

And the kids were there, in simple white clothes, bare feet over damp earth, the girl's head covered by a heavy white veil. There were a lot of people present at the funeral, but no one came close to the two little ones, as if some invisible line separated them. Neither of them said a word, they just stood there… until several men began covering the bodies with dirt, then the little girl dropped to her knees before the graves and began sobbing. She said not a word, just kept crying for a long while. The boy beside her did not speak either, he just stood there, by her side.

The rain was gaining strength when a light-skinned hand touched the girl's shoulder, she turned to look at him in silence. It was as if they could communicate without any need for words, after a few seconds she nodded her head slightly and allowed him to help her up, paying no heed to the mud on her dress. They both walked in silence out of the cemetery and all the way to the house, apparently without noticing the flowers beginning to pop over the graves at their backs.

The children sat at the front porch of the house, still without talking, simply sitting beside one another, keeping each other company.

It took a while but eventually a woman arrived, a foreigner who claimed to be the boy's godmother, she was taking him with her, 'for his own good'. The little girl's eyes opened wide, at the same time the hand holding the boy's own tightened, she didn't want to let him go… he got closer to her then, pressing his lips to her ear briefly before shifting a bit and placing a kiss on her temple.

It took a moment longer, but eventually she let go of his hand, allowing the boy to leave with the woman; she remained for much longer without moving from her spot, dark eyes fixed on the dirt-road where he'd walked away. What no one knew were the words they had exchanged, which she held carefully inside her:

"We'll meet again," he'd told her. *"It's a promise."*

"Yes," she'd nodded immediately. *"A promise."*

Eighteen years later, remembering what had happened that day, Xochitl couldn't help but think about how naive she'd been back then.

<As if there were any chance of us ever meeting again, someday,> she thought to herself. *<We didn't even share our names...>*

Just like all those years before, the time came for a group of men to begin covering the grave. But unlike then, Xochitl didn't drop to her knees, or begin sobbing. Whatever tears she might have shed, had been cried the previous night.

When the ceremony finally came to its end and the people began leaving, directing just the briefest of glances toward the young woman, Xochitl bent before the grave, placing a hand over it briefly.

"Goodbye nana..." she said her own farewell softly.

And with nothing further to say she straightened up, shook the dirt off her hands quickly and left the cemetery without looking back even once... she never noticed the flowers beginning to bloom over the grave.

The following day Xochitl was getting ready to leave when she received the unexpected visit of a man in suit and tie. Which was something more than a little unusual in the village, the young woman couldn't remember having ever seen someone in a suit in town, except perhaps the doctor that would visit from Tula in extraordinary cases, and even then, they weren't suits quite like the one the man was wearing.

"Do you need anything?" she asked him, standing on the door.

"Miss Yolol?" the man inquired in a pompous tone.

"It's Yolotl, and yes, that's me," she corrected him.

She didn't know what it was, exactly, but there was something about that man she just didn't like, not in the slightest. The gal wasn't distrustful by nature, but there was an instinct inside her screaming not to trust him.

"Yes, Yolotl." The man nodded, dismissing it as unimportant. "I'm Mr. Ahumada, attorney at law, I'm here to see to the matter of your grandmother's last will and testament."

"Last Will and Testament?" Fiore arched a brow. "With all due respect mister lawyer, I very much doubt my grandmother left any will whatsoever. Here things are inherited through family lines; deals are made by word and that's enough. There's no need for signatures, sealed documents or intermediaries."

"You mean to say you have no papers that prove these lands belong to you or that they belonged to your grandmother?"

"I mean to say that we don't need them." She still had that bad feeling, had no idea why but it couldn't be anything good. "This house and the lands surrounding it have belonged to my family for more than fifteen generations. Almost everyone here in the village are descended from people who've lived here for over five centuries."

"Then I'm afraid, in your case, we have a problem miss. Since my client has documents that prove these lands do, in fact, belong to him."

"What did you say?" She wasn't expecting that.

"No reason for you to be upset miss. My client is fully aware that you were not informed regarding the legal situation of the property which is why, even though I've tried to persuade him against it, he's decided to offer you an economic compensation for the house and land. If you accept all you need to do is sign the papers and that will be it, we'd be able to avoid all legal issues."

Xochitl thought it over for a minute. If she was honest with herself, she had no special interest in the house or the property; it wasn't like she was going to stay and live there, or plan on spending any vacations there. The only family she'd left was an aunt, perhaps a cousin, but she hadn't seen anyone except her grandmother since her parent's funeral.

<My aunt was never here to help grandma and I out,> she thought. *<I can't even remember her name... or her face.>*

"I accept," the woman announced seriously. "Where do I need to sign?"

"Here." The lawyer immediately pulled a file with several papers out of his briefcase and handed it over, along with a pen.

Xochitl didn't even think about it, she carried the papers to the nearest table, took the pen the man offered her and signed as many times as was necessary. And so, the deal was made.

A few hours after sealing the deal Xochitl found herself going through her grandmother's possessions. The lawyer had told her she could keep or do whatever else she wanted with Azalea's personal belongings, all his client was truly interested in were the house and the land.

Xochitl had already decided that the clothes, trinkets, and most of the stuff she'd be leaving to the people in the village, allow them to distribute them as they saw fit; a last memento of the woman they held in such high regard.

It took no time for the young woman to notice that, just as expected, most of her grandmother's possessions were simple things, of little economical value. She'd almost considered her inspection finished when she discovered something she'd never seen before: at the bottom of an old trunk was a small chest of finely carved wood with silver inlays and what looked like quartz and semi-precious stones forming a design she couldn't quite make out.

Xochitl couldn't understand how her grandmother could own something like that without her having known about it. Just the chest, even without knowing what might be inside, or if there was even anything at all, must be worth a lot. Why then had her grandmother chosen to live so humbly? Why had she condemned herself to working for a living even at her advanced age? Something just did not fit in her mind.

Defeated by curiosity, she wanted to know what was inside the small chest and began looking for a way to open it; the problem being that there were no padlocks, or latches or anything like that in sight.

Almost giving up, Xochitl began observing more closely the surface of the chest. What at first had seemed like an erratic design, perhaps even abstract seemed to almost change before her eyes, or maybe it instead was that the more she looked at it, she slowly began to understand what it was she was looking at exactly: pieces of obsidian and onyx together seemed to form an animal, perhaps a dragon, with wings somewhat odd looking, as they appeared more like those of a bird, than what one would expect from a dragon; and then there were the small pieces of fire opal that took the place of eyes. The animal formed a half-circle and beneath it there was a flower, each petal a piece of quartz of a slightly different hue, the stem and leaves formed by finely carved jade. Also, the whole design was highlighted by polished silver filigree, and on the corners, pieces of amber seemed to almost glow, giving the design an almost mystical air. Xochitl had never seen something so beautiful...

Almost without thinking, the girl ran a hand over the design, the tips of her fingers very lightly gracing the flower... and then something happened. It was as if the flower's petals opened at the same time the dragon unfurled in the opposite direction. The girl couldn't even imagine the kind of work that must have gone into creating a design that could open in such a way... it almost seemed like magic.

The first thing she noticed was the strong smell of flowers, and it was that the inside of the chest was almost filled with big petals and small flowers, all dry, though not any less aromatic. It took a few moments, but eventually she noticed the only thing different: silver. A delicate chain and hanging from it a medallion, a beautiful bird with tail-feathers that were bigger than the rest of its body; it was all done completely in silver, a silver that was even shinier and more beautiful than the insets on the chest.

"*It's gorgeous*..." Xochitl couldn't help but whisper out-loud, fascinated.

Hesitant, she extended a hand, and the moment the touched the object a scene seemed to hit her mind, like some kind of vision:

A woman, kneeling in between hundreds of flowers in all colors; a man standing before her, extending a hand to let an object fall into her own.

"It's beautiful…" She whispered in admiration.

"It's for you." He replied without a doubt. "A token of my promise…"

Xochitl pulled her hand back immediately, almost as if she'd just been burned.

"Promise?" she asked out-loud, confused. "What was that? I must be dreaming or something like that. Not drinking coffee in the mornings is taking its toll on me." She turned her eyes to the necklace again. "Strange as it might seem, I cannot help but feel drawn to this object. Almost as if it were mine… as if it had always been…"

A minute later she was standing before her grandmother's only mirror, beside the wardrobe, the medallion hanging from her neck.

In another city, in another house, the lights were off as it was late, and all the inhabitants of the place were sleeping… or at least they were supposed to.

The quiet was suddenly interrupted by a female cry originating in the small sitting room in the ground floor. The house was old, colonial style, with a variety of staircases and halls that at times seemed to lead everywhere and nowhere at the same time. It had been rented out to students for several years, but at moment it was being used by a group that had a few things in common, things that most people could never comprehend…

The sound of doors opening and slamming against walls violently filled the house for several seconds, right after the cry, followed by multiple rushed footsteps, most of them given by bare feet; right before five individuals, two women and three men, all of them between the ages of nineteen and twenty-one, made it to the sitting room's entrance.

"What happened?" the first of the men asked, while holding a golf club as an improvised weapon.

"The grains..." the

girl who had cried out mumbled as she was in the very middle of the room, kneeling before a low wooden table, framed by colorful candles and with a smoking container filled with copalli on the opposite side of the table. In the middle of it was a fistful of grains laid out in such a manner that most would consider it haphazard or careless... to everyone but the young woman kneeling before them.

"The grains say so," she insisted, at the others' silence.

"Such a ruckus over some grains?" the first guy asked, tossing the golf club into a corner and turning around to leave. "It's too late for this... this nonsense."

"Or early," another of the guys offered from the other side.

"I'm going back to sleep," the first insisted.

"Shut your mouth," the shortest of the girls, who was also the oldest, interrupted them.

With one hand she took hold of the first guy's ear, pulling on it just enough to keep him from even thinking about leaving, and completely ignoring his exclamation of pain, she knew he always exaggerated. Regarding the other boy a hand signal from her was enough to make him raise his hands in surrender. No one wanted to defy her when she got serious.

"If we're understanding each other now..." The young woman nodded, satisfied, before turning all her attention to the one still kneeling. "What do the grains say Hyacinth?"

"She's awoken..." Hyacinth murmured without taking her eyes from the grains on the table.

"I could have told you that," the guy with the ear still being held by the one beside him muttered. "How could we not awaken after such a scream?"

"Shush I told you," the gal pulled on his ear.

"Ouch... Bella..." he whimpered.

Ironically, he was also the eldest among the men living in the house; though if anyone were to ask the one named Bella, he behaved as if he were the youngest...

"Valiant guardian..." she hissed between gritted teeth with evident sarcasm, choosing to focus on Hyacinth instead. "Who's woken?"

"Our Mistress..." Hyacinth answered in a sigh.

The response was immediate, nothing great or exaggerated, but it wasn't necessary in the end. The young adults simply turned to look at each other in complete silence. None of them spoke, they didn't need to, they all knew perfectly what the others were thinking, for it was the same: that which they'd been waiting for anxiously for years had finally happened...

In a small apartment a girl was sitting on the floor beside a window, an old laptop on her lap. The light of the nearby street-lamp the only help, aside from the light from the screen itself; and a mug of hot chocolate on the floor beside her.

"You're still working?" a masculine voice asked from behind her.

"Did I wake you up?" she inquired, concerned, turning to look over her shoulder. "Forgive me, it's just that I need to finish this assignment in order to accredit the subject."

"You're going quite fast," he complimented her.

"Yes well, it's an open high-school and I'd really like to get as up to date as possible... after all, I dropped out two years ago."

"That's in the past. What matters is now, the fact that you're trying, that you're willing to keep studying, keep improving yourself."

"It's all thanks to you. It was you who motivated me into going back to school. You're the one who has supported me, the only one who's been with me these last few years..."

"It's what anyone would have done in my place..."

"But not anyone did it, only you."

"It's nothing, really. You know how much I enjoy your company."

"I don't know what I would have done without you."

Without another word being said he closed the laptop and pushed it aside, holding her by the waist to pull her up and once they were on their feet he moved his arms just enough to embrace her. The street lamp illuminated them both, their darkly tanned skin, short brunette hair, so closely cropped his head was almost shaved, in their sleeping clothes.

They spent several minutes like that, just hugging, their bodies fitting perfectly together with one another. Until he took hold of her chin, tipping her face up enough to place a short peck on her lips.

"No… we shouldn't…" she murmured weakly.

"So, you say every time I kiss you," he commented with a small exhalation. "And yet you don't stop me from doing it again."

And as if to prove his point, he kissed her again. She sighed, but just like he'd said, didn't stop him.

<Why is it that even with how amazing this feels, a part of me cannot help but think I shouldn't be feeling it?> she wondered quietly, resting her head on his bare chest.

Right then they both experienced a very peculiar sensation. It was as if they suddenly knew that somewhere, very far from there, something very important had just happened, even if they hadn't the slightest idea what it was exactly; one thing they knew for sure, whatever it was, it would change their life for good.

Fiore finally returned to the capital on Sunday afternoon, after having settled all remaining affairs. In the end all she had kept from her grandmother was the delicate silver necklace and the chest where she'd found it, dried flowers and all. The smell reminded her of old times… better times.

She was in no hurry to get to the penthouse. Jessica and Rick would surely be there, having fun, and she didn't want to be the third wheel. Besides, while she'd never say it out-loud, Jessica could be a difficult person at times, always wanting to know everything, to control everything and Fiore didn't want any trouble right now; Rick on the other hand… Rick was the kind of man who liked to 'admire' women, all women, and Fiore sometimes felt uneasy when he looked at her. It was better not to go to the penthouse until it was completely necessary.

Thus, the young woman left the bus-stop and began walking almost aimless, simply killing some time. Eventually she arrived at a small park full of gardens and a few benches. She placed her suitcase to a side as she sat on one of the benches, pulling her legs up until she could rest her head on her knees.

The surroundings felt sad in a way that was hard to fully explain; the day was clouded, gray, the sun couldn't be seen and something, either mist, dust or even smog made everything in the city look somber. Even the flowers in the little gardens seemed to be part of it all, bent and half-wilted as they were.

"So dark, so… lifeless…" Fiore whispered quietly, her eyes fixed straight on the plants while she kept holding onto her legs. "So different from the village," she sighed. "The village… why am I thinking about it just now? Now that I've finally broken all the bonds I had to that place, now that I've decided there's nothing that could make me go back… Now I can't forget about it."

And as if things weren't depressing enough already, it began to rain at precisely that moment. It was a light shower, and while most people around began picking up their stuff and leaving; Fiore didn't so much as move, it was as if she weren't aware of the rain, or simply didn't care about it, she made no effort to move from her spot.

It would be impossible to know exactly how much time she spent in that place, when she suddenly felt a hand on her shoulder, and not just any hand; it was big, strong, a man's hand.

Bewildered by the sudden contact Fiore looked over her shoulder and upwards to see who was touching her, and then her surprise grew when she noticed that it was not just any man, but the school's guest, the doctorate aspirant: Draco…

Neither of them said a word, Fiore couldn't think of something to say, and it seemed he couldn't either. It didn't seem to be necessary, the silence wasn't awkward. After several moments Draco offered Fiore his other hand, who took it without comment and allowed him to help her up.

In that moment, and almost without intention, Fiore couldn't help but wonder about the great similarity that very moment had with another one that had taken place seventeen years prior…

<What are the chances?> she wondered. <For even the most unlikely promises to be fulfilled? What are the chances that ancient prophecies might come true?>

The answer was a multitude of bright flowers swaying to the rhythm of the wind in the gardens the two were leaving behind.

Chapter 4
Begonia

After the unexpected encounter in the park, Draco insisted on accompanying Fiore to her place, lending her his jacket when it became evident she wasn't properly bundled up. That was how, almost an hour later, Jessica saw Fiore arrive completely soaked, with locks of jet black hair sticking to her face and neck and a dark leather jacket that wasn't hers, she also vaguely managed to see the back of a man with messy dark hair as he walked away. Of course, being the kind of person she was, Jessica did her best to 'interrogate' Fiore on the jacket, the man who'd escorted her, she wanted to know everything. However, Fiore was just so tired, mentally more than physically, that she pretended not to hear a word.

By the time the first class began on Monday, everyone in their group knew already that a hot guy had escorted Fiore to the penthouse, and he'd also left her his jacket. Gossip which got drastically worse when they saw the young woman hand the jacket to none other than Draco.

"Forgot to give it back to you yesterday," Fiore excused herself.

"No problem," Draco assured her, taking the garment. "You needed it more than I did. By the way, I never asked what exactly you were doing in that park in the middle of the rain."

"I just… I needed to think," Fiore answered honestly though somewhat vaguely. "The park seemed like a good place and I really wasn't paying much attention when it began raining. It didn't seem important…"

"Then it was probably lucky that I was passing by," he decided. "I don't think it'd have been a good idea for you to get soaked much longer, you probably would have ended sick."

"Yeah, that definitely wouldn't have been good," Fiore admitted, bowing her head slightly in a move that seemed to be completely instinctive, and which she didn't quite notice. "But really, thanks Mr. Yao."

"Draco please. Mr. Yao is unnecessarily formal."

"Very well, Draco."

"And you're Fiore, correct? May I call you that?"

"Yes and of course you may call me that, no problem."

"Good." Draco smiled at her.

"Why don't you introduce your friend to us Fiore?" one of her classmates, Ximena, asked in a fake, overly cheerful, tone, interrupting the conversation.

Behind her there were other gals, including Isabel, at least half of the women of the group Fiore used to 'lead'.

"My name is Draco Yao Tamay ladies," he decided to introduce himself. "And I believe I'd been introduced to you all already last week, on the day of my arrival."

"True," Carlota, another of the girls, nodded. "It's just that we never imagine the two of you to already knew each other."

"But it was to be expected," Jessica intervened, in apparent defense of her friend. "They both come from Europe! Surely, they must have met there. Maybe during a summer in the Mediterranean, or a weekend in Paris, skiing in Switzerland..."

Fiore made no comment, there was no way she could have met Draco in Europe, since she'd never been there; truth be told, she'd never left Mexico. Though of course no one knew that, everyone was convinced that she'd spent more than half of her life in that continent, that her father was Italian and so many other things that Fiore had no idea where they'd even come from half the time. She'd begun the lie, that was true, though she'd never gone beyond the name of Fiore and implying that she'd spent a year in between finishing her High School studies and going into college in another country. The truth was she'd spent that time in the southeast corner of the country. She had been very evasive regarding her past, her parents, Jessica had assumed things and Fiore chose not to correct her… it had just grown from there.

The most incredible part though, at least in that moment, was that Fiore did feel as if she'd known Draco before, somehow.

"I don't think it was like that." Draco's words surprised everyone. "I'm sure we have met before, but it wasn't in Europe."

Everyone, including Fiore herself, were in equal parts surprised and confused with such an affirmation. If not Europe, where could they have met then? Thankfully, or not, depending on what side of the conversation they each were, the professor for the next class arrived right then and there was no more time for chatting.

After the last class that same day Fiore inwardly cursed the frequent weather changes the autumn brought. When she'd left the apartment that morning the sun had been shining bright, making her decide to leave her umbrella behind, which had proven to be a serious mistake considering the harsh downpour they had now. Besides, Rick and Jessica had had their last class a couple of hours earlier, so there was no one to drive Fiore to the apartment.

"Need a ride?" a familiar voice asked.

Fiore turned around abruptly, the last thing she expected to see was Draco standing beside her, a black umbrella in hand.

"Huh?" The surprise was such that for a moment she'd no idea how to answer.

"My car is right over there." He signaled to the left side of the parking-lot. "If you want I can take you to your apartment so you won't get wet. I don't want you to get sick."

"I…Thank you." Fiore couldn't help but blush, and lower her head slightly, embarrassed.

It was something completely new for her, feeling flushed. Ever since beginning university boys had been noticing her, a few of them had complimented her, there had been flirting, and at times even catcalls; none of them had ever made her feel the way Draco did simply by offering her a ride. He made her feel different, and not in a bad way. There was something about him that made her feel incapable of faking in front him, but more than that, she didn't want to, not the way she did with everyone else. She felt natural, almost… free.

And as Fiore got a bit closer to Draco, at his own insistence, so the umbrella might cover them both as they made their way to the car, someone was observing them from the shadow of a column: a young woman with chocolate-brown eyes and light brunette hair that curled at the tips, the expression on Veronica's face seemed to express that she saw something others could not:

"It's incredible…" she murmured under her breath. "Those two… again…"

The black-haired woman was kneeling on the dirt ground, surrounded by beautiful flowers of many colors; behind her an imposing white-stone temple. She was facing the east and she could see the sun beginning to rise in the distance, its light highlighting the silhouette of that mysterious man with the odd and elegant attire that looked like a completely strange and perfectly familiar at the same time.

But then the scene, instead of following the same sequence as before, shifted unexpectedly:

It was as if the sun had vanished in an instant, and with it practically all the light in the world. The man too disappeared in the shadows.

She stood immediately, without thought, surprised and confused by what was happening, without paying attention to the clothes she was wearing, the long dress and bare feet… and it didn't end there, the flowers around her began wilting very fast, and when she turned around she could see the temple collapsing before her eyes.

Eight individuals were there among the ruins, four men and four women, they too vanished.

And then everything else around her vanished too, leaving the woman in absolute darkness. She couldn't understand where she was, or what that had meant, though a gut feeling told her it couldn't be good.

Suddenly, a dark voice echoed all around her:

"I will destroy you little flower. I will destroy you, just as I did so long ago, except this time you will have no way of coming back."

She had no idea what he meant with that; neither did she get the opportunity to ask, for right then she felt as if she couldn't breathe, as if an invisible hand were suffocating her.

Seconds that seemed eternal passed, and right as she thought she'd die, a silver silhouette came from nowhere, enveloping her, protecting her, taking her away from that malignant presence. It was a brilliant light that somehow didn't blind her and carried a warmth, like the most perfect embrace…

She could feel how everything around her became progressively brighter, it still didn't blind her, but an instinct made her close her eyes anyway, only for a moment…

She sat up in bed so abruptly that she almost fell out of it in the process. Her skin was damp with sweat, the images of her dream still fresh in her mind, the same as the fear, the absolute terror, having felt just one step from death.

Slowly she rose from the bed and went to the en-suite bathroom to wash her face.

<*What's the meaning of all that?*> Fiore wondered as her mind cleared. <*That man… I'd seen him before, in another dream… and I think in another place as well… and then that garden, and the temple and those people…*> She sighed tiredly. <*So many figures and not even one face. How am I supposed to understand what I'm dream if I don't even know who those people are? Or were? And that man at the end… he desired my death so intensely…*>

She brought a hand to her neck, it still hurt. And then, as she straightened and looked at herself on the mirror above the sink she could see something that unsettled her profoundly: her neck was bruised, a big, ugly mark in the shape of a hand pressing on her throat, the invisible hand that had choked her in her dream…

Fiore had to wear turtle-necks and scarves the rest of the week to hide the marks on her neck. She didn't want to be interrogated; and anyway, she doubted that 'being injured by a man in a dream' was a believable explanation.

Friday had finally come, Fiore was wearing a royal blue blouse, it didn't have a high neckline, but the white scarf she wore covered her neck, and it went well with the white skirt she was wearing.

For some reason even she couldn't comprehend, over the past few weeks she'd taken to walking from the subway station to the penthouse instead of taking the tram or finding someone to take her all the way from the school, as she used to. She'd been walking for a few minutes when she got the feeling that someone was following her. As discreetly as she could she increased her speed, even crossed the street a couple of times, but the sensation of being followed just wouldn't disappear.

<Who's following me?> She wondered while turning a corner. *<And why?>*

It was too late when she noticed she'd taken a turn in the wrong street, finding herself in a dead-end.

<I don't think this is good...> she thought to herself.

Her fear grew upon turning around, blocking the entrance to the alley was the one who had been following her all along. But what really frightened her was that it didn't seem like a normal person... or even a person at all. The being, with a vaguely female form, hit Fiore with the back of its hand, making her crash violently against the alley wall.

<What is going on?> Fiore asked, swallowing a pained cry. *<I don't understand. Who, or what, is she?>*

Her head ached, as did her left shoulder and the part of her back that had impacted against the wall. Besides, because of the hit her eyesight had become a tad blurry. That was why she couldn't see how a silvery glow enveloped her suddenly, creating a barrier made of light which protected her from her attacker. It took a couple of minutes, but eventually the odd being seemed to give up and leave.

Fiore fell to her knees, feeling somewhere between relieved and stunned, she'd no idea what had just happened exactly, but that didn't stop fear from invading her. She remained in that place, without moving, for a long while that seemed like hours until eventually, in a state that could be defined as semi-unconsciousness, she got on her feet and walked the rest of the way to the penthouse. She didn't want to think about what had just happened, to wonder about how insane it all seemed, or if maybe it was all really just in her head and she was crazy.

Several hours later, two individuals arrived at that same alley. The first was a woman, young, about eighteen years old, a bit tall, slim, darkly tanned skin, her hair of a copper brown shade, very short and somewhat messy, eyes of an amber brown and dressed in a loose long-sleeve beige top, a brown vest, washed-out light-denim shorts, gray leggings and ankle boots of the same brown as the vest. Right behind her was a guy, perhaps a year or two older than her, about her same height, skin a bit darker, hair dark and cropped very short, chocolate eyes, a wide back, narrow waist and not too bulky, athletic, he was wearing what looked like a gray wife-beater, old and somewhat worn out jeans, especially on one knee, and what looked like old dark-gray combat boots. They both work biker gloves.

"Are you sure the power came from here Lils?" he inquired, observing around him carefully. "I see nothing…"

"Don't look, feel," the girl replied, placing a hand on the wall. "I can feel it."

He didn't argue, simply closed his eyes and focused; just a few seconds later he snapped them open, an exhalation showing his surprise.

"This power…" he murmured, sensing what she had. "It's the shade's…"

"Yes, the damned monstrosities that we've been pursuing the last eighteen months." Her mouth twisted in a sneer as she said that, though her tone changed abruptly as she added. "But that's not the only trace. There's another power here, the vestige is minimum, but I can still sense it."

"That's true." It took him a moment later to make it out, but eventually he managed. "It's a power like yours."

"No, not like mine." She shook her head. "Greater, much greater. Even with how small the remnants are it's obvious that it wasn't used for long, it's also obvious that the energy is a very powerful one."

"You think someone else is hunting the shades?"

"No, I..." Her voice turned darker as she declared: "I think the shades are hunting them..."

Chapter 5
Petunia

Fiore woke abruptly, sitting up harshly, her breathing was rough enough she was at risk of hyperventilating and her dark eyes shifted relentlessly, thoroughly analyzing each and every centimeter of the room; her whole-body tense, as if she expected an attack to come at any moment.

There was a very good reason for her to be like that, once again that same odd individual had appeared in her dreams and tried to murder her; except that time, he hadn't been able to touch her, the silver silhouette had made an appearance earlier and protected her.

<*What does all this mean?*> Fiore wondered, eyes fixed right then on her own hand, remembering what it'd looked like with the layer of silver glow enveloping her. <*The dreams, the attacks, they feel so real. I don't understand it…*>

The sun had risen and on the rooftop of an apartment building a young woman could be seen seated on a small mat, legs crossed, arms resting on them and eyes closed. She seemed to be meditating. Some meters away, laying against the small door that lead to the roof, stood the same guy that had been with her before. He didn't speak, just stood on his spot, waiting.

It was until hours later that she finally opened her eyes again; then her whole body seemed to relax in an instant, so suddenly it looked like she might collapse.

"Lils!" the young man cried out, placing a knee on the ground behind her and holding her by her back just in time.

"I'm fine." She tried to convince him, though she couldn't help but rest her weight against him. "Don't worry about me."

"Of course, I worry," he insisted, seriously. "You've been at this for hours, since dawn in fact. And you were at it almost all day yesterday. You've barely eaten or slept these last few days. You'll get sick if you continue on like this."

"I'm sorry." She lowered her eyes, embarrassed. "It's just that I can't seem to find that energy and I feel that I must. I need to find the one who has all that power before the shades do."

The girl breathed in deeply once, before straightening up, trying to get back into a meditative position.

"No, no way," he refused. "You're not doing that again until you've had some rest and eaten at least something!"

"But Chris..." she began.

She didn't get to finish her sentence, and it wasn't even because he scooped her up, or forced her in any other way to move from her spot, but because something else had thoroughly captured her attention.

"There it is!" she cried out unexpectedly. "The energy... and there's a shade heading in the exact same direction!"

"I-Damnit, alright, let's go then," he declared some hesitation.

With nothing further to say they both went down one floor to the apartment where they lived, took a couple of old denim hoodies and then rushed out in the direction where Lils had detected the energy.

Fiore couldn't believe it, it was happening again. Was her luck really that bad? Again, she'd felt like someone or something was following her, she'd tried to lose them, but once she made it to some rarely used streets she found herself being openly pursued. From that point on all she could do was run. She ran and ran as fast as her legs could carry her, and no matter how hard she tried, she couldn't seem to shake her pursuer. At least, ever since she'd begun walking home she'd taken to carrying a pair of ballet-flats in her bag, she would have never been able to run so much in heels.

There were some differences from the previous time when she'd been pursued. The being after her was smaller than the one from before, though it looked just as bad, just as inhuman. It was like a mix of ghost, a shadow, and something else she couldn't quite describe except to say it wouldn't have been out of place in one of those murdering-alien movies Rick seemed to like so much.

Fiore was so terrified she wasn't paying enough attention to where she was stepping, she didn't notice the uneven ground in time before she found herself hitting the pavement hard. The shade leapt at her, pouncing on the moment of weakness, and the girl reacted instinctively, rolling to a side, she tried to get up but a sharp pain in her ankle made it impossible.

The shade noticed her difficulties and threw itself again at her. Fiore could do nothing except close her eyes tight and brace for the pain that was surely coming... except the attack never came.

Several seconds passed though it felt like forever, but when Fiore finally dared open her eyes again, she was stunned, surprised to find the shade that had intended to attack her was now locked in hand-to-hand combat with a tanned young man with average-height, very short hair and a presence Fiore found both nearly intimidating and familiar at the same time.

"Are you alright?" a female voice asked her.

Fiore turned her head to a side to find a girl, about five years younger than her, crouched beside her. Even more incredible was the fact that, despite having never seen her before, Fiore didn't fear her, but the exact opposite.

"Yes," Fiore answered honestly. "But I can't stand."

She'd no idea what it was exactly, but there was something that just made Fiore trust the girl and her partner blindly.

The fight took a turn then, as the shade managed to get the guy off itself, throwing him against the farthest wall.

"Chris!" the girl cried out in fright.

A part of Fiore expected her to rush to help her friend, it was the logical choice, wasn't it? But she didn't, instead the girl threw herself at the shade, dealing punches and kicks as fast as she could, doing her best not to give the other a chance for a counterattack.

Fiore was speechless, everything that was happening had her beyond impressed.

<The way that girl... the way they both fight, it's amazing,> Fiore thought. *<But what I cannot get out of my head is the idea that I'd witnessed such a confrontation before...>*

Even she had no idea what that could mean exactly, and thus she decided it was better not to say a word about it.

Minutes later the shade was thrown violently against one of the alley's walls, beside a dumpster; the impact didn't seem to affect the wall or the trashcans in the slightest. It was odd, as if the shade were physical, and not, at the same time. By that point the two newcomers had been fighting together, it was what had allowed them to achieve victory. What left Fiore in shock was when just for an instant, barely a fraction of a second, in the place of that sinister being that had been pursuing her earlier, that had attacked her for no apparent reason, she thought she could see a child weeping...

The girl, whom her companion had referred to as Lils, tensed, probably preparing to give a coup de grace, or something, when Fiore unexpectedly intervened.

"No!" she cried out, voice more intense than even she planned for.

Lils seemed to freeze completely; she and the boy, Chris, turned to look at her in silence, not understanding her attitude.

With some effort, seeking to put as little of her own weight on her left foot as possible, Fiore stood, then half limped, half hopped towards the shade, which hadn't gotten up from its position on the ground, against the wall and the dumpster.

"Don't be a fool!" Chris spat at her. "Do you want it to kill you?"

"You must not get any closer, it's dangerous," Lils added with more cordiality, reaching out as if trying to hold her back.

"No, it's not," Fiore contradicted calmly, slowly approaching the fallen being.

"Are you insane?" Lils inquired, she really didn't understand where the older girl had come from, or why she was suddenly so serene... the monster had almost killed her less than a quarter of an hour before!

"How do you know you're not putting yourself in danger by approaching?" Chris sounded honestly intrigued at the sudden attitude shift of the unknown girl.

"I just know," Fiore answered simply.

Truth was even she didn't have the slightest idea where her sudden trust that everything would be alright was coming from. There was no logic to the matter; though truth was there was no logic in a creature like that existing either so...

It took a few moments, but eventually she got close enough to the shade, she could almost touch it. With some effort she got down on one knee, settling herself so as not to hurt her twisted ankle any further. Though it already hurt less than it had before, she just didn't want to risk it. While the being before her still held that inhuman appearance, that most might even define as monstrous, inside her head Fiore simply couldn't stop seeing that scared little boy, weeping... It was insane, the image had last barely a fraction of a second, she couldn't even know if it had been more than just a hallucination of her confused and tired mind, but the same part of her that had given her the confidence to stand up and move, that made her blindly trust the two young people... that same part was telling her that she was right in this too.

"It's alright..." Fiore whispered quietly. "I don't wanna hurt you..."

There was no direct answer, but Fiore could hear it mumbling, voice so quiet it took great effort to listen, much less understand.

"You are nuts if you really think you can reason with those things," Lils said with evident dislike.

"Shush..." Fiore directed at her.

Lils took offense, but Chris just raised a hand in silent request for them to wait, to see what happened.

Fiore ignored them, focusing completely on the shade before her, trying to listen to it, to make out what was being said.

It took her a while, but eventually she began to understand. The shade was praying, and in a language that wasn't English.

"Nahuatl..." Fiore whispered, not quite believing it. "It's praying in Nahuatl."

Lils opened her mouth, about to exclaim something, but Chris covered it with a hand before she could say a single word.

Fiore kept her focus on the shade.

"Everything is alright," she assured the shade, the child, softly in Nahuatl. *"You need not be afraid, I will not hurt you."*

The words, and in that language, seemed to make the shade react, as it stopped praying and lifted what might have been its head, turning in her direction.

Lils brought both hands to her mouth to hold back her scream, at the same time Chris held her by the shoulders to keep her from moving, either willing or unwillingly. And it was that from one breath to the next the terrible enemy had vanished, leaving in its place a small boy of no more than ten or eleven years of age, wounded and scared; his clothes were odd, simple and looking like they came from a different time, his feet were bare, and, in his eyes, one could see the shadow of someone who's suffered more than if they'd been in hell itself. The most striking was, perhaps, the chained hands, big and heavy chains, terrible.

Fiore didn't even know where the words came from, she just began pronouncing them at the same time she reached out a hand until she could almost graze the child's face:

"May chains be broken, may sufferings be soothed. I'm here to dry your tears and heal your wounds. I call upon the powers of the light to free your soul..."

The chains, which seemed to keep the child prisoner shattered without a sound and both the tears and wounds vanished, as if they'd never been there at all. The boy was suddenly standing before her, smiling almost shyly.

"Thank you..." he whispered with a bow.

An instant later he was gone, leaving behind a little flower... a petunia.

Consciousness returned to Fiore little by little, and even before opening her eyes she could tell she was no longer in the alley; she couldn't feel the coolness from the end of October and the surface beneath her back was too soft and smooth for it to be the street. She'd been taken somewhere else, probably by the two youngsters.

Without opening her eyes just yet, she concentrated on remembering what had happened before falling unconscious. It took a few seconds, but her mind slowly cleared: her mysterious pursuer, the attack, the two young people who'd intervened to help her and finally the abrupt change in situation once she'd managed to see through the monstrous shade to the scared little child... the last thing she remembered was him disappearing in a haze of white light. Fiore hoped that meant something good, that she'd been able to help.

Fiore sharpened her senses, trying to get some idea as to where she might be exactly, and then a strange sensation filled her. Something impossible to describe with words, it reminded her of a very particular place: the village, the garden at her grandmother's place. The sensation that went through her was very similar to what she felt whenever she was there, yet more intense, somehow, at the same time.

Slowly, to make sure that the movement wouldn't cause her pain or dizziness or something else, Fiore sat up and opened her eyes and immediately met a pair of amber ones fixated on her.

"Ah, you're awake," a masculine voice called, entering the room. "Are you alright?"

Fiore nodded in silence, she could see she was in a mix of living room and sitting room, simple in design, laying on a mat. Somewhere, beyond this room, a teapot whistled.

"Lils, the water is ready, could you go get it?" the boy asked the girl who was sitting on her heels beside Fiore, nodded in silence, standing fluidly and walking in the direction of the very room the boy came from; the kitchen, guessed Fiore.

They spent several seconds in a somewhat awkward silence before Lils came back out of the kitchen, carrying a teapot and three cups. She served the liquid in all three, added something from a different jar to one, and then offered that cup to Fiore. Unsure, but not wishing to be rude, she took the offered beverage, smelled it briefly and took a sip, immediately identifying what was in it.

"Rosemary tea," Fiore commented surprised.

"So, you know what it is," Lils replied, nodding her head. "I thought it might work in case you had a headache."

"Thank you," Fiore mumbled taking another sip.

She'd begun feeling melancholic suddenly, she'd had that kind of tea before, when she'd suffered headaches as a child, and her grandmother would prepare it. They spent several minutes in complete silence, all three simply drinking tea. Eventually it was Fiore who broke it, deciding there were things she simply needed to know and wouldn't unless someone began talking.

"Where am I?" she decided to start with that.

"In our apartment," the young man answered. "As we've no idea what your name is or where you live… We decided it was for the best, for both us and you, to bring you here rather than leave you in that alley."

"Right, thank you for that." Fiore inclined her head slightly.

"It's not precisely the 'residential zone' of the capital, but at least it's safer than some dead-end, especially once it gets dark."

"Thank you," Fiore repeated. "My name is Xo-… Fiore, pleased to meet you."

She'd almost said Xochitl, almost… and she hadn't the slightest idea as to why.

"I'm Chris," the boy introduced himself. "And she's…"

"Lily, call me Lily," the girl intervened.

"Again, thanks for helping me." Fiore had no idea what else to say, how to even begin to phrase all the questions swimming around in her head.

"No problem," Chris assured her.

"One could say that dealing with these things is something of a 'self-appointed mission' of ours," Lily added in an indifferent tone.

"Could you tell me what that thing, or person or whatever, was exactly?" Fiore wanted to know.

"I thought you'd know." The younger girl arched a brow. "Considering how you handled the situation."

"I've no idea what I did, I only did it because it felt right," the jet-black haired one admitted.

"Are you gonna tell me you don't know why it was pursuing you either?" Lily didn't believe a word that was being said. "Or the one from a few days ago." At the surprised look from the older girl, she added: "Yes, I know that you were attacked a few days ago too. Regretfully we didn't not make it there in time." The silence upset her fast. "Please! You cannot expect me to believe that you've been harassed, pursued, and even attacked more than once by the shades and you've no idea why."

Fiore just shook her head but didn't say anything.

"I think she's telling the truth Lils," Chris offered before the girl could go into another rant.

"What?!" Lils still couldn't believe it. "But the power... she has it, I could feel it. And I saw it, we both saw it, the way she vanquished that shade... or what was the shade..."

"I freed him," Fiore interrupted.

"What?" For a moment Lily seemed lost.

"I didn't vanquish him, I freed him," Fiore clarified. "And before you ask, no, I've no idea how I did it, or why I did it. Like I mentioned before, it just felt right, like it was what needed to be done. It was as if the words came to my mind on their own, all I did was pronounce them. I know it sounds strange, but that's how it was, I swear."

"We believe you," Chris assured her, once more attempting to be the calm one.

The both turned to look at Lily who, after several seconds, exhaled and nodded.

"We'd be hypocrites if we didn't," she admitted belatedly. "We aren't exactly what you'd call normal either."

The girl with the short copper hair extended her right hand then, she twisted her wrist to one side and then the other, as if to show she had nothing on it; then he snapped her fingers once. The effect was instantaneous, a spark, not just the sound, but something real, that could be seen, a violet-gray spark that Fiore couldn't help but follow with her eyes when Lily twisted her wrist again, opening her hand slowly, the small spark grew until there was a small sphere of about an inch in diameter at most, floating in the middle of her palm.

Fiore observed everything in perfect silence. Remembering the battle, she could see that was the same kind of energy Lily had used to throw the shade against the wall, back when he'd still looked like a monstrous being, before revealing the scared child inside.

"You have magical powers?" Fiore finally inquired.

"Well… that's a way to describe it, yes," Chris nodded.

"Since when?" Fiore wanted to know.

"Ever since I can remember, really." Chris shrugged briefly. "Though for the longest time I didn't use them, and there was even a time when I wanted to deny I had them but eventually I accepted them as part of me."

Lily just nodded, Fiore guessed her story was similar enough that she felt no need to explain it.

"And how long have you been fighting these… beings… zombies… shades, whatever?" Fiore asked next.

"A year and a half?" Chris answered, head tilting up as he made some mental calculations before nodding. "Yeah, a year and a half, more or less."

He turned to look at his partner then, a shadow of worry in his face but she didn't react; Fiore didn't seem to notice.

"What about you?" Lily surprised her by asking.

"About me?" Even Fiore was confused by that.

"Yes," the other gal insisted. "Since when have you had powers? Where did you learn that spell from earlier?"

"Nowhere, I told you already," Fiore replied. "This morning I didn't know I had magic, or that magic even existed. Nothing even remotely magical had ever happened to me before…"

But the moment those words passed her lips, Fiore knew they weren't true. There were memories that came back to her, one after the other: the previous attack, her odd dreams, the marks that had appeared on her neck following that nightmare. And as she allowed her mind to stray further into the past, more scenes came:

teas and creams that seemed to fix everything, songs that helped to heal depression, plants and flowers that would recover or bloom at the slightest touch… the flowers on top of her parents' graves, which seemed to have appeared from one day, looking like they'd been there for months.

"Well, you're quite good for a newbie." Lily's words pulled the other gal from her thoughts.

Fiore couldn't help the smile as she registered those words, she liked the amber-eyed girl.

The silence held for a long while; it was obvious for the three young adults in the sitting room that not all had been said, there was still more than one secret to be revealed. And all three understood that when it came to secrets, real secrets, the kind that aren't named even in solitude, it was next to impossible to trust someone enough to reveal them; they'd have time to get to that point.

Meanwhile, that didn't stop them from getting along. All three understood enough about secrets to accept that they didn't know everything about the other and yet they could still form a friendship, and that was something good.

"Well, so will you help us?" Chris inquired suddenly.

Fiore raised a brow, not quite comprehending where that was coming from.

"You've seen that we fight those beings, the shades," Chris explained calmly. "Will you help us?"

Fiore contemplated her answer for a few moments. She didn't want to offend them, not by denying them, or even by accepting right away, without first considering the consequences of her choice. She didn't like the idea of placing herself in harm's way, but just like when she'd chosen to approach that shade, she couldn't help the instinct pushing her in that direction.

"I will," she finally announced, "I'll help you."

Chapter 6
Allium

A haze of white light rose into the sky, leaving on the ground a small pink flower.

"*Rest in peace...*" Fiore murmured quietly.

"There," Lily announced dusting of her hands. "We're done."

"You mean Fiore's done," Chris chided with a smirk, "You spent half the battle laid out on the floor."

"Hey!" Lily whined at the same time she ran a hand through her short hair, trying to get out all the dust. "Give me some credit! I wasn't on the ground just for kicks!"

Fiore covered her mouth with her hand to hide her light chuckle.

<*Those two really are the perfect couple,*> she thought to herself, watching the two who in a short time had become her best friends. <*Why haven't they made it official then? Why aren't they dating?*>

That was the question that had been going around her head ever since she'd gotten the chance to know them, and she still hadn't the slightest idea of what the answer might be. Except that it was something important, and part of the secrets that remained between them.

It had been three and a half weeks since Fiore met Chris and Lily, the day they'd saved her from that shade-child and she'd discovered she had the gift to free his soul. Days later they'd discovered she could also create magical shields.

Along with the sparks and energy spheres that could sometimes be turned into something close to lightning Lily was very skilled in martial arts, though with no formal technique, not that she really needed it anyway. Chris was also quite good at hand-to-hand combat. He seemed to be stronger than the average human being and the earth sometimes reacted to his actions, moving, vibrating; it was a gift that seemed to still be growing, developing, perhaps one day he might actually be able to control the earth.

After Fiore had made the choice of helping them fight against the shades, they'd found themselves fighting them twice or thrice a week, one at a time. Sometimes the fight would happen when they came upon a shade by chance, but there had also been those occasions when she would find herself pursued by one of them. They'd found all kinds; women, men, children, adults, elderly; and the trio of friends still hadn't the slightest idea of what they all could have in common, or what turned them into shades exactly. It was clear they were all dead, they were spirits, and had been so for at least five hundred years, quite possibly longer; but that was all they could deduce. There were too many things still to be discovered.

Back in Chris's and Lily's apartment, all three were drinking cups of rosemary tea for the tiredness and headache they got when they used their gifts too much; especially Fiore, who wasn't used to it all yet.

"You did very good today Flower," Lils complimented her.

Fiore had no idea why, but Lily had taken to calling her that, and there was something in it, in the fact that the girl was giving her a nickname, a pet-name, that the older gal liked.

"You've improved a lot in your fighting skill, and your ability with magic," the teenager went on. "Who could ever imagine that just a month ago you knew nothing about it... I certainly wouldn't believe it hadn't I seen it with my own eyes."

"It's all thanks to you," Fiore assured them with a smile.

"Lies," Chris denied emphatically. "Your talent for both is innate. Believe me, I've seen talented people and you... well."

Fiore just curled up a bit into herself, flushing.

"Just look at the difference," Lils added. "Three weeks ago, you lost so much energy freeing a soul you passed out. Now you can handle a good fight, free the spirit and still remain standing at the end of it all."

"I'm still not as good as you," Fiore insisted.

"That's only because you lack experience," Chris declared. "You have the power. Lils has told you already, your power is much greater than our own."

"That's what I don't understand," the eldest of the group frowned. "You've had these powers your whole lives, you've trained for years, and used them consistently for over a year. Me on the other hand, I suddenly discovered I had them, not even a month ago. How can my power possibly be greater than yours?"

"Time is independent to the amount of power." Chris tried to explain things as he understood them. "Training gives you experience, sure, and through that you can perfect the power; but the amount of that same power and the kind of it you have already inside you. It's a part of you, like your eye-color, or hair-color, it's something that's in your blood..."

Chris's last words gave the young dark-eyed woman a revelation, though those eyes were still hidden by turquoise lenses. Her magic was something that she carried in her blood, like the true color of her eyes, her straight hair, her indigenous ancestry, her parents' and grandmother's ancestry... the name of Xochitl.

"Flower, are you alright?" Lily inquired looking at her with a hint of honest concern.

"Yes, of course I am," Fiore answered with a jolt, suddenly drawn from her thoughts.

But she was lying, and they both knew it. Fiore wasn't alright, and she wouldn't be until she faced her greatest fear once and for all: her past.

The young woman rose from the bed in silence, went to the bathroom, where she washed her face and then carefully checked herself thoroughly in search for new marks, scratches or bruises, there was nothing.

<At least that's a relief,> Fiore thought. *<I hate having to hide the marks of the attacks from that bastard.>*

The attacks in her dreams, the murder attempts, not only hadn't ceased, but they'd pretty much become an every night event. Same as the appearance of the silver silhouette that protected her. And of course, each morning that followed Fiore had to check herself in the bathroom in case there were any new marks to hide, she didn't even want to think how she would explain them to Jessica.

Fiore took her time under the shower, contemplating everything that had happened in recent weeks.

When she was finally dressed, with her hair curled, contact lenses in and her usual make-up the young woman stepped out of the bedroom and went down the stairs into the kitchen. The penthouse was basically a two-floor apartment, with the lower floor holding all common areas while the upper one held three bedrooms with en-suite bathroom, dresser and balcony. Once in the kitchen Fiore pulled a bottle of orange juice out of the refrigerator, she'd bought it herself in the market days earlier and to it she added some nasturtium for its revitalizing effects and all the ways it helped promote good health; she needed it after the previous day's fight and then the night attack. There was a limit, after all, to how much good rosemary could do on its own.

Jessica entered a little while later and went straight to turn on the coffee-pot; they could both remember a time when the second girl would enter the kitchen to find the coffee already prepared and Fiore drinking her first cup; but all that had changed. Fiore didn't even drink coffee anymore, only teas and juices with the added herbs. Jessica really didn't want to know what those were, it was all too weird for her; the hot cocoa was less strange, but even then, completely different from what had been the usual for so long.

Jessica could see that the other woman was changing more and more every day, and it had all begun almost a month earlier. Since then it was normal for Fiore to disappear for hours at a time for no apparent reason, sometimes even during class-hours; it had been a while since she'd asked Rick for a ride, always choosing to go on her own using public transport or walking. And Jessica really couldn't imagine someone preferring public transport to Rick's luxurious car! She truly suspected something was going on with her roommate, though she'd no idea what.

In another apartment still in Mexico City; a simple one with a small living-room, kitchenette, counter, main bedroom, bathroom and a second room that acted as both office and guest bedroom at the same time, a young woman with light brunette hair that was just slightly curled and went to her shoulder-blades, pulled back with a couple of barrettes, was holding a phone in her hand, her whole attention focused on an intense argument with the person on the other end of the line:

"Of course, it's them… I know it's them," The girl stressed impatiently. "How do I know? Because I see them. I see their 'true image'… That's my gift, have you forgotten? It's why you gave me this name… What do you mean what am I going to do with this information? I'll do what I must do… To hell with prophecies, I too have a right to be a part of this… I'm not alone, the others support me… Maybe not, but we'll never give up. We'll continue till the end…"

In the modest apartment in the outskirts of the capital, Lily seemed to be quite thoughtful as she drank a cup of tea.

"Everything alright Lils?" Chris asked, as if able to feel her tension.

"Yes… no… I don't know." Lily put aside her tea. "Chris, what do you think about Fiore?"

The use of that name, rather than her nickname, made it evident that the question was serious.

"Why do you ask?" The young man was confused.

"Just because." She shrugged in an attempt at nonchalance.

"I think she's a very kind young woman, one of the few I consider truly good in this world, though she harbors many secrets."

"We have our secrets too."

"So that's what this is about. Have you thought about telling her the truth?"

"I've been contemplating the possibility. You know I consider her a true friend, and you don't lie to your friends."

"And?"

"What do you mean 'and'?"

"What's the other reason?"

"What makes you think there's another reason?"

"Because I know you Lils, that's why."

"Alright... I wanna ask her to help me."

"You mean you want her to help you find Esteban." It wasn't a question.

"I know you might think that I shouldn't have any hope, but I cannot help it. My heart tells me he's alive and I have to find him."

"I know Lils. But you also know I'll always support you."

"Yeah, thank you."

Chris took her face in his hands, pulling her to him until he could press a kiss to the corner of her lips; short but charged with as much emotion as any other they might have shared before.

In the State of Mexico, in the living-room of an old restored house six young people between the ages of nineteen and twenty-one were gathered; three men and three women. The women with lightly tanned skin, average height, generous curves in their bodies, dark brunette almost fully straight and brown eyes with a hint of green that became more evident in very specific circumstances. The males had darker skin, were a bit taller than the girls, not exactly thin but evidently athletic, with brown hair lightened to different levels by the sun and brown eyes so dark they were almost black.

The first woman was the eldest in age and the shortest in height. Sitting on a chair, enveloped by an air of serious authority, her hair was pulled back in a high ponytail that reached nearly to the middle of her back; dressed in a reddish-brown skirt, black ankle-boots, and a simple blouse also in black. Around her left wrist she wore a knitted armband with no color except for a small painted flower, a belladonna blossom. Leaning slightly against the back of that same chair was a man who was also the eldest of the group, the same height as the other men, in a simple striped button-up in dark blue, open over a light blue t-shirt, khaki pants and dark brown boots.

The second man and second woman were on a side sofa, sitting side by side. She in plain washed-out jeans, yellow polo-shirt and sneakers; her hair went down to her shoulders and was fixed with a clip in a half-ponytail. She was wearing a knitted armband identical to that of the first woman, except with a different flower painted: A Magnolia. The boy, for his part, was wearing dark jeans, a dark-red long-sleeved collared shirt and sport shoes. Unlike the other guys he wore looser clothing, though even that did not hide that he was just as athletic as the others.

The third boy remained on his feet, standing straight and with his eyes fixed on the young woman before him. They were both the youngest of the group, she the tallest among the women, even though the difference was minimum. He was dressed in black slacks and a pale-blue button-up shirt, black dress shoes finished his attire. And finally, the last girl was wearing a lacy sand colored skirt and a coral pink V-necked blouse with decorations on the elbow-length sleeves, a pair of platform shoes had been put aside as in that moment she was kneeling before the living room's low table. Her hair was long almost to her waist, in a loose braid tied with colorful ribbons. Her armband had a Hyacinth painted on it.

The eyes of them all were fixed on the last girl. A small knocking broke the silence at the same time small dried grains were scattered over the table, which was suddenly covered by small wallflowers. The girl, on her knees before the table, moved her hand slowly over the grains without quite touching them at the same time she whispered a prayer in another language.

"I see her..." she murmured after a while. "The Maiden of the North... the Protege of the Earth..."

She broke off and even with her eyes closed it was obvious to her companions that she was making a great effort to achieve something, something she wasn't managing. Until after about a minute, when she was forced to give up. She let her arm drop and let herself fall backwards, where the other man dropped on one knee immediately and caught her before she ended on her back.

"Hyacinth!" the girl on the sofa, Magnolia, exclaimed with worry.

She didn't throw herself at her friend only because the guy beside her took her arm, holding her back.

"What happened Hyacinth?" the first gal asked, she was the leader of the group, Belladonna, and apparently the only one not to be affected in the slightest by what had just happened.

"I saw our sister," Hyacinth announced, forcing herself to gather her wits. "And I thought I could detect on her a trace of our mistress, but when I tried to get closer something blocked me."

"Something?" the guy on the sofa inquired, arching a brow.

"Yes," Hyacinth nodded vehemently. "I don't know what it was exactly, but it was strong; more than me, more than any of us."

That statement left them all stupefied.

"Could you determine the location of our mistress?" Belladonna asked.

"Not with precision," Hyacinth admitted, embarrassed. "She's in the capital, that's all I know for sure, same with our sister." She made a pause before adding. "I'm convinced, though, that if I were to feel her again I would be able to follow her trace and locate her."

"We'll have to make do with that for the moment," the boy in the blue shirt said, though it sounded more like a question than an affirmation.

"At least we now know they're both here," the one in red commented. "And if the fourth is here, the last one of us will surely be with her."

"That means that soon we'll all be together," the first of the guys declared, trying to contain his excitement.

There was no response to his words, suddenly all eyes were fixed on Belladonna, still on her chair.

"What's the plan Bella?" It was Hyacinth who finally pronounced the question that was probably in everyone's minds.

"We'll wait," Belladonna decided after several seconds of contemplation. "We'll wait for those damned beings to appear again, and then we'll act. Remember that our priority is to find the Lady of the Flowers and reunite with her, serve her like we did in the other life."

The others could only nod in silence. The decision had been made, the path traced, all left to do was find her...

Chapter 7
Bluebell

Fiore was putting away her French school books, the only class she had on Saturdays, when suddenly her cellphone rang. Since the class was over already and most of the students were busy talking about what they'd be doing during the weekend no one paid any attention when she began talking quietly.

"Hello? … Lily? … Again, where? … Yes, yes, I know where that is… I'm on my way. I'll be there in twenty minutes."

With nothing more to say Fiore took off at a run, she threw her bag with the books into her locker, stopping barely long enough to take off her heels and throw them inside, take the flats and put them on at the same time she slammed the locker closed harshly. Several people looked at her either surprised or confused but she paid them no mind and she left the university as fast as she could. She had to take the bus, since the place of the attack wasn't close enough for her to just run there. She spent the whole time mentally cursing herself for not having a car, or some other form of transportation that might allow her to get faster to where she was needed. The attacks were becoming increasingly common and tougher; she really didn't want to imagine the possibility of one day not making it in time to help.

When finally making it to the right area she took a deep breath, concentrating like Lily had taught her, seeking the younger woman's essence. It took a few seconds, but eventually she found her, in a half-finished construction area, the entrance but a few yards away. She took off running immediately. The place was a mess, with incomplete walls, unsupported roofs and construction materials everywhere, it looked like the worst class of labyrinth.

Fiore refused to give up, keeping her focus on the essence of Lily she'd detected and using that as a guide.

Eventually she took a turn, only to halt violently when seeing the scene before her: Lily was on the floor, hands and legs tied; a few feet away Chris was locked in a duel, not with one shade, but five. That last part was what had frozen Fiore; the previous time they'd had to go against two shades and that had been a complication, never could she have imagined facing five, nor could she understand why they were being attacked by so many at the same time.

As discreetly as possible, Fiore approached Lily, being careful not to step on or hit anything that might alert the shades to her presence. The amber-eyed girl kept struggling against her bindings, which only hurt her further, but even that wouldn't make her stop. Nothing could make her give up.

Fiore found a decent sized piece of glass and got closer to her friend.

"Do not move," she whispered under her breath.

"F...!" Fiore barely managed to shush her friend with her free hand.

"Sh... I don't want to call attention to myself." Fiore murmured. "Not yet at least. Don't move, I'm going to try and cut the ropes."

The short haired girl showed neither doubt nor nervousness, she simply halted her movements and waited, trusting completely the jet-black haired woman. Fiore worked with all the speed and care she could, using the piece of glass as an improvised blade to cut the ropes, while at the same time doing her best not to cut her friend. She ended with a few minor cuts on the palms of her own hands and the base of her fingers, but nothing serious and chose not to mention it.

It took a long minute, but eventually the ropes were severed, Lily jumped onto her feet then.

"We have to go help Chris," she said, ready to throw herself into the fight.

"I know," Fiore nodded. "But we should try to formulate some kind of plan first. After all we're outnumbered, and they probably have superior strength too so..."

There was no doubt that the older girl was right in her reasoning, but circumstances were against her. In that precise moment Chris was violently thrown past them and against a pile of wooden planks, going straight through half of them.

"Chris!" Lils yelled in fright, and without even thinking about it rushed straight to her partner.

At the yell, the nearly half dozen shades turned their attention to the gals, moving against the first of them: Lily.

Fiore noticed what was about to happen and she had but a fraction of second to act before it was too late. She stepped directly before her two friends, extending her hands to the sides, palms out, concentrating. Three of the five shades leaped into attack at the same time, but in the last moment a barrier that to the naked eye looked as if it were made of transparent crystal with a slight silver-tinted glow materialized, forming a cupola around all three.

Seconds passed slowly and drops of sweat began forming on Fiore's forehead. That shield was harder than the basic one she could conjure, but the other one was a simpler barrier, with which she would have risked their enemies attacking them from a side. It wasn't easy to hold the shield, especially with constant attacks.

Behind her, Lily convinced Chris to lean some of his weight on her, so they could stand. Fortunately, his injuries weren't serious and after a few moments he could stand on his own, mentally preparing to continue the fight.

"Guys..." Fiore murmured eventually, her arms trembling with effort. "I won't be able to hold on for much... longer..."

The shield fell, and in the same instant Lils jumped, with some assistance from Chris to achieve a height above Fiore. The moment she hit the highest point she extended her hands, shooting energy spheres from both palms.

The battle went on then. Chris did his part, though his ability over earth was limited, not so much by his own power or wounds, but by his fear, fear of hurting the girls; or worse yet, making the building they were in come down on top of them. He'd never forgive himself were he ever to hurt the girls.

At some point one of the shades ended beneath a half-finished archway of red brick. Chris took the opportunity to hit the right-side column, sending out his power to make the archway collapse over the shade, taking it out of the fight.

"Finally," Lily declared, relieved.

"Don't crow victory just yet, there's still four of them and I cannot concentrate on freeing one with the others still upon us," Fiore reminded her.

"And how are we gonna make sure that one doesn't try to kill us again when it wakes up?" Chris wanted to know.

"Well," Fiore looked around her, trying to plan, she was still on that when, without thinking it over much, she added. "I'll handle it."

The remaining shades seemed to come out of their stupor then and threw themselves back into the fight, Chris and Lily preparing to face them; though truth was they were beginning to really tire.

Fiore was chastising herself for being no good in a direct fight; and it was that as much as Chris and Lils might try to teach her, truth was that hand-to-hand combat just wasn't her forte. Then there was the fact that her attire, almost always with a short skirt, did not help much. Even then her friends had assured her many times that it did not matter, she had talent and helped them in other ways, like with her shield and the releasing spell, that was enough.

Fiore sought with her eyes something that might help her hold the fallen opponent. It took a moment, but eventually she noticed a bunch of straw, which put an idea into her head...

<Seems insane,> Fiore told herself as she scooped a fistful of long, wholly unbroken sticks. <But if it works... Besides, magic is supposed to be capable of anything>

With nothing further, Fiore knelt beside the still unconscious enemy, she split the fistful of sticks into two bundles, placing one over the shade's arms and the other over its ankles; then she concentrated, trying to find inside her the words that might allow her to achieve what she desired.

"*Sticks of humility…*" she recited, running a finger lightly over each bundle of straw. "*…become chains of unity.*"

The moment she pronounced the last words the straw became something that looked like a cross between a rope and chains, though the texture was still like that of hay. The shade was bound in a matter of seconds.

Lily and Chris were surprised when seeing Fiore join them in dealing out blows, or at least try, against the remaining shades.

"Where's the other one?" Chris asked, doubtful.

"Back there." The long-haired girl gestured vaguely, as she stuck a foot out to trip one of their opponents. "Don't worry, he won't be getting free any time soon."

Fiore wasn't too sure of the how or the why, but something told her that was the truth. The bindings would hold.

Right then, a scream distracted Fiore from her thoughts, which might have been a good thing. Fiore hated losing herself in circles, trying to understand how her magic was supposed to work, how she had it and how exactly she could have known nothing about it until a few weeks ago… it was a vicious circle.

"Lily!" she cried out instantly, recognizing the voice that had screamed.

"Elena!" Chris's yell got lost a midst Fiore's.

Chris moved just in time to catch the amber eyed girl after she was thrown through the air by one of their enemies. The young man was infuriated the moment he saw his partner, who had an ugly wound on her left forearm that was bleeding profusely.

Fiore concentrated as much as possible, raising a new shield before her friends; a simple shield, half a circle, she didn't believe she could raise a full one that might last more than a few seconds. She knew it wouldn't last long against four enemies, but she hoped to at least buy enough time for Chris to gather his wits and for her to come up with a plan. It was clear that Lily couldn't keep fighting with such a wound and it would be very hard to continue without her help.

Fiore made a great effort to concentrate on the fight, pull her mind away from the negative ideas of what would happen if she couldn't hold the shield up. She raised her eyes then, fixing her dark eyes, still hidden behind turquoise lenses, and could see the three opponents banging against the shield. Wait... three?

"Flower look out!" Lily screamed in terror.

Fiore turned her head to the right just in time to see the fourth enemy which, having gone around the silver-tinted shield, was about to attack the black-haired girl.

None of them had time to move. Fiore knew there was nothing more she could do; if she tried to protect herself from that shade the barrier holding the other three back would fall, leaving her friends vulnerable. She could feel every fraction of second passing as she waited for the attack, a part of her praying that Chris and Lils would be ready; except the attack never came.

Fiore opened her eyes slowly, a corner of her mind wondering when exactly she'd closed them, she hadn't noticed. She opened them in time to see the shade that had been stalking towards her being thrown away to smash against a wall.

"Mess with someone your own size damned abominations!" a female voice called from the other side in an authoritarian tone.

Fiore, Chris and Lily turned to see who'd just intervened, and they were surprised on seeing it wasn't one person, but six. There was the girl who'd just spoken, who seemed to be the leader of the group, she was also the one holding her hand up, holding the shade who'd just tried to attack Fiore, against the wall.

The moment Fiore's eyes found those of the six newcomers an image filled her mind momentarily:

An imposing white temple with eight individuals in ancient attires. The women in a blouse and skirt ensembles made of raw manta with flowers embroidered; the men in pants and vests made of leather. Suddenly the temple crumbled, burying all eight beneath its ruins.

Fiore inhaled deeply, she had no idea what it was she'd just seen exactly, but she didn't like it in the slightest. It was awful and filled her with a grief so big it was as if she couldn't breathe for a moment.

The shades, all four of them, were still being held against a wall, though judging by the way they managed to move every so often, it was obvious that the one holding them there was beginning to have difficulties doing so.

"Eddie!" the leader of the newcomers called, she had an embroidered armband on her wrist, with a painted flower, a Belladonna...

"I've told you not to call me Eddie!" the man directly behind her complained.

"Then stop complaining and start helping me," Belladonna replied, in between annoyed and mocking.

The man in khaki pants only sighed and raised his arms, instantly wind began to blow, getting stronger and stronger, until it turned into gusts which soon substituted the woman's invisible energy holding two of the shades.

Maybe in other circumstances Chris, Lily or Fiore would have doubted the newcomers' intentions, whether they themselves were truly good or bad, but in that moment all that mattered was that they were in trouble and the newcomers were helping them.

Fiore knelt beside Chris and Lily.

"Go and help them," she told Chris. "I'll take care of Lils."

After a couple of seconds of hesitation Chris nodded and left the injured Lils in Fiore's arms to join the battle that had unleashed the moment the newcomers stopped holding the four shades against the walls.

Fiore used a scarf she'd been wearing as an accessory to cover her friend's wound and stop the hemorrhage.

Chris was furious, that was evident in every line of his body while he advanced to the other side of the construction, where the battle was taking place; a predator in the midst of a hunt. Those beings had dared hurt the most important person in the world to him, and for that he'd make them pay.

The girl that the other three had been able to deduce was the leader noticed Chris getting closer and tried to stop him.

"Go back to your friends," she told him in a low tone. "Let us handle this matter."

"No," Chris refused with cold seriousness. "Those bastards hurt Lils... I'm gonna make them pay."

"And how do you expect to manage that, smart guy?" Belladonna asked.

For all answer Chris dropped to his knees at the same time he hit the ground with open palms in quite a violent manner.

"Lia! David! Get out of the way!" Belladonna ordered strongly, apparently deducing what was about to happen.

And just in time, the two newcomers leaped in the opposite direction, right before the floor they'd been standing on cracked and pieces of concrete and metal jumped in various directions. Bella's partner used his power over wind to deviate any material that could have injured his companions; it wasn't much, even in his fury Chris had enough conscience to direct his attack as much as possible.

"What was that?!" yelled Lia, who was wearing around her wrist an armband adorned with a magnolia, and the male-leader, who didn't like to be called Eddie, at the same time.

"The power of the Earth," Belladonna answered as if it were the most obvious thing, and for her perhaps it was.

"He's one of us," the broadest of the men, David, declared.

"The fourth guardian," added the other girl, in the long skirt, with an armband with a Hyacinth on her wrist, with a sigh.

"Then one of the girls accompanying him must be..." such was the shock that the last guy didn't even manage to finish the sentence.

On the other side of the floor Lily was slowly getting on her feet, with a little help from Fiore. No matter how hard the black-haired young woman might try to stop her, to convince her to stay out of the battle, the amber-eyed one was simply too stubborn. Fiore was truly worried, for while the injury seemed to have stopped bleeding for the time being, they did not know how deep it might be, nor how likely it was that it might bleed again, especially if Lils moved her arms too much.

But Lily didn't seem to worry about any of that, didn't even seem to care in that moment; the only thing in her mind was Chris and the danger he was in, she had to help him...

Fortunately for the badly wounded Lily and a very concerned Fiore, in the end her intervention wasn't needed, for the other seven combatants managed to dominate their opponents completely with a big water blow summoned by the man in dressy clothes, from some nearby water tank; the attack seemed to leave the shades breathless, or at least stunned.

As soon as they were sure that the shades didn't have the strength to rise again, Chris rushed to help Lily, who could barely stand, tired as she was. The other six took formation before the fallen enemies.

"David." Belladonna called without a hint of emotion. "Take care of the rest."

"Right away Bella," the man in question nodded.

Fiore had no idea how or why, but the moment she saw the man step forward and raise his hand, as if getting ready for an important attack, lethal, something inside told her she couldn't allow it.

"No!" she yelled, running without thinking about it, to stand between the man and the shades. "Don't do it."

The young man barely managed to give a step back, closing his fist as tight as possible to stop his attack and not injure the woman.

"Are you insane?!" Bella bellowed with obvious anger. "Why protect them like that?"

"I cannot allow you to destroy them," Fiore explained, as serenely as she could.

She knew that the six before her had power, she'd seen it. The one called David hadn't used magic before, but after what the others had done it wasn't hard for the black-haired girl to deduce what he must be capable of. In the same way, an instinct made it impossible for her to fear them, a voice inside her head assured her that no matter what happened they would never hurt her. And so there she was, standing, trusting her instincts and the fact that, once again, instead of the terrible fallen shades she was seeing people in ancient clothing, curled upon themselves, injured and very, very scared. The scene made her heart ache.

It was so illogical, Fiore would never be able to explain why she worried so much about them, where that need to help them, save them, came from; that conviction that she was the only one who could do something… maybe one day she'd understand it, but even if that never happened, nothing would stop her.

"Why do you want to protect these monsters?" the leader of the men asked with obvious incredulity.

"Because they're not monsters," Fiore answered sadly.

Saying nothing further she spun on her heel and approached the first of the opponents, the one still tied up…

"Don't be a fool…" Bella began, putting all the authority she could in her tone of voice, it was useless.

"Let her," Lily interrupted sharply, as she and Chris approached the others. "She knows what she's doing."

Fiore extended a hand then and with simple motions broke the bindings holding the being, turning them again into straw, cracked; which she then pushed aside carelessly. She knew all eyes were on her, but she chose to ignore them, they weren't important in that moment, only the souls that needed her were. Then she settled herself before the first, on her knees and sitting on her heels, she put her hands together and breathed deeply; the moment she did, it was as if some invisible veil had fallen, everyone present could see the true image of the supposed monsters. For Chris and Lily that was normal, but it hit the others pretty hard.

"*May chains be broken, may sufferings be soothed,*" Fiore recited, though unlike previous occasions, she moved softly, taking a moment to touch the forehead of each of the spirits. "*I'm here to dry your tears and heal your wounds. I call upon the powers of the light to free your soul…*"

The chains seemed to turn into dust and the shades/spirits transformed into hazes of light that rose into the sky in silence, leaving behind each of them a small petunia in different colors.

The shock of the six new individuals was so big most of them didn't seem capable of saying a word.

"That was… a high-level spell," David murmured after a bout of silence.

"She has so much power," his partner beside him, Magnolia, added.

The same question came to both leaders at the same time:
"Who is she?"

Chapter 8
Nightshade

The six newcomers were still looking at Fiore as if she'd just grown another head. While Fiore herself was trying to stay on her feet after having freed five spirits simultaneously and that was without considering how long and hard the battle against the shades had been.

"She just did a high-level spell," David repeated.

"Something like that… it's impossible," his partner, Magnolia, murmured.

"It's not," the woman in the long skirt, Hyacinth, countered.

"But for her to be able to do something like that she'd have to be…" Her protector became speechless at the mere idea.

"The Enchantress," the other man finished.

They all turned to look at Belladonna immediately, waiting for her opinion before believing or not something.

Chris and Lily stood close to Fiore on either side of her, who was laying against one of the columns still standing, her breathing irregular.

"You alright Flower?" Lily asked.

"Tired," Fiore answered honestly. "But I suppose it's normal, considering the battle we just fought."

"None of us are used to a battle as long as today's nor to having to fight so many shades at the same time," Chris pointed out.

"True," Fiore nodded, only to then turn slightly to look at the others. "We were lucky they got here."

"Were we really?" Lils inquired, brow arched.

Fiore directed a look of incomprehension at her, she didn't understand what exactly it was her friend suspected, or why.

"Think about it guys," the gal with short hair said. "We've been battling the shades for weeks, just the three of us. Weeks, only us and before Flower showed up, it was just me and Chris. And now suddenly they appear?"

"I too appeared suddenly," Fiore reminded her.

"But it was just you," Lily pointed out calmly. "And when it all began even you didn't know what your powers were all about, or how to use them. Even with us, until today Chris had never been able to truly command the Earth like that. Now there's six more, and from what I've seen they have perfect knowledge and control of their abilities, all of them. People like that don't just come out of nowhere."

Chris and Fiore had to admit, at least to themselves, that there was a certain logic to what Lily was saying.

"Besides," Lils went on, still in disbelief. "Chris and I had been on this for more than a year before we met you, and not even then did we know that other people with powers like ours existed, much less that they might be battling the shades just like us."

"You're right about that," Chris admitted. "For them to have the same level of control over their gift as we do over ours, or even a better one, they'd need to have had and been using their powers for years."

"And if it is so, why didn't they appear before?" Lils added. "Why now? Why exactly now?" As she spoke she put emphasis in the last two words.

When Fiore understood what her friend was saying her concern just went up.

"You think this has something to do with me." Fiore's words weren't really a question but an affirmation. "You think they're here because of me.

"I don't know," Lily admitted. "But we'd do well not to trust them blindly."

"I agree," Chris supported. "As long as we don't know who they really are or what they might be planning, we have to be careful."

The three of them had just reached their conclusions and had the basis of a plan, even though it basically consisted of keeping their guard up when in presence of the other group.

It was then the sextet approached them slowly. Belladonna at the front of the group, pausing but a few steps before Fiore where, without warning, she dropped on one knee and bowed her head in deep reverence, and act that was promptly imitated by the other five.

"Mistress..." Bella murmured in a tone of near adoration.

"W... What do you mean?! Mistress?!" Fiore cried out, moving back in a hurry, she probably would have jumped if she just had had the energy to do so.

The move was so sudden she became dizzy, stumbled and her body began swaying without her being able to control it; her two friends held her up just in time to keep her from falling and hitting the ground.

"It means we're here to serve you, my lady," the man at the right of the leader explained, he was the one with dominion over air. "We're your faithful servants, just like we were centuries ago."

"No... it can't be..." Fiore denied, tensing up and becoming very, very nervous for reasons even she didn't fully comprehend. "I don't know what you're talking about."

"But mistress..." Hyacinth began.

"No!" Fiore screamed, sounding like she was on the edge of a breakdown. "I'm not your mistress, I can't be. I don't even know you!"

That was enough for Lily; neither she nor Chris were about to tolerate for a bunch of complete unknowns to harass their friend like that. And so, without further ado, Lils rubbed her hands together and then extended them harshly, releasing several bolts of lightning in multiple directions. It wasn't a technique designed for attack, the bolts were very small and too weak to do any true damage, but it was good enough to give them a very necessary distraction.

While the six strangers concentrated on dodging or deviating the small bolts, Chris took hold of both girls, one with each arm and summoned his power. The floor beneath his feet moved, but it was not an uncontrolled hole like the ones he'd created during the battle, instead he created an exit and the moment they reached the ground level the earth beneath his feet kept giving him its support, allowing him to cover more distance, until the trio left the construction area and reached the street, where they could take a cab to Chris's and Lily's apartment.

By the time the other six understood what was happening it was too late, they had no way to catch up.

"Are you sure you know what you're doing?" Chris asked Fiore with a hint of insecurity.

They were in the kitchen, where Fiore had just prepared an infusion using ingredients Chris had never seen, hence his nervousness.

"Of course," Fiore assured him as she got to work on other things. "You just make sure Lils drinks that tea."

Fiore kept working several minutes longer. Eventually she came out with a small tray, except that what she carried on it wasn't food, at least not in the strict sense of the term. A deep bowl held clean, warm water, beside that there were two towels and on a smaller plate an odd brown-colored paste.

"What's in this tea?" Lily asked when seeing her, after taking another sip. "Because I'm sure it's not rosemary."

"No, it's not," Fiore admitted. "It's yellow valerian. I got some in the greenhouses a block away from here."

"What's the valerian for?" Chris asked with curiosity at the same time he drank his own tea, which was of rosemary.

"One of the uses for the valerian is as a relaxant, a minor sedative," Fiore explained. "It seemed to me that it'd be useful while I treat her injuries, especially the one on her forearm."

Chris and Lily asked no more questions, instead they were content enough with observing Fiore work. She for her part untied the scarf covering the wound on Lily's arm, it wasn't bleeding in that moment, but still looked serious. In normal circumstances one of them would have insisted on a hospital, or at least one of those cheap clinics, seeing how neither of the two younger adults had health insurance. The problem with that idea was that they had no way to explain an injury like that without getting in trouble, and quite probably getting someone else in trouble too. It was a miracle that the confrontations against the shades had gone unnoticed until then, and they couldn't risk civilians getting involved.

"The wound isn't too deep," Fiore announced after observing it carefully. "I don't think it needs stitches, we'll be able to handle things with steri-strips. All the same, you will need to be careful, avoid movements that might re-open your wound, at least for a few days. I know that all three of us heal faster than most people, but even so, this will take a bit longer than you're used to. The wound was quite deep."

"How long?" Lily wanted to know.

"Five days?" Fiore offered, she couldn't be sure. "A week would be most recommended, to be sure that your muscles healed and not just your skin."

Having said that Fiore got to work. With one of the towels and the warm water she cleaned the injury carefully, as well as the skin on both sides, being particularly careful to not start the bleeding again. Then she used the other to dry.

Lily observed fascinated, trying to ignore the stinging in her arm. She saw Fiore join both sides of the skin carefully with the steri-strips. Then the black-haired woman squeezed a couple of yellow flowers in her hands and proceeded to rub the substance she got on both sides of the cut; she also used her fingers to spread the brown paste that had been on the other plate, as a sort of poultice. Finally, she took the bandage Chris offered her and used it to cover Lily's injury and the rest of her forearm completely, not too tight, but just enough to make sure the wound wouldn't open easily or get infected.

"There," Fiore announced with satisfaction.

"Incredible," Lily said, surprised. "I can barely feel it, though whatever it was you put on it feels weird."

"That's normal," Fiore assured her with a small smile. "Because you're not used to this kind of remedies."

"What did you use exactly?" Chris inquired.

"Well, the flower is the valerian," Fiore explained. "I used it for its effects as analgesic and noninflammatory, also to sedate the area a bit so you wouldn't feel so much pain. The paste is a chamomile poultice."

"Chamomile?!" Both younger adults exclaimed surprised.

"Yes," Fiore nodded, smiling at her friends' reaction, she knew that when most people thought of chamomile they only thought about the commercial tea bags. "Chamomile is very good for promoting healing, scarring... of course there are other plants and fruits that give better results, but they require more preparation. The chamomile is easy to get your hands on and gives good results."

"Where did you learn to do all of this stuff?" Chris was very interested in everything Fiore was explaining.

It was as if a shadow settled over Fiore, a hint of sadness invading her after hearing those words.

"Flower?" Lils called, doubtful. "What is it? Is there any trouble?"

"The one who taught me everything about plants, from their meaning to the medicinal properties of every flower, stalk, root, leaf, and fruit was my grandmother... in the village," Fiore explained very quietly. "She passed away a little over a month ago."

"Oh Flower..." Lily whispered, ashamed for having summoned sad memories on her dear friend.

"Did you say village?" It was Chris who noticed the other detail. "But I thought you were Italian, or at least European, and since you're called Fiore..."

"Actually... no..." Fiore hesitated for a few moments, she wasn't sure if she could do it, could take the risk and reveal the truth, or if it would be better to keep the secret. In the end she took a deep breath and risked it: "I'm not Italian, nor of any other country in Europe; and my name is not Fiore... it's Xochitl."

What had once been a half-finished building had turned into a zone in ruins after the supernatural battle that had taken place barely a few hours earlier; though what fit the least with it all were the dozens of petals and different small flowers in all the colors of the rainbow, which seemed to be scattered everywhere, especially the second level, which was also the most damaged.

Over the next few days the owners of the lot would visit the place, as they planned what to do since the project had been canceled. The destruction would be blamed on the recent activity of criminal groups in the area, and in the end the place would be fully shut down, not that big a surprise considering that, due to the owner's economic problems, there had already been delays and finally a full stop in the project weeks earlier. No one would have any reason to suspect what had really happened.

The owners hadn't arrived yet, though the place wasn't empty either; six individuals in their late teens to very early twenties were still there, the same ones who'd helped Fiore, Lily and Chris to combat the shades. They were studying the petals left behind by the confrontation, especially those they'd never seen before.

"Have you discovered anything else?" Belladonna inquired eventually.

"Basically, what we knew already." Magnolia answered. "The petunias are a result of liberation spells, a sign of comfort. We have white and pink petals of what might be lilies, we're not fully sure right now, seeing as they're a tad burnt…"

"Scorched, I would say," David commented in an almost mischievous tone.

"We also found several broken pieces of straw and sticks that seem to have been used for some kind of spell, though we cannot know what exactly," Lia went on, ignoring her partner.

"Anything else?" Bella wanted to know.

"No," the other woman shook her head. "The rest of the petals and flowers we found came from the three of us."

"What about Hyacinth?" the leader asked then. "Has she been able to find out anything else?"

"She says the same energy from before is protecting the one we believe to be our mistress, but not the other two," Belladonna's guardian, called Eduardo, explained. "She thinks we might be able to track the girl using the lightning."

"And Julian?" David asked, looking around.

"Where do you think?" Eduardo said for all answer, as if it should be obvious. "Standing guard behind Hyacinth as she tries to obtain a clearer reading from the grains."

"Even though the battle is over he's still on guard, as if something were about to attack Hyacinth at any moment," Lia added, somewhere between curious and entertained.

"Like any guardian worth his salt should." There was an evident hint of approval in Bella's tone.

"Are you insinuating something?" Ed inquiring, raising a brow in doubt.

"No," his partner denied, making a pause before adding: "I don't imply, I only establish a fact."

Eduardo's expression transformed in ways that would be hard to describe, bewildered offense would fit but there was a fair amount of hurt and more there.

Anticipating another battle, one less evident but perhaps more violent, was about to start, the rest decided to intervene before it happened.

"So that means we're finished with what we had to do here?" David wanted to know.

"Yes," Bella nodded. "Call Hyacinth and Julian, let's go back home. Tomorrow we'll get to work on tracking down those three."

"Xochitl?" Chris and Lils inquired in unison.

"Yes," the young woman nodded, closing her eyes for a moment. "Xochitl Yolotl Nahui."

"Yolotl?" Chris repeated. "Isn't that surname…? I mean… well…"

"Indigene?" the black-haired girl finished for him. "Yes, it is, the Nahui surname too, to tell you the truth. My whole bloodline, going back to before the Conquest, even before the rise and fall of the Aztec Empire, has been natives."

"But the whole being from Italy thing..." Lils murmured without understanding.

"It's a lie," the older gal admitted. "The funniest part is that I wasn't even the one who started it. I changed my name the summer before starting university; my classmates have a few foreigners among them and many who've spent time in Spain, the United Kingdom and other European Countries. They thought I was one of them and I chose not to correct that idea, it was easier. Truth is I've never left Mexico. The most I did was spend a year in Yucatan in the Southeastern Languages Center, where I finished learning Spanish and Italian. That was after leaving the village but before starting college. To tell you the truth, before I turned eighteen I'd never left our little town."

As she talked, Fiore brought a hand to her eyes and very carefully took out her contact lenses one by one. Looking at them for a moment before throwing them into trashcan, they were almost a month old anyway, she'd need to open a new package once she got back to the penthouse. She didn't need to do much with her hair, it had already straightened up for the most part due to how much she'd been moving in the last few hours; and the make-up had been gone when she washed her face once they got to the apartment. And so, in that moment it became clear the woman before Chris and Lily wasn't Fiore, but Xochitl.

When seeing her two friends saying nothing about it Xochitl decided that it might be a good idea to tell her story.

"I was born in a little town a bit over a quarter of an hour away from Tula," she began to explain. "The kind of village that you won't find in any map, or the internet. I've always been convinced that only those who live there know the place even exists... The town has a single road, I wouldn't call it a street, no car would fit there. People walk, and those with enough resources use horses, or sometimes bicycles. They all know each other, for good and for ill... most of those who're born there, die there. Of course, there are those of us who're the few exceptions." Like her... like her aunt... "My mother was a basic education teacher and expert gardener, my father a renowned blacksmith. Neither of them went to college, nor did they have much money, two things that didn't seem to matter much in the village. It's the kind of place where status isn't measured by the number of zeros in a bank account, or the jewels or the number of diplomas with your name, but by the blood running through your veins. Blood that carries centuries of history and tradition."

It was the first time in more than half a decade that the dark-eyed young woman allowed herself to speak about her little town, her people with someone, anyone, with so much sincerity and feeling. It was as if some unknown force made her want to put all masks aside and finally show herself as she was, with no modesty or unease.

"My parents died when I was six," Xochitl went on. "In a highway accident, in the mountains. Another couple died in that same accident, friends of theirs who'd come to visit them from overseas. I have an aunt, though she left the village years prior, the last time I saw her was in the funeral, and the last thing I knew was that she changed her name, hers and her daughter's, for her new husband's, she never came back to the town. I was raised by my paternal grandmother: Azalea."

It seemed like Lily was about to say something, but Chris stopped her; he'd a feeling that the other woman was venting all the thoughts and feelings she had been keeping bottled up for a long time and that they shouldn't stop her. There would be time to show their support after she was done.

"I studied as far as high-school in the village," Xochitl continued explaining, "It was two years, very basic in comparison to what I found here in the capital. I always wanted more than what the town could offer, and for a long time I convinced myself that was wrong. That it was an insult to my heritage, to my parents, wanting more than I could have in the village..."

She exhaled, "It was a professor who convinced me that I was wrong, that I could aspire to more. She was the one who signed me up for the exams to validate high-school here in the capital. That was the summer after I turned eighteen. The first day... one of the guys saw me and called me Indian. That was the first time someone made me feel less for my looks, my descent. I thought it would be a one-time thing, but it went on for the rest of the week, there were exams in all the basic subjects and some for extra courses, to see what year we should start in and how many credits we could validate. I did pretty well, even with all the mocking and insults from the other students. I thought I could handle it, that I could simply ignore them, convince myself that their words did not affect me… But I was wrong."

She kept her eyes firmly down, hands clenched together, pain in her voice evident, "Eventually I couldn't handle it anymore. The day before the last exam I went to a beauty salon to have them teach me how to do my make-up and hair in a way that would show my features less. Then I used the money from my part-time job to buy new clothes, heels, and the make-up I'd been recommended. The next day I went to the school like that, it was as if they were all seeing me for the first time. The guys admired me and directed compliments my way, the girls would make small talk and even the teachers seemed more willing to listen to me, to my questions and doubts. As if I were a different person, as if I were worth more… and I liked that."

She sighed, "The whole thing with curling my hair, the colored lenses and even the name came later, after the year I spent in Yucatan. But it all started then, after that first week here in the city. After that day… truth is I liked the attention and didn't want to stop receiving it. My grandmother didn't like it, though truth is she never agreed with me coming to the capital. I think she was hoping I'd spend the rest of my life in the village, like her son…" She shook her head. "We had a very…bad argument that summer and once my acceptance papers for my last year of high-school here came in I decided to move and not go back to the town. And I didn't; at least not until I got the call letting me know she was very sick. I went to see her, to find out how she was, try to convince her to come with me to the city, to see better doctors… she wouldn't listen to me. She died the next day and I… I couldn't even say goodbye to her." She began sobbing quietly. "The last time I talked to her we argued again about how much I'd changed, about how I wasn't myself anymore. It was the last time I spoke to her and I couldn't even tell her how much I loved her…"

Xochitl couldn't go on talking, all her masks fell in that moment and she broke into tears in Lily's arms, who whispered words of comfort into her ear, though Xochitl wasn't listening, all she could do was cry, all the tears that hadn't been shed in so long...

It was obvious that change couldn't happen overnight, the change from Xochitl to Fiore had taken almost two years, after all, even though the first part had happened over a few days; but at least Xochitl had taken the first step, with time the world would get the opportunity to see who she really was.

Chapter 9
Geranium

The same white stone temple, mostly surrounded by a garden with the most varied and beautiful flowers, each of them representing an idea, a thought, a feeling... the same four women dressed in raw manta ensembles with flowers embroidered, a single flower adorning their hair. The same four men dressed in treated leather attires, proper clothing for warriors, even if their weapons were different from traditional ones.

But there was something new in that scene, not something physical but spiritual, an understanding of who those eight individuals were and the links that united them:

The maidens of the four cardinal points...

The warriors of the four elements...

Priestesses and guardians...

The eight custodians of the Flower Temple...

The eight disciples of the Enchantress...

And in the middle of all that, an object falls, a small figurine, delicate, of a bird with very long tail feathers, carved from silver...

Arguing voices woke Xochitl. It took her a little time to recover consciousness completely and remember where she was exactly, why the mattress underneath her felt so different from her bed and she couldn't recognize the room she was in. She remembered the battle, Chris's and Lil's apartment, how they'd insisted on her spending the night, exhausted as she was after using so much magic. It had taken a while, but eventually Lily had convinced her to take her bed, instead of sleeping on the couch, as had been the older girl's original idea. She wasn't sure if Chris had surrendered his bed to Lily or if they'd shared, it was really none of her business what her friends did or didn't do in private.

The volume on the argument kept rising, and eventually Xochitl decided it was better to intervene before things got out of control. She got dressed in a thin strapped top and denim shorts that Lily had lent her; while Xochitl was older than her, Lily was taller, so the clothes weren't too big or too small on her. Though they weren't the style the black-haired gal usually favored. She was no longer wearing contact lenses, as the new packages were in her room in Jessica's penthouse and she decided there wasn't much reason for any makeup, and after brushing her hair it had recovered its natural state, completely straight. She considered things for a few moments, and eventually decided to go out like that.

She was just stepping into the sitting-room/dining-room when she felt Lily's aura rise, signal that she was preparing to use her power, the dark-eyed woman broke into a run.

"I've told you already." She heard Chris said right in that moment, voice hard and cold. "You're not getting into my apartment."

"We came here looking for our mistress," one of the men outside stated. "We'll come in whether you like it or not."

"Wanna bet?" Lily dared them, her hand sparking as she prepared to fight against the newcomers.

"David." Belladonna called.

At the mere mention of his name, the young man in question closed his fist and twisted his wrist; it took several seconds, his hand acquiring an orange-red aura that began to grow until it almost looked like a flame…

"Stop it!" Xochitl yelled, passing her friends without thinking about it and taking a position between both groups. "Do you wanna kill us all? Or perhaps you want the neighbors to come out and see what's going on and discover us?"

Eyes dark like cacao seeds directed hard looks at David's hand and then at Lily's. Nothing more needed to be said, in an instant both attacks vanished as if they had never existed.

"Now," Xochitl went on, calmer than before. "Could you calm down just a minute and tell me what's going on here?"

"We've come looking for you, mistress," Belladonna announced with a deep bow.

The other five followed her lead.

"There you go with that again," Xochitl muttered with annoyance, turning to look at Chris over her shoulder. "Could we continue this conversation inside please? I know you didn't want them in your home, and normally I wouldn't ask, but I have a feeling they won't leave us alone until we talk, and I don't wanna risk one of the neighbors peeking, seeing us all here… We'll be lucky if no one saw us yesterday in that construction site, the last thing we need is to call attention to ourselves."

"Sure," Chris nodded in resignation.

He didn't much like giving in, but he got her point.

"But if you dare say or do something that hurts us in the slightest I will not be held responsible for my actions," Lily hissed, upset by the situation.

They all stepped into the apartment, sitting down in the sitting-room/dining-room, though no one relaxed, it was as if everyone were on their guard, preparing for another battle. Xochitl couldn't help but think it was ridiculous. That did not stop her from placing a heather branch on the door, murmuring something that was more a wish than an actual spell, for things to go well, though she'd be content with the magic keeping the neighbors from listening in or having any other reason to suspect that something was going on.

"Alright." Seeing that no one else was doing anything, Xochitl decided to take control of the situation. "Before anything, who are you?"

"I'm the priestess Belladonna, guide of the East," the leader of the sextet introduced herself, "my guardian is Eduardo of the Air. The others are Magnolia of the South, with her guardian David of the Fire, and Hyacinth of the West, with her guardian Julian of the Water."

"Priestesses? Guardians?" Lily inquired, unable to hide her confusion.

Xochitl didn't say anything, the phrases that she'd heard at the end of her dream echoed inside her mind as she tried to comprehend their meaning, their importance. That did not stop her from noticing that they all had names of flowers, but only the women... she wondered if it was for the same reason that her grandmother had taken the name of Azalea... Xochitl had never fully understood that; she knew her grandmother hadn't been born with that name, she'd taken it and made it her own when she'd taken her place as one of the leaders of the village, a guide...

"Yes." The voice of Eduardo pulled her from her thoughts. "We are part of a legendary group that guarded the Flower Temple and the Enchantress that inhabited it."

"We?" Chris repeated with an arched brow. "Are we a cult now or what?"

"Yes, you're part of this too," Hyacinth confirmed. "With my gifts I've seen your past, that of you two: the fourth priestess, guide of the North, who's protected by the Earth..."

Though during the first part of her declaration the woman in the long skirt had kept her eyes fixed on Lily, for the second half she turned to look at Chris.

"It's insane." Lily shook her head, as if that could give more power to her words, to her denial. "It's complete madness, I've never even heard anything about a Flower Temple. Sounds like something out of a cheesy fantasy novel!"

"Not a fantasy, though not something openly known either, not nowadays at least," Magnolia pointed out. "The Flower Temple existed more than a thousand years ago... Due to a series of events that aren't important right now it fell, and us with it. And now we're in the world again."

"Reincarnations?" Lily snorted. "I don't even believe in any of that."

"There must be a mistake," Chris added.

"There isn't," Julian assured them with complete seriousness. "Both of your gifts prove it. The power of the Earth can only belong to one of us, a guardian, an Atlante..."

"And what about me?" Lils inquired, still refusing to accept it. "I haven't seen any of you showing an ability that looks anything like mine." As if to prove her point, she made a spark dance over the palm of her hand. "Actually, aside from the telekinesis I haven't seen anything special from you, only them."

"Telekinesis is my gift," Belladonna pointed out, "while precognition is Hyacinth's. Magnolia for her part can conjure illusions." She made a pause before adding: "And regarding your ability... that power is the greatest confirmation of your identity. The Priestess of the North, protege of the Earth, who wasn't born Toltec but embraced our culture and swore fealty to the Enchantress... the only one of us who defied customs and traditions to receive the same training as the warriors, to be at the front of the battlefield and not behind." Her voice was reduced to a whisper as she added: "The favorite of our mistress..."

"Let's suppose what you're saying is true." Chris still didn't believe it but was willing to go along with it for the time being. "That we believe you. What happens with X... Flower? What part is she supposed to play in all this? Flower is our friend and she's helped us a lot, we won't abandon her now."

"You won't," Eduardo assured her. "And of course, she's a part of all this. Otherwise she wouldn't be here."

That only managed to confuse all three friends.

"What Ed means is that it's no coincidence, her being a part of this," David added. "Her powers, her ability, the fact that those monstrosities pursue her, her being capable of using magic at all... it's all due to a single and simple fact."

"She's our mistress," Lia finalized with a big smile turning to look at the girl in question.

"What?" Xochitl got on her feet but couldn't move more than that, the shock was too great for her to know what to do. "No, that's impossible."

"It's not impossible," Julian said, standing slowly, trying not to upset her any more. "We're the wardens of the Flower Temple, loyal servants of the Enchantress, our mistress..."

"No!" Xochitl cried out, finally recovering enough to give a step back.

"But..." Hyacinth began.

She and Magnolia stood, tried to get close, but just then something happened that no one was expecting. Without Xochitl moving a haze of silvery light appeared, taking the form of a half-moon shield, separating the three friends from the other six individuals; and especially, preventing any of them from touching the black-haired young woman, who seemed to be vibrating with nervousness.

"Enough!" Lily yelled losing her patience. "You've upset Flower enough for one day. Now go, get out of my house."

"We won't leave without talking with our mistress first..." Bella stated.

"You have spoken, and you've heard what she said, she wants nothing to do with you," Chris growled. "Lily warned you when you came in and you did not do your part. We have no reason to endure your presence here."

"It's up to you," Lily declared, energy sphere in hand. "You leave, or I will not be held accountable for what may happen to you."

"You cannot ma-" Belladonna began.

Eduardo barely managed to push her aside in time and use the wind to keep the energy sphere from touching her, though he ended with a scratch on his wrist for his trouble.

"Bella, I think it would be better if we were to leave, at least for the time being," Hyacinth suggested in a low tone.

Quite reluctantly the leader acquiesced, and the group took their leave, though not before directing some very disconcerted looks at a silent and very stressed out Flower, who was being guided to a chair by both Chris and Lily.

Xochitl threw the set of emergency keys onto the small table in the lobby, she'd had to take them from the decoration outside, where they kept them for those days when Jessica would lose hers, was asleep or too drunk to remember where she'd left them, or for when Rick arrived and would rather not knock; Xochitl needed them because she'd left hers in her purse in the school locker.

Her head was still spinning after everything that had happened: the exhausting battle, the memory of her past that she'd finally shared with her friends, and then those six… everything they'd said. Priestesses, guardians, enchantress… the words kept turning nonstop in the black-haired girl's mind.

<Why did my life have to be so complicated?> she wondered.

"Fi!" Jessica called from the living-room when she saw Fiore walking in the direction of the staircase to the second level of the penthouse. "Where have you been? I was so worried about you. If you weren't going to come home last night, you should've let me know so-"

"I'm sorry Jessica," the other girl interrupted her without thinking. "Something came up and I couldn't make it back last night."

Truth was Xochitl didn't much believe that Jessica's worry was sincere. Jessica was a lot of things, and while she wasn't a bad person, she wasn't the kind to worry about the welfare of others; mainly because she was one of those who lived under the belief that their name, their money, and status somehow were enough to protect them from anything that could happen, things that only happened to others. It was also why she'd never suspect that something bad might have happened, in fact, she was sure to believe Fiore had gone on some date or to a bar and had then spent the night with some guy. That was Jessica's world, the world she understood. She couldn't begin to imagine the reality her roommate was living. Fiore herself couldn't quite believe it.

Xochitl said nothing further and went straight to her bedroom, since she had her hair pulled up into a twist and the jacket had the hood up, Jessica had been unable to appreciate how different she looked in that moment, in comparison to the Fiore she was used to; that would have scandalized her too much.

It was barely noon, and Xochitl knew Jess didn't accept tiredness as an excuse not to leave the bedroom; so, with resignation she took a quick shower, dressed in her usual style of clothing, curled her hair, put on some make-up and after pulling a new package of contact lenses from the drawer she slipped them in. Then she stepped before the mirror to make sure everything was in its place. She almost couldn't believe what she saw.

"How is it that I changed so much?" the young woman wondered out-loud. "When exactly did I become like this?"

Her questions went unanswered.

Weeks passed and there had been no more battles, or at least the trio of friends hadn't been there for any.

"You think they might have given up?" Chris asked Lily one night.

The girl in question was laying against a window frame, observing the outside world with an expression of profound melancholy. The silence extended for several seconds and Chris began thinking that she hadn't heard him, or if she had she'd no intention to answer him, it wasn't so.

"No," Lily finally answered. "They haven't given up, the exact opposite in fact."

"If so why haven't we seen them?" Chris inquired, not liking that idea.

"Because 'they' are interfering." Lily knew there was no need to specify what 'they'. "I've told you I can feel the shade's presence, but they always disappear before we get there. I think that's why, they're battling them, defeating them before we arrive."

"But they don't have Flower, and I don't think just anyone can do the freedom spell..." Chris's voice faded as he understood. "They aren't vanishing them, they cannot. They defeat them, but cannot destroy them..."

"If we're right and the shades are souls that have been corrupted or cursed in some way, you cannot believe that one of them, or of us, could really have the power to destroy a soul, can you?" The amber eyed girl might not be exactly religious, but in some things, she did believe, like the immortality of a soul. No way would she believe that one of them could ever destroy them.

"They do defeat them but cannot destroy them... They're only angering them, and then there's the chance that the numbers might grow." Chris went on, beginning to understand the gravity of the situation.

"And none of them will stop trying to get what they want, who they want... Flower..." Lily murmured, tense.

"You think they truly are after her?"

"I'm sure of it."

"I wonder if they might know more about all this. I mean, reincarnations, custodians of a temple... It sounds way too fantastical. I suppose they might just be lies."

"I don't think they are."

"Lily..."

"I know it sounds strange, especially because of how I treated them when they were here, but I think I'm beginning to accept it. I've seen it in my dreams Chris... That place, the one they call the Flower Temple. I've seen us there, the two of us... I'm always dressed in a top and skirt ensemble of a thick but fresh bone-colored cloth, with flowers embroidered, lilies... My feet are always bare, there's a veil on my head, and my hair is longer, and I don't like it, but I get the feeling that that's how it has to be. And you... you're dressed in leather, pants and a vest, and you're always close, looking after me and..."

"And..."

"I've seen her too, Flower. In a gorgeous long white tunic and a knitted veil over her head. You believe me, right? You don't think I'm hallucinating or insane...?"

"Of course, not Lils. And I've gotta confess something, all that you've mentioned... I've seen it too."

"Really? Why didn't you tell me before?

"I didn't want to put pressure on you. You were so reluctant to believe... I didn't want to become yet another person pushing you into being something or someone you don't want to be. But what about you? Why didn't you talk to me about these dreams of yours?"

"Because I was afraid." It shamed her to admit it, but she knew it was necessary. "I didn't want to accept... To tell the truth I still don't want to accept what's going on. Because accepting it means we're involved in something much bigger and more dangerous than what it seemed at the beginning. Something that could cost us our lives, again. And that's something else, if we accept they're telling the truth, that we are these custodians, reincarnations... how much control do we have over our own lives then?" She sobbed, "I don't wanna lose you Chris, not you or Flower... I already lost Esteban and believing that those dreams might be real... Then that means I already lost everything once, including my own life. If we don't manage to win this time, if something happens to you..."

"You won't lose us Lils, not Flower and not me. And Esteban... Some time ago I promised you I'd help you find him, that together we'd find the way to bring your brother back. And that's a promise I plan on keeping. You'll see, everything will be alright."

She didn't answer, just embraced him tightly as she kept crying in silence.

"Nothing and no one will separate us Lily... my Elena... I swear to you..."

She was running as fast as her legs could carry her, though her feet made no sound, perhaps because they were touching no ground at all. Everything was darkness around her, impossible to make out an up or down, a beginning or an end; all that seemed to indicate she was moving at all was the fact that her pursuer hadn't caught up with her yet.

"You won't be able to run from me forever, little princess," the dark voice of the one hunting her, not just that night but every night, said.

"I've told you I'm no princess and have no interest in being such!" Xochitl yelled without stopping or even thinking about looking back; much as she might not want to accept it, she was completely terrified.

"Maybe not now," a voice replied. "But a princess you once were, and you shall be again unless I prevent it."

In that moment, it was as if the girl tripped on something invisible, impossible as it should have been without a ground with anything to trip over. She tried to get up, but it was impossible, she was exhausted beyond comprehension, night after night, fleeing from the same dark hunter… and to end like that. It made a part of her wonder what the point had been of running in the first place, if it would always end like this. It was a darkness of thought such that, had Xochitl been thinking clearly, she wouldn't have recognized herself in that moment, she didn't remember having ever acted or felt like that in her whole life.

Her pursuer caught up to her and held her up without the slightest effort, his hand around her neck, in no time he was asphyxiating her.

"No… let me go…" she pleaded quietly.

She used her own hands, trying to make him let go of her, going as far as digging her nails on her attacker, but it was pointless; and as her body ran out of oxygen, both her voice and her body weakened.

"I cannot allow you to reunite with your king…" her attacker insisted, a man that seemed to be made of smoke.

<King,> she thought with desperation. <What the hell is he talking about?>

Xochitl felt she was reaching her limit, her lungs seemed to burn with lack of oxygen and her mind was clouding up. A part of her was beginning to wonder if dying in a dream, or a nightmare, meant that she'd also die in real life. It seemed impossible, but the memory of those marks on her neck after the first nightmare gave her the idea. One that would terrify her, if she had energy for even that. She was about to lose all hope when a tiny voice was heard wailing:

"NO!"

It was as if the voice came from every direction at the same time, Xochitl could have almost sworn that she heard it even from inside herself…

So surprised was he, hearing someone else in that plane, that the smoke-man slackened the pressure on Xochitl's neck, just enough for her to take a deep breath, her lungs filling with air. An invisible force then threw the attacker away, before he could hurt Xochitl again.

Still completely exhausted, the black-haired woman wasn't capable of offering any resistance, she couldn't even stand up; she could only think about breathing. Slowly she managed to straighten up, just enough to end up sitting with her legs up, she immediately began looking for her pursuer with her eyes. What she found confused and terrified her in equal measure, and it was that the being that had tried to assassinate her in that moment was pointing at what looked vaguely like a human figure, small, formed by silver light, at the same time as he pronounced words in a dark tongue that the black-haired couldn't understand, though it still froze her blood.

"You won't be interfering in my plans again brat," the man hissed in English, before adding something else in the other tongue.

"No!!" Xochitl screamed, feeling a sudden panic.

She had no idea what was going on, all she knew was that it was terrible. But it was too late already, from one moment to the next the silhouette seemed to shatter, the fragments falling on Xochitl's hands, like petals made of light...

When Xochitl woke up she was still grasping those petals in her hands.

Chapter 10
Daisy

Fiore was running to Mater University at her top speed. Jessica had decided to play hooky for her first class that morning, and thus Rick hadn't gone to pick her up. Nobody knew it, but Fiore was a scholarship student, which meant that she couldn't have more than a certain percentage of absences. With the shades situation she already had several late days and there was always the risk that one day she'd miss class, so she couldn't do it just because. Without Rick to take her, she'd been forced to take the subway; the problem was that, with so many people she'd been delayed and missed the tram that took the students who used the subway, so they wouldn't have to walk the seven blocks separating them from Campus, forcing her to run.

A block away from the university there was a park, one the dark-eyed young woman particularly liked due to its beautiful gardens, the only one she'd seen that was well taken care of. It was also, a convenient shortcut.

She was rushing through it when she found a little girl, no more than five or six years of age, hair ebony black and eyes that seemed to be both dark and bright at the same time; dressed in a simple tunic of raw manta. In between her fingers the little one held a white rose, of an oddly bright white, and she was crying.

There was something in that little girl, Fiore had no idea what it was exactly, but she couldn't help but stop running and approach her.

"Are you alright?" Fiore asked her with as soft a voice as she could.

But her question went unanswered.

It was then that Fiore noticed that the rose in the girl's hands still had its thorns, the little one had pricked her fingers.

"Allow me," Fiore said with a small smile, taking the flower.

She made sure to move slowly, not wanting the child to think she wanted to take away her flower. The little one just watched in silence how Fiore took the rose in her hands and with great care stripped away its thorns; the same way her mother had once done, many years earlier.

<Why is it that nowadays everything I do reminds me of someone in my family or of the village?> Fiore wondered, though she did not expect an answer.

Having finished taking off the thorns, Fiore gave the flower back to the little girl, at the same time she smiled at her, a smile the child returned before sprinting away; the young woman vaguely noticed her feet were bare.

<Blessed be the children,> Fiore thought with a soft smiled. *<They have no worries in the world but playing and being happy...>* She sighed, and her eyes laid almost without wanting, on her watch. *<Damn it!>*

She straightened up with a jump, after having been on a crouching position for a while and ignoring the brief pain in her knees for the harsh movement she resumed her interrupted race, mentally praying that she'd make it to class in time.

Fiore was a bit late for class, but since it was Professor Solis, he let her in without trouble. That's just how the teacher was, showing favoritism not only for things but also for people from other countries, especially European. And since he, just like everyone in the school, except perhaps whoever worked in the Administration Area and had access to the young woman's documents, had the belief that she was Italian... there was also of course the fact that everyone in her clique tended to support all the malinchistic comments the professor made, and thus Fiore was considered part of that support as well.

That kind of comments… Fiore had noticed she liked them less and less every time she heard them. Things that might have once seemed funny to her, and that she'd felt were very real, she began feeling them as not only something negative, but a little deserved insult. Even then she preferred not to say a thing about it.

Classes passed, and Fiore couldn't take from her mind a foreboding feeling regarding the girl she'd seen that morning. She didn't know what it was she was feeling exactly, but something in her mind told her that wouldn't be the last time she saw the little one, just like a part of her felt that hadn't been the first either. Though the latter was harder to explain than the former.

Those strange premonitions, thoughts, feelings… She didn't know why she had them, though she knew they weren't new, she'd been having them for a long time, perhaps since forever. The difference was that she was finally paying attention to them, doing something about them.

The day had come to an end, at least as far as classes were concerned, and it was then that Fiore noticed Jessica hadn't been around all day.

<Surely Rick convinced her that they should spend the day together, go hang out or something,> Fiore thought. <Or she simply wasn't in the mood to come.>

Fiore knew that was how things were with her roommate. Daughter of a rich family, heiress of a good number of shares from a great businessman; she was only attending university to make her mother happy. Regardless of her grades, she'd still be the heiress of the Favre family. And if she didn't get a passing grade in one or more classes, there would come a check with a generous donation for the university signed by Etienne Favre, and all would be solved.

Knowing that if she wanted to reach the subway station before it filled with people, which, consequently, would probably have her not getting a place in the subway train itself and end up stuck for hours waiting for the next, she needed to hurry. So, Fiore picked up the pace.

It didn't take her long to get to the exit where those who, like her, were there thanks to scholarships and not because they belonged to wealthy families, were hurrying to board the transport that would take them to the station. Fiore was going in the same direction, when a mob caught her attention. A lot of people seemed to have gathered on the other side of the street, around a car and one or more people.

<Looks like there was an accident,> Fiore thought to herself.

She was about to ignore the whole thing and climb on the transport when something called her attention: a sobbing, shrill voice calling for help among the crowd, in a language that wasn't English. In the space of a heartbeat the young woman completely forgot the transport, the subway, going back to the penthouse; she didn't even pay attention to the murmurs of those who began moving past her, a couple even bumping against her shoulders, to get on the vehicle. She ignored them completely and instead began walking towards the mob, she didn't stop when getting there, instead making her way through the people. Once she got there her surprise grew as she discovered the owner of the voice, the same little girl from that morning.

"What's going on here?" Fiore asked the man beside the car, who seemed to be at the core of the matter, in a tone of firm authority she didn't know she possessed.

The man, of average height, broad built, tanned skinned, brunette slightly grizzled hair and dark eyes, seemed to be in his forties, perhaps fifties. The young woman could tell he was nervous, perhaps even afraid, though it was impossible to tell the reason.

Some others in the crowd, mainly students and even a few professors for the university, they all turned to look at her attentively. Most probably had no idea what her name was even, but it was as if they instinctively answered to her tone of voice.

"Miss..." the man addressed her. "I don't know what happened. That kid came out of nowhere. I don't think I hit her, I hit the brakes just in time. But she hasn't moved from there, hasn't stopped crying and muttering, but no one here understands what it is she's saying."

"No one?" Fiore inquired, raising a brow.

"No one miss," the man insisted.

Fiore could still hear the little girl murmur and she was having no trouble at all understanding her. She was looking for help, for her mom, she was afraid and feeling lonely. Making a sudden decision Fiore went straight to the child, leaving her bag to a side and holding her skirt in place so it wouldn't rise inappropriately she crouched beside the little one.

"*Hello,*" she greeted her directly in Nahuatl. "*You remember me? I'm the one who stripped the thorns from your flower this morning.*"

The girl stopped crying right away and fixed her dark eyes on Fiore's. She seemed to contemplate her words for a few moments before nodding fervently.

"*Are you alright?*" Fiore asked her then. "*The car didn't hurt you?*"

As she said the last part she signaled to the vehicle, in case the girl wasn't familiar with the word.

"*No,*" the little one finally spoke to her. "*It just scared me. But I'm tired and hungry.*"

"*Where's your family?*" Fiore inquired then.

The child seemed to almost curl upon herself but refused to express whatever it was she was thinking, Fiore could almost sense her fear.

"*Everything will be alright, I promise you.*" Fiore assured her with a soft voice and a small smile. "*I'm going to help you.*"

The girl hugged her immediately, and the embrace was strong enough Fiore ended sitting on the edge of the sidewalk, but she did not mind.

"You're right," Fiore said, switching to English and turning her attention to the driver. "You didn't hit her. But she's scared, that's why she's still here and wouldn't stop crying."

"You understand her miss?" the man inquired, intrigued. "What language is it she's speaking?"

"Nahuatl," Fiore answered honestly. "But that's the least of it. What worries me is that she cannot seem to be able to tell me where her family is, and I'd seen her already this morning in the park, early, also alone."

"You think she's been alone all day?" The man sounded honestly worried. "What kind of mother or father would leave their daughter alone for so long? And in the streets?!"

"I don't know," Fiore admitted, making a choice right that moment. "But I think I'm going to find out."

"You'll be taking her with you?"

"I'm the only one here who understands her, so I think it's the best thing for her. At least until I find someone who can help her more."

"If you want, I can take you to the DIF or the Public Ministry."

Fiore hadn't been paying enough attention before, but the man turned out to be a cab driver.

"Yes, thank you, that's a great idea," Fiore agreed. "The subway train probably already left and I'm not even sure how I'd be able to handle things with her if she happens to be afraid of being with so many people."

"I can take you wherever you need, free of charge," the cab driver assured her. "Consider it a thank you for your help. I honestly had no idea what to do to help her."

"It's normal. There aren't many people left who speak Nahuatl nowadays."

"Where do you wish me to take you then?"

"I think..." She made a pause to look at her watch. "My place. It's past seven, the DIF office will already be closed, and I honestly have serious doubts that the Public Ministry or a hospital will be any more successful in understanding her. I'll be taking her to the DIF tomorrow."

"Shall we leave now then?"

"Yes please."

It was until then that Fiore became aware of the fact that the little girl in question had fallen asleep in her lap.

"Could you carry my bag for me please?" she asked the man as she settled the girl in her arms and stood very carefully so as not to awaken her.

"Of course, miss." The man did as ask immediately.

"You truly surprise me Fiore," Ximena called from the decreasing mob.

"Why do you say that?" Fiore asked quietly, not really turning to look at Ximena.

"I didn't know you to speak that odd language," the other girl explained in a tone that could almost be called disdain.

"What's so strange about it?" Fiore inquired, looking over her shoulder. "If we learn to speak Spanish, French, German, Italian… why not Nahuatl?"

"Because it's the language of Indians, that's why."

"You don't belong here. You're nothing more than an Indian!"

The voices echoed inside Fiore's memories, those voices that had tortured her so cruelly when she'd first arrived at the capital… she wasn't that person anymore. And not only because no one knew she was indigene, but because, in that moment, those words didn't make her tremble, or want to hide. No, instead they woke an instinct of protection, of defense, a desire to shield the one who Ximena, directly or indirectly, was insulting. She managed to hold herself back and said nothing, instead she followed the man waiting for her beside the open door of the taxi. She vaguely heard her classmate calling to her but paid her no mind. Ximena would surely have a lot to say about what had just happened, but Fiore honestly found that she didn't care. Gossip and insults were not important right now, nothing except the little girl sleeping in her arms was important.

It was just past eight at night when Fiore entered the apartment. It was a huge feat to be able to open the penthouse door while balancing the girl on one arm, her handbag on the opposite shoulder, and a bag with some basic things she'd stopped to buy on the way, especially to feed the little one. Eventually she managed, she'd just closed the door when she found herself face to face with Jessica.

"Who's that?" her roommate asked with evident surprise when seeing the child in Fiore's arms.

"It's my…charge," Fiore answered.

For a moment she thought about telling Jessica some white lie, but Ximena had been there when everything had happened, and without a doubt would take no time in letting everyone know, if she hadn't already.

"She has no family, and if she does we don't know where they are," Fiore explained briefly. "Until someone claims her I'll be looking after her."

What she failed to explain to Jessica was how difficult it'd be for something like that to happen, since she hadn't reported her to anyone yet, and didn't plan to. Fiore knew it was crazy and she couldn't even explain it to herself, not yet, but the same instinct that had pushed her to going into that mob made her think it wasn't a good idea to involve the DIF, or any other authority, not yet at least.

"Why you?" Jess wanted to know.

"Because she doesn't speak Spanish, only Nahuatl," Fiore explained. "I speak it too. So, for the time being I'm the only one who understands her."

"So, it turned out to be useful then, having to learn your mother's tongue."

Jessica, like everyone in their little group, and most of those in the university still believed that Fiore was of mixed-blood, from a Mexican mother and a European father, quite probably Italian. It wasn't something she'd ever said, not really, but it was so common in their group. Most were children of marriages where at least one was foreigner, or of foreign descent. It was why no one found it odd for Fiore's skin to be dark even when compared to her turquoise eyes and curled hair.

Fiore only shrugged at Jessica's comment, too tired to feel offended.

"I'll be in charge of her for a while, I hope you don't mind," she said eventually.

"As long as she doesn't break anything." Jessica didn't seem fully convinced, but she probably couldn't think of a reason to say no either.

Fiore knew Jess could refuse, in which case she'd need to make use of the money the man had given her after she'd signed the papers surrendering her rights over her grandmother's house and land, of which she hadn't spent a single peso, to get a place to stay. That was something that might still happen, seeing how she hadn't the slightest idea of how things might progress.

One thing the young woman was sure of: She wasn't going to leave that little girl. Even without knowing what made her want to hold onto her like that, there was something in the child that invoked a very strong protective instinct in Fiore, she was answering to that. Eventually she'd have to think of a permanent solution, but for the time being all she wanted was to rest.

"She can stay in your room," Jessica finally said. "As long as you make it clear that she can't go around the apartment and get into everything, and I don't want her to come into my room and make a mess for any reason." She made a pause and then added in a tone of displeasure: "I don't want her getting into my makeup or perfumes. They're high-quality and very expensive."

"You don't need to say it in that tone," Fiore told her, having noticed that the girl was awake and looking at them in silence. "I can explain all that to her without you needing to say it that way."

"What's the problem?" Jess didn't give see it as important. "You said it yourself that she doesn't speak English, she won't understand a word of what I say regardless of what it may be exactly."

"Even so," Fiore insisted. "Her not understanding the words doesn't mean she doesn't understand the feelings behind them. Even babies, before learning to talk, can tell if they're loved or not."

"Who told you that?"

"My mother."

In that moment Fiore didn't remember that she had once implied that she didn't like her mother, nor did she get along with her father; or if she remembered, she didn't care. Anything she might have once said or implied, years ago, when nothing seemed to be more important than fitting in with Jessica, Ximena, Carlota and everyone else… well, there were much more important things in her life.

"You've changed Fi, changed a lot," Jess commented, almost melancholic.

"I don't know what you're talking about," Fiore lied.

"Yes, you do," the amber-eyed girl contradicted. "You don't drink coffee anymore or go to the parties like we used to. Our games from before, where we'd flirt with all the handsome guys and enjoy watching them try everything to win us over until we grew bored with them… You're not interested in that either. You won't even go shopping with me anymore."

"Maybe I have other interests now."

"And that's not all. There are days when you disappear for whole afternoons and I don't know where you are. The other day you didn't even come to home to sleep. Rick told me you said we no longer had to pick you up the days you have French class."

"And? So, what?"

"You're changing a lot Fiore, and I'd like to know why. I'd like to know what it is that has made you be so different now."

Fiore was saved from answering when the little one began making small noises, as if she were just waking up. Jessica reacted, giving a step back, it was obvious she hadn't noticed the girl had been awake for a while already. For a moment the black haired young woman even wondered if it was a coincidence, or if somehow the child was reacting to her own mood.

"If you'll excuse me Jess, I'm taking Rose to bed and then I'll be going to sleep as well," Fiore declared.

She'd no idea where the name had come from, though she did think it was quite appropriate; considering that even in that moment the little girl was holding in her hands the very white rose Fiore had stripped of thorns that morning.

Jessica just nodded in silence.

With no further ado Fiore settled Rose better into her arms and sorted out a way of getting up the stairs and to the bedroom.

She dressed the girl in one of her old tops, so she'd sleep better, before getting into her own sleep-clothes. Mentally adding things to the list necessities she'd have to acquire for Rose. She was settling into bed, eyes fixed straight on the little one who'd already gone back to sleep, when she remembered the last thing her friend had said.

"Maybe not," Fiore whispered into the darkness. "It's not that I'm becoming different… I'm just going back to who I used to be…"

Chapter 11
Heather

Fiore left the university campus almost running, schoolbag on one hand, while with the other she did her best to put her jacket on. Fortunately, she wasn't wearing heels, or she would have probably fallen. Little by little she stopped wearing them, opting for flats instead. She still wore colored contact lenses and curled her hair, but was less obsessive about it, and the amount of makeup she used was also a lot less than before. A bit at a time, others noticed the change; and while some seemed confused, or even curious... not everyone seemed to like it.

"Why the hurry?" Carlota asked as she watched her pass.

"Don't you know?" Ximena asked without giving Fiore the opportunity to talk. "Ever since she began looking after that Indian girl Fiore has time for nothing else."

"I don't know why she takes such troubles for an Indian..." another began to say, brunette with Californian highlights, Marlene.

That was the last straw.

"That's enough!" Fiore exclaimed. "I forbid you from referring to Rose in that manner."

"Who do you think you are to forbid me anything?" Marlene spat in a shrill tone.

"I'm Rose's temporary guardian," Fiore replied firmly. "It's my duty and my right to watch out for her well-being."

"Jess is right," Ximena decided. "You're changing a lot Fi. Until recently you'd have never bothered over an In..."

"I told you not to call her that!" Fiore snapped at her, her posture changed in an instant, her back straight, body tense, the rest of the girls almost gave a step back instinctively. "How dare you... How dare you all speak so contemptuously of that which you do not know! You call her Indian with such scorn, without knowing at all what being descended from a native community truly implies." For a moment it seemed like she'd say something else, but in the end, she changed her mind and shook her head. "There's no point. I'd better go now. There's someone waiting for me."

The others had no chance to say anything else before Fiore left, too stunned by the sudden change in Fiore to respond to it. They didn't understand, and that was something they didn't like.

Fiore had made a deal with a florist in the park who knew a bit of Nahuatl, so she'd watch over Rose in exchange of a bit of money. The woman claimed to be of mixed-blood, which was why she knew some of the language, and she loved to take care of Rose. Assured that when the little one was present she sold more flowers than at any other point of the day. And Rose herself seemed to enjoy being there, among all the flowers; she also had a special charm that seemed to attract people to her and, consequently, to the flower-shop too.

And as she walked to where she knew Rose awaited her, Fiore couldn't help but think about what had made her react so vehemently to the words said by her classmates:

An eighteen-year-old Xochitl, still with her eyes as dark as cacao seeds and hair as black as obsidian, long and straight, dressed in a skirt made of light-brown dyed manta and a white blouse of the same material with flowers embroidered, leather sandals on her feet, arrived at the place where she was to present her high-school test.

She had the best scores of the village. Several of her teachers had insisted on her leaving the town to continue her studies, insisting that she deserved more than what they had to offer. It was through their recommendations that she was there. The two-year high-school program in the village was too basic to allow her to enter any university, which was why she was going to take a high-school test; according to her score they'd know what semester she could start in. She'd studied a lot, with the hope of advancing soon. She also hoped to achieve enough points to earn a scholarship, knew that her grandmother would never be able to pay the fees for a school in the capital; she didn't even agree with Xochitl wanting to leave the town.

"Who are you brat?" someone who'd just stepped into her path asked her coldly.

It was then that the black-haired girl looked up and found before her a bit over half a dozen either blonde or red-haired girls with white skin, designer clothes and make-up. Xochitl blinked, confused by the stranger's tone and the way she was looking at her, a look that was making the dark-eyed girl feel uncomfortable, though she didn't understand it.

"My friend asked, who are you?" another insisted, in the same tone.

"Xochitl Yolotl Nahui, at your service," Xochitl introduced herself as she'd been taught, with a smile and a small dip of her head.

"Well of course you're here to serve us, I don't think you'd be good for much else," the one who appeared to be the leader of the group said in a derogatory tone. "I suppose you're the new maid; and if so, let me tell you there's no reason for servants to go strolling down the halls, you should be working.

"I'm not a servant," Xochitl replied, clenching her teeth to control her indignation. "I am here to study, I'm taking my entrance exam today."

"Really?" one of the girls from the back inquired.

"What a waste of time," another declared with a grimace. "There's no way someone like you will ever be accepted in a school like this one."

"That's true," a third one agreed. "Only the right people study here… the important people. You get my drift, right?"

Xochitl was going to say something in her defense, but the leader of the group gave her a push, making the black-haired girl stumble; then she spoke with an air of superiority and haughtiness:

"Go back to your little town, Indian," she said cruelly. "There's no place for your kind here."

Those last few words from the other gal had been the beginning of everything. They'd left their mark in ways that, even years later, she couldn't quite explain. It didn't matter how many people or how many times they told her that no one could make her feel bad without her consent, and all those phrases designed to help, made by people who surely must have never been through the experience of being cruelly insulted for no reason.

It was because of those words that by the end of the week Xochitl was using makeup, doing her hair and had bought new clothes. And then came the day when the results came in:

She'd been in a dark blue knee-length skirt, elegant white button-up, pantyhose and black heels with black hair in an elaborate twist pulled together with blue ribbons, with makeup that made her eyes look lighter than they were, was walking through the university's halls.

It was what she had been able to get with the money from her half-time job. It had been necessary to make some sacrifices in regard to her meals and transport, but she believed it was worth it. The difference wasn't great, but it was a good start.

"Good morning, are you new here?" someone asked her.

When Xochitl turned to her left she could see a gal about her age, dressed and adorned in the same way as the girls the black-haired young woman had seen her first day; there was even the possibility of her being one of those same women, though she didn't seem to recognize Xochitl.

<It's incredible how much a person's attitude can change once they see you dressed like them...> Xochitl thought with a mix of annoyance and irony.

"Excuse me, my name is Mireya Valverde," the other girl introduced herself, offering her hand. "I'm new, and you?"

"Me too," Xochitl finally answered. "My name is X..." The decision was made in an instant, without allowing herself to think much about it. "Fiore, my name is Fiore."

And that's how it had all begun; the fake name, the clothes, the lies. She managed to finish high-school in a year, and then the Language Center in the Southeast made her an offer she couldn't turn down, an exchange, the possibility of learning a language if she were to teach another. That lasted a year. It had been in Yucatan, spending so much time among all kinds of people, many of them foreigners or of foreign descent, where she'd begun to create her new persona. Back in Mexico City she had entered University and at the end of the summer had stopped working altogether. She met Jessica during the orientation and she always insisted on paying for everything, claiming that's what the money was for. And when she'd offered up her home for them to live together that had simplified things a lot for Fiore. She didn't need to pay tuition, thanks to the fact that she had a full scholarship, and the money she'd saved was enough for any other possible expense.

Fiore's line of thought was interrupted harshly when she felt two small arms grasp her waist, not quite managing to envelope her completely.

"Mommy Flower *is back*," the little one declared with a big smile that marked the dimples in her cheeks.

Mommy Flower... those were the only two words the girl had learned to say in English, and only because she didn't seem to be able to pronounce Fiore.

"*Yes baby... I'm back*," the woman assured her as she scooped her up into her arms and smiled just as brightly.

Yes... that little one made everything worth it. A smile from Rose was enough to make the young black-haired woman's day, because to her there were no Xochitl, or Fiore... only Flower.

It was Friday, four days since Fiore had met Rose and decided to take care of her. Everyone around her had the belief that Fiore had been registered as guardian until the DIF found a more permanent situation for her, either her family or an orphanage with space; no one knew that Fiore had never reported Rose, nor did she plan to. She knew the situation couldn't go on forever, and not only because sooner or later someone would force her hand, probably Jessica. There had been certain difficulties, as was to be expected; it wouldn't be easy for anyone to take care of herself, a child and not neglect school, but Fiore did not regret the decision she'd taken.

Fiore had her reasons for the decision she'd made. The easiest to explain was that she knew how unlikely it was that the DIF would be able to do anything to help the little one. But that was only the simple reason, the one Fiore had prepared in case anyone were to ask for explanations. Truth was there was something about the child that made it impossible for Fiore to even think about leaving her. As if some kind of power pushed her to keep Rose with her. It wasn't normal, but Fiore knew that the little girl was more than she seemed. Besides, it was clear that Rose felt the same, that connection, that need to remain together; it was the reason why she'd taken to Fiore so quickly, even calling her Mommy… something that would never stop both marveling and terrifying Fiore at the same time.

Considering that on Friday she finished her classes a bit early, and that she hadn't seen Lily and Chris in over a week, Fiore decided it was a good day to pay them a visit. It was also an opportunity for them to meet Rose. She had to take the subway, a bus, cross several streets very carefully for Rose's own good, while at the same time explaining to her everything she had to do: like looking to both sides of a road before crossing, using footbridges when they were available, being careful of cars that may be going too fast, and many other things.

Fiore was aware of several people looking at her oddly because she was always speaking Nahuatl, but she simply ignored them, keeping her whole attention on Rose.

Finally, they arrived at the right building and Fiore took the little one by the hand all the way to the apartment door on the fourth floor. The bell rang and almost a minute later the door was opened, Chris behind it.

"Hey Flower," he greeted her happily. "Long time no see. How have you been?"

"Marvelous Chris," she answered with a smile. "How about you and Lils?"

"Great as well," Chris nodded. "A bit bored even, honestly. But I'm being rude, come in, come in."

"Thanks." Fiore smiled before adding: *"Come on Rosie."*

It was until that moment that Chris noticed the little one in a white pleated skirt, light-colored flower-printed top, pink shoes, a sweater in the same color and a simple white headband, who seemed to be trying to hide behind the black-haired young woman.

"I'll explain inside," Fiore assured him.

Chris just nodded and urged them in with a wave of his hand.

"Hey Lils!" he called as he guided the two dark haired girls into the sitting-room. "Come and see who's come visit us!"

"Who...?" Lily began, stepping out of her kitchen, her casual clothes covered by an apron. "Flower! I'm so happy to see you."

"I'm happy to see you too Lils," Fiore replied.

And then Lily noticed the kid.

"And who's this munchkin?" Lily inquired, crouching to be more at the girl's height.

"Her name is Rose," Fiore explained, "and she only speaks Nahuatl." She turned her attention to the little girl. "*Rose, baby, say hello. These are Lily and Chris, very good friends of mine.*"

"*Friends of* Mommy Flower?" the child inquired.

"Mommy Flower?" Chris repeated, between surprised and confused.

"*Yes Rosie, they're my friends,*" Fiore assured her with a warm smile. "*And they'll be your friends too if you want.*"

"*I want,*" Rose nodded with obvious enthusiasm, running to stand before the two young adults, dipping her head slightly as she introduced herself. "*Rose, to serve you and God.*"

The two young adults' surprise was great when they heard the child introduce herself with those words, and a perfect intonation, almost as if she were an adult in a small body and not a little one of barely five years old or so; even then, nothing could compare with Fiore's expression of total stupefaction. It reminded her so much of the way her own grandmother had taught her to introduce herself, once, seemingly so long ago.

"*It's a pleasure to meet you, little miss. A friend of Flower's is a friend of ours.*" Chris was the first to recover, speaking to Rose in perfect Nahuatl.

"*Chris is right Rosie,*" Lily added, pulling herself together instantly and speaking Nahuatl as well. "*All of Flower's friends are our friends as well.*"

Rose smiled brightly, a smile that seemed to illuminate the room.

"*I'm making some cookies,*" Lily commented then with a small smile directed at the child. "*How about you help me?*"

Excited, the little girl immediately followed the short-haired girl into the kitchen, where the ingredients awaited them.

"Why don't you take a seat?" Chris offered Fiore.

"I didn't know you and Lily spoke Nahuatl," Fiore commented as she sat.

"It's from my father's side," Chris explained, shrugging a bit, as if giving the whole thing little importance. "His family is indigenous. Koli, my grandfather taught me Nahuatl when I was little. Lily… she said she learned the basics when she was little, and I helped her perfect it shortly after we met, when she wanted something with which to distract herself…" He trailed off, he'd been about to say something private. "I suppose she has a gift for languages."

Fiore of course noticed that Chris was holding back, avoiding saying something, something big, but chose not to comment on it. As much as a part of her might hurt at the lack of trust, she didn't feel with the right to dig, she herself had kept a secret for a good while, after all.

Fiore was still half lost in her own thoughts when she felt Rose's little arms hugging her legs. The young woman's response was automatic, as she took the child in her arms, pulling her to her lap to better hug her.

"*My child…*" she whispered into the girl's ear. "*Don't worry little one, mommy Flower is alright. I will always be alright with you.*"

It took a while, but eventually the cookies were ready. Chris insisted on some hot chocolate to go with them, a discovery that seemed to fascinate Rose, who apparently had only drunk juices, teas, and water until then. And so, between jokes and stories exaggerated to comical extents in order to entertain one another, they passed the time. Eventually, Rose fell asleep with her head on Fiore's lap, her feet against Lily, it was then when the three young adults began talking seriously in Spanish.

"Who's this kid really Flower?" Lily inquired, completely serious.

"My daughter," Fiore reiterated. "At least for now."

She explained with as much detail as possible what had happened the day she'd met the little girl in the park. Then she took a few minutes to focus on her chocolate, giving her friends time to process it all.

"You told the cab driver that you'd take her to the DIF the next day... but you never did." Chris was the first to comment. "Why?"

"Because it'd have been pointless," Fiore answered honestly. "Rose won't be in any database, not from the DIF, or anyone else's. Her parents probably won't be either, whoever they might be."

"You sound very sure." Chris arched a brow, curious.

"I was the same," the black-haired gal explained calmly. "When I arrived at the capital I had no papers, not even a birth certificate. I still remember when I went to register for school. They ask me for my CURP and I'd no idea what they were talking about. I had to go to the civil registry and spend hours filling papers and answering questions. That's how I got the necessary papers."

"You had nothing?" Lily still couldn't believe it. "Nothing at all?"

"No," Fiore shook her head. "They're not necessary in the village. We're so few... everyone knows everybody else, and most never leave the town. I don't know if I've mentioned this before, but the place I come from... it doesn't have a name, at least not one outside of the legends some of the old ladies love to tell everyone, and you can't find it on any map. Someone I knew once said you can only get to it if you know it's there, otherwise you'd pass right by it without even knowing."

An insanity that all three would probably declare an exaggeration and fantasy if it weren't for everything they'd already seen up to that moment. After elements, flowers, shades and magic, the idea of a little village somehow existing outside of the perception of most people wasn't that hard to accept.

"Then you didn't take her to the authorities because that wouldn't work, how can we help her then?" Chris wanted to know.

"I've no idea." Fiore ran a hand through her head, paying no heed to the fact that such actions undid her curls, each time she cared less and less about such details. "This goes beyond my belief of them being unable to help her, or not wanting her to end up in an orphanage or something like that. An instinct is telling me that she needs to stay with me, that I have to take care of her. That I'm the only one… the only one who can help." She exhaled loudly. "It's complete madness, I know."

"I don't think it is," Lily assured her, tilting her head to a side as she seemed to contemplate something. "Flower… I don't know if you've noticed but this little one…"

"I know," Fiore interrupted her softly, before placing a little kiss of Rose's brow. "She's special, as much as us, perhaps even more."

The night had fallen already when Fiore took the subway back to the penthouse. Chris and Lily had offered her to stay, but Fiore hadn't wanted to inconvenience them. Besides, the last thing she needed was Jessica interrogating her over her absence, again.

She'd just stepped off the subway when the sleepy Rose seemed to react, holding with all her strength to the legs of the young woman taking her by the hand.

"*Rosie…*" she didn't understand what was making her act like that.

Before she could ask what was going on a noise interrupted them, it was something odd, the sound of an animal, part mewl, part growl, except Fiore did not believe dogs mewled or cats growled. There was the possibility that it was both animals, fighting somewhere relatively close, it was a possibility Fiore did not like. Especially considering Rose's reaction to the noise, clinging with all the strength in her small body, practically shaking in fear.

"*Easy...*" Fiore didn't even need to think about it, she scooped the girl up, cradling her against her chest. "*You have nothing to fear. It's just dogs and cats fighting in some alley. No one's going to hurt you.*"

"*You promise* Mommy Flower?" the little one inquired, and in her eyes the young woman saw something she could only define as authentic fear.

"*I promise.*" Fiore didn't even doubt.

She'd do whatever was necessary to protect the little girl, anything.

Meanwhile, in a small wooden house outside the city, a very peculiar meeting was taking place. Two women were together in the room, illuminated solely by candle-light. The first woman was of advanced age, with her skin darkened by the sun and wrinkled by age, her hair completely white in a long braid, dressed in a robe made of dyed manta with tiny white flowers embroidered in the hem. She was sitting on a rocking chair in the center of the room, observing the second woman, younger, with dark eyes, dark hair to her shoulders in a wide, pale-pink skirt, an off-white blouse with tiny flowers the same color of the skirt embroidered around the neckline and the elbow-length sleeves; she was beside a window, under the light of the moon, in a wheelchair.

The silence was broken by an animal noise, a mix of a dog-like growl and a cat-like mewl... except they both seemed to flow together, as if they were the same sound, coming from a single animal...

"*You hear them?*" the older woman inquired.

"*Clearly,*" the younger one replied without taking her eyes off the outside, the hills in the distance. "*The beasts have gone, they're on the hunt for the 'most beautiful flower'...*"

"*You're planning something...*" It wasn't a question and the tone of voice made it evident how much the elder woman disapproved of the idea.

"*It's necessary,*" the one on the wheelchair replied. "*I must go to the city. If the cardinal points remain ununited they won't be able to protect the Enchantress as they ought to. We cannot risk losing her, not now.*"

"*And you think you alone can make the difference? You really believe you have the strength to stop those beasts Camellia? We've already lost so much...*"

"*I know exactly what we've lost mother, I see it when I look at myself every day.*" Her hand closed tight into a fist, pressing against a leg that couldn't feel the contact. "*I don't know how much of a difference I can make, but I will not stand back. We've spent too long hiding, waiting for others to end this war for us and that's not fair, not for them, and not for us. We're a part of this too...*"

The old woman's eyes narrowed, but she said nothing more about it. She'd spent years protecting her daughter as much as possible, fearing she'd lose her just like she'd lost her husband, like others had lost their loved ones, entire families had been lost... but she couldn't forbid her from going down the path she herself had chosen. And who knew? Maybe that was how it was supposed to be.

Camellia seemed to understand where her mother's thoughts had gone, she smiled at her once, placing a hand on the old lady's wrinkled cheek, placing a kiss on that same cheek before extending the hand a little more to take the wooden box on the small table beside the rocking chair.

There were no words of farewell, they weren't needed, Camellia just nodded one more time and rolled herself out of the room, and the cabin, the beautiful carved wooden box on her lap. She had a trip to go onto, her destiny awaited her...

Chapter 12
Mistletoe

In a room softly lit by the light of several torches placed in strategic locations, a group of people had reunited. They all wore modern clothing in different colors and styles, though mostly casual; the only thing they had in common was the rebozo all women wore, a hand-span in width, in diverse colors; they used it either around their waists as some kind of sash, around their neck as a scarf or behind their back and around their elbows, which was the most traditional manner; the men all wore a leather band with a design engraved either around their wrists or high on their arms. The only exception was the young woman in the center of the room, her rebozo was wider and longer than anyone else's, and she used it as a shawl.

"I've called you here today because we must prepare," she announced seriously, as the leader she was to those present. "The powers that had remained asleep have now awoken. We must stop them."

"Why us?" a female voice asked from the crowd.

"Because that's why we've gathered, not only tonight, but ever since our group was created," the leader declared, not upset in the least. "Or will you tell me there were other reasons that brought you to us Poppy?"

The Poppy did not insist.

"But why us?" it was a man who insisted then. "Didn't the prophecies speak also of another power that would come solve this?"

"That's right," the leader nodded. "But as long as they continue with their inner conflict they will be unable to fulfill the divine duty they've been tasked with; and things are getting out of control." She shook her head emphatically. "No… truth is that this problem began years ago, and it's impossible to be sure that they will be enough to stop it this time; particularly while there's no harmony between them. No, we must act now, be strong and decisive; demonstrate that we will not allow he who claims to be king and god to rule over our lands again. That's how it's been decided, and that's how it shall be done."

"That's how it shall be done!" The rest of those present echoed.

The torches went off in an instant, plunging the room into darkness and marking the end of that little and mysterious meeting.

It was instinct, more than any noise, that woke up Fiore. Though once awake she couldn't help but hear the tiny whimpers coming from the other side of the bed. The sound and noticing who it was coming from was more effective than a bucket of freezing water to make her wake up fully.

"*Rose?*" Fiore called immediately. "*Rosie? Baby are you okay?*"

"*Mommy!*" the girl shrieked, waking up.

The moment her eyes opened, the little one threw herself into Fiore's arms, bawling.

"*Everything's alright baby, everything's fine,*" she assured the child.

"*No mommy, the monsters want to eat me!*" Rose replied.

"*Monsters?*" Fiore wasn't expecting that. "*It was just a dream, little one.*"

"*A dream?*"

"*A nightmare. You're here with me. And there are no monsters here, we're safe. Go back to sleep, I'll be here with you.*"

It took a while, but eventually Rose went back to sleep. Fiore waited until she was sure she wouldn't wake up, then she stood from the bed and without thinking about it put on the house-robe over her pajamas and, with her feet still bare, stepped out of the room. She found Jessica standing at her bedroom door.

"What the hell was all that racket Fi?" the redhead demanded.

"I'm sorry Jess," Fiore ran a hand through her hair, wishing she could ignore Jessica, all while knowing that wasn't an option. "It was just a nightmare."

"That wasn't 'just' anything Fi," Jessica insisted.

"It won't happen again, I promise," Fiore assured her. "Now, if you don't mind I'm going to fix myself a cup of tea..." She'd taken a few steps when she looked over her shoulder. "Do you want anything?"

"No... you go," Jess waved her hand in a simile of goodbye.

Fiore just shrugged and made her way down the stairs. She didn't notice the way Jessica's eyes remained fixed on her as she did, or more precisely, on her long, straight hair...

The week was total madness, with final evaluations. Most consisted on essays and papers fortunately; though even that could be a lot of work, especially when the fights against the shades had delayed Fiore more than planned. And then there were Rose's nightmares. They hadn't stopped since that first night. Ever since, it was common for her to wake up whimpering a few times in the middle of the night. Her nightmares were always the same, exactly like the first night. Fiore tried everything to help her, reassuring her that it was just a nightmare, that she'd protect her... she'd have liked to tell her monsters didn't exist, but she regretfully knew that would be a lie.

On Friday afternoon Lily offered to take care of the child, she could see how exhausted Flower was, and she still had to study for her final exam: Her French test the following morning. Rose was very excited about going to a 'pajama party' with the friends of Mommy Flower. Fiore for her part felt bad about not being able to do something to help Rose, but she had to keep her grades up, keep her scholarship, otherwise she wouldn't be able to graduate.

She barely slept on Friday night, but at least she was prepared for the exam. It was long, and hard, and Fiore really hated French. A part of her wondered what she'd been thinking exactly when she decided it was a good idea to take that as her language elective. The exam lasted two hours and Fiore, like most of the students in that class, chose to stay in campus for an extra hour as they awaited results, which were promptly posted on a board beside the classroom door.

Fiore exhaled in relief when seeing her results, 85%, not her best mark, but it was enough to pass the class. With that finished she had no more classes. The campus would be open for an additional week, for those who needed to present extraordinary exams, or wanted to clarify a grade. Fiore had no need of the first, nor interest in the second, which meant she was officially free. The next semester wouldn't begin until February, which meant she had the next six weeks free...

"Fi!" Jessica called her right then. "All good?"

"Yes, of course," Fiore answered almost automatically, wondering what Jessica was doing there, she had no more exams, nor any interest in changing grades.

"Then your daddy gave you permission already?" she asked then.

The confusion must have shown on the black-haired gal's face, because Jessica rolled her eyes before elaborating:

"The trip to France?"

The trip to France... Fiore had completely forgotten about the trip to France. Ever since she'd met her, Jessica had always talked about the beautiful property her father's family owned in Lyon, the perfect house, the vineyard... she always talked about taking Fiore to see it. Finally, at the start of the semester they'd gone from a mere idea to an actual invitation. If Fiore could get permission they'd spend the Winter break in the Favre house in Lyon... of course, that plan had been made before her grandmother had passed away, before people like Lily and Chris had entered her life, the shades, the magic, Rose...

Fiore had totally forgotten that journey, and truth was, even if she hadn't forgotten, she simply couldn't imagine herself making the trip, not right now. Not with everything going on. For so many years she had wanted nothing more than an opportunity to see the world, or at least a part of the world beyond her country... but not like this.

"Fi!" Jessica exclaimed. "Tell me!"

"I'm afraid I won't be able to go with you Jess," she finally said.

"But your daddy said that if you passed all the classes he'd let you go," Jessica whined, obviously upset about the change in plans.

"I know but... things have changed," Fiore exhaled, trying to think of something to say, without having to explain the truth. "My grandmother... things aren't good right now Jess."

"Fiore! We've been planning this trip the whole semester. Months!"

"I know Jess, I know. I don't like this anymore than you do. Believe me. It's just that... it's not a good time. I can't leave the country now; my family needs me."

The young woman knew that at some point Jessica would probably find out the truth, at least as far as the lies concerning Fiore's origins and family were concerned; but she couldn't worry about such things in that moment. And what she'd just said wasn't actually a lie. Rose needed her, Rosie was family.

For a moment it seemed like Jessica was going to say something more, but in the end, she kept it to herself; instead of talking she simply got into Rick's car, who was waiting for her, and they both left. A part of Fiore wondered if that was the last time she'd see the one she'd once considered her best friend. Although, could one consider another as such when that person didn't even know her real name?

The young woman chose to try not to think further about it. She still wasn't sure what she'd be doing the following six weeks, one thing was for sure though, unless by some miracle she found Rose's parents and gave her back in that time, she wouldn't be going back to live with Jessica; even then she probably wouldn't.

She didn't even stop to regret her and Rick's departure, them not taking her with, in the last few weeks she'd grown used to it. So, she simply crossed the campus on foot and left the university in route to the subway station. The last thing she expected was meeting none other than Draco Yao Tamay in the middle of the park a block away from campus.

"Mr. Yao!" Fiore exclaimed, completely surprised to see him.

Draco said not a word, just observed her in silence, an eyebrow raised, waiting for something.

"Oh! Draco!" she corrected herself with a little smile.

"Miss Fiore," he replied with an elegant inclination of the head.

"Just Fiore," she corrected him, smiling and inclining her own head.

"Would you like to walk with me?" he asked suddenly, offering her his arm.

A part of Fiore couldn't help but think about how odd the whole exchange was, and not just for the old-fashioned factor of it all. Though she chose not to focus on that. Draco was just being kind, after all, and she could appreciate the attention he gave her, so she accepted his arm and the two began a slow stroll around the park.

"Wasn't expecting to see you here," the girl admitted after a while. "Did you have any exams today?"

"No," he shook his head. "I'm only here for my research, I've finished the rest of my studies, so I actually don't have any exams to do, just my thesis."

"I see," she nodded. "And how's that going?" She contemplated something before adding. "To tell the truth, I don't even know what's the topic of your thesis."

"Identity," the young man answered seriously. "The way the national and cultural identity of a society shapes an individual… It's something fascinating, especially in a country with a society as varied as ours."

Professor Solis came to Fiore's mind without her being able to help it. And not just him, but the fact that the comments made by him that had once seemed funny to her, she'd begun seeing like what they really were, words of disdain, insults. She wondered if she was changing, perhaps due to everything she'd lived through recently, or maybe it was just that she hadn't dared to express her discontent before. Even in that moment she hadn't said anything openly, though most of her classmates had noticed she didn't support the professor like she used to.

"Have you considered the influence certain individuals in positions of authority may have during the formation of someone's national and cultural identity?"

"Of course," he assured her. "The topic is very wide, and I've had to limit the specifications of my study repeatedly so as not to try and cover more than I can honestly handle. It's still a very interesting topic."

"I've no doubt."

They talked a little more about Draco's thesis, Fiore's works. She felt quite comfortable talking to him, like she had with no one else, not even with Lily. Even then, it took her completely by surprise when he changed the conversation.

"You know?" he said. "Ever since I came to the city I've been hearing all kinds of rumors, about all sorts of things. The most interesting, are about you."

"Really?" Fiore had no idea what else to say.

"Really," the man nodded. "There are so many people in campus convinced about things related to you, some completely incompatible."

"Like what?" she couldn't help the almost defensive tone in her voice.

"The conviction that you're Italian, and at the same time one of your parents is indigenous and has taught you Nahuatl."

"One thing does not exclude the other. It's very possible that I'm Italian and my mother indigene and she taught me the language."

"But that's not it, is it?"

Fiore didn't even think about it:

"People tend to assume things, and I've never been interested in clarifying my personal life. My family, my past, are none of their business."

"That's very true," he admitted. "I'm curious about something else, the Indian girl you're taking care of."

"Rose?" Fiore's voice turned abruptly cold. "What does she have to do with any of this?"

"I don't seek to do harm," Draco assured her. "To you or the little one. I'm only curious about how you ended up as her guardian."

"I was the one who found her," Fiore answered, still defensive. "Promised I'd take care of her until I could reunite her with her family."

Fiore knew she was being somewhat vague, but that was intentional, the last thing she needed was someone pointing out the fact that she hadn't taken the girl to the DIF, or some orphanage or even a hospital. Lily and Chris had understood her logic, at least enough not to argue with her actions, she couldn't say the same about someone like Draco.

"I think it's very brave," the young man surprised her with his next words. "Making yourself responsible of a little girl, taking care of her, guiding her… it must not be easy."

"To tell you the truth, it hasn't been as hard as I thought it'd be," Fiore admitted, her expression softening a bit. "Rose is very well behaved, a sweetheart really."

"Had you looked after kids before?"

"Never, I'm an only child, grew up alone. The only cousin I have lived in another town, haven't seen her since I was really little."

"Ah… I'm an only child too. My godmother had kids, I consider them my cousins, but we were never too close. Truth is I've never felt any important bond to anyone in my whole life… Not since the death of my parents. I know some people have tried to connect with me, but I simply cannot help but feel like I'm…"

"Alone even when surrounded by a sea of people," she finished.

"Exactly."

Images crossed Fiore's mind. She, at six years of age, and then again at 23, standing before graves, dressed in white, with a veil over her head, surrounded by people, and completely alone… Except it hadn't always been like that. The first time, when she'd been six, she hadn't been alone, not at first. He had been there… Until they'd taken him away, it had been then that the loneliness began.

"Fiore?"

The young woman blinked at the sound of her name. She couldn't help but notice how lost in her own thoughts she'd been, embarrassed by what her friend might think about it. She opened her mouth to apologize, and it was then that she noticed how close they were. She didn't know if it had been her, or him, but in that moment, they were so close. She could feel the heat of his body, could almost feel his breath. Without even stopping to think about it she closed the distance a bit more, their lips were almost brushing… and then Draco stepped back.

Fiore froze abruptly. Draco's distance making her react with a flinch, she almost felt as if someone had dumped a bucket of iced water over her head.

"I'm sorry," he apologized, extending a hand to take hers.

"No, I..." It was Fiore who gave a step back then, keeping him from touching her. "It was my fault. I shouldn't have presumed."

"It wasn't your fault Fiore," he assured her, though fortunately he didn't try again to touch her. "I didn't mean to offend you, and I take no offense. It's just… It wouldn't be fair for me to take advantage in such a way."

Fiore really didn't understand… she was the one to almost kiss him, that wasn't what she'd consider taking advantage, at least not on his part.

"It's not that I don't want to kiss you," he assured her. "You're a very beautiful woman, and I really wish I could, but it wouldn't be fair to either of us."

"I don't understand," she finally admitted.

"I made a promise to someone a long time ago… I can't break it."

"A promise? What kind of promise?"

"On my honor, I suppose. I'm a man of my word. I will not forsake my promise, will not betray her, or disrespect you, beginning something I know I won't be able to see through. It wouldn't be fair to either of us."

"No… it wouldn't..."

Cold. Fiore suddenly felt very cold, and she didn't even know why. Only one thing she was sure of, she needed to get away from Draco, and fast.

"I have to go," she announced suddenly.

"Fiore?" Draco obviously wasn't expecting that.

"They're expecting me at home and I'm late already," she explained, forcing herself to keep her composure as she made her way to the edge of the park.

"Fiore, if I've offended you..."

"Not at all Draco. Maybe I'm the one who should apologize, I never wanted to push you into breaking a promise... I know how important they can be."

A bright object falls, shattering into a thousand pieces, with the sound of glass breaking and it's as if someone has just buried their fist into her chest and pulled her heart out whole, still beating.

Fiore ignored Draco's voice calling her, a hand holding tightly onto the pendant underneath her blouse, walking as fast as she could, fighting to ignore the tears pooling in her eyes. She didn't even know why the rejection had affected her so much. Men had turned her down before, it wasn't common, but neither was it a complete novelty, and it wasn't as if she was dying out of love for him, that was completely illogical. She and Draco barely knew each other at all! There was no reason for her to react so intensely to his rejection, no reason at all... no...

Chapter 13
Lily of the Valley

By the time she stepped off the subway Fiore had managed to convince herself that she must be hormonal, sick or something like that. It was the only logical reason to have reacted in such an exaggerated manner to a man refusing to kiss her. It wasn't important, she could forget about the whole thing. She wasn't sure who she was trying to convince.

She was about to leave the station when a voice called her attention:

"Mommy Flower!" It was Rose.

Fiore couldn't help it, the moment she heard that little voice her whole face lit up, anything else she might have been thinking about before disappeared.

A second later, a groan like that of metal under too much pressure preceded the sound of glass breaking into pieces at the same time several lights seemed to blow up without any apparent reason... no reason except that which Fiore could feel... and she wasn't the only one. Her eyes met Lily's, who was standing beside Rose, holding the child's hand, they were both sensing the same thing.

"Run!" they both yelled at the same time.

The people, who'd been quite frightened with the lights popping and sending the room into darkness, went into absolute panic right then, they all began running, trying to abandon the station as fast as possible. Lily, understanding what was coming, took Rose in her arms and pressed herself to the closest column, protecting the girl in between the concrete and her body to make sure the mob wouldn't hurt her. Fiore let the people push her until she was as close as possible to Rose; that made it difficult to get out of it once she got to where she wanted to be, but it took no time for her to notice that if she touched people and asked them to leave her alone, they did. Even amid the panic and madness there was something about her, in her voice, that persuaded people to listening to her. She'd no idea where it came from but chose simply to take advantage of it to get to Lily and Rose.

She'd barely managed to get to them when a piece of concrete from the ceiling fell but a few feet from them. The girls couldn't help but jump.

"Where's Chris?" Fiore asked, right then noticing the absence.

"In the Mall," Lily answered, signaling vaguely in the right direction. "We thought it was perfect, I'd come get you and then we could all have dinner together, maybe catch a movie... Rosie insisted on coming with me. We never thought there would be an attack."

They hadn't thought about it in the strictest sense; but if they were honest, they'd both known it was only a matter of time before such an attack took place. No way were the shades going to give up, and the other six gifted individuals did not have Fiore's ability to free them. Fiore knew the battle wasn't going to be easy, but what she truly regretted was Rose being there. She'd promised herself to protect the child and now she was the cause of her being at risk.

"We need to deal with this and we need to be fast," Fiore declared, forcing herself to focus on what was going on. The rest could wait. "With all the people that fled it will take no time for the police to come. We can't risk being discovered."

Lily just nodded once, passed the girl to her, before throwing herself into combat.

It took nearly ten minutes for Chris to arrive. The ten longest minutes of Fiore's life who, with Rose in her arms, couldn't help Lily in the battle, instead all her concentration went into keeping the girl and herself safe.

There were at least a dozen shades, the place was small and with only two people capable of fighting... They weren't prepared for something like that.

The sound Lily's body made as it crashed against a column, cracking the concrete, was horrific, same as Rose's shrill cry at seeing her friend fall unconscious to the ground. The little one didn't even think about it, she ran towards Lily; Fiore, terrified, screamed her name as she ran after her.

"Fiore look out!" she vaguely heard Chris call out behind her.

Her reaction was instinctive: the moment she reached her little girl and the unconscious Lily, Fiore dropped on one knee, spun on it and raised both arms while invoking a shield to protect all three of them. It didn't last long, but it was enough to shield them from attack.

Chris threw himself against the shade who had attacked her, attracting its attention. He was doing the impossible, but it was obvious that he alone couldn't handle so many opponents.

It was then Fiore noticed it, almost without thinking about it, a hint of green... They were perilously close to the subway tracks; Fiore had no idea when the next one might come, but that didn't change the fact that it was dangerous. And the green... the green was coming from beneath the platform, plants... creeper vines! Suddenly Fiore had an idea.

"Chris!" she yelled as the plan took form in her mind. "Try to guide as many shades as you can towards the tracks."

"You expect the subway to come and run them over or what?" Chris replied even as he began trying to do exactly that.

A nearly hysterical laugh escaped Fiore's lips, but she chose to ignore that, instead she laid down on the floor, close to the edge of the platform, taking hold of the vines with both hands, she closed her eyes and concentrated. Images ran through her mind: empty graves filling with flowers, dried gardens blooming again, a white rose in a glass in her night table, still fresh even after more than a week...

The effect wasn't fully evident at first. Not until one of the shades tried to take advantage of Chris's blind spot to kick him and found it impossible, as its leg was being held by a creeper that kept growing.

Fiore used the energy to make the vines grow, and to guide them into doing exactly what she wanted. She'd no idea how it was working, but it was, and that was what mattered.

When Chris discovered that the number of enemies was dropping and why, that seemed to give him a second wind, realizing that not all was lost, there was still a way to win the battle.

Soon the battle ended, they managed it somehow, it wasn't easy, but they did. The moment the creeper touched the last shade, they all changed abruptly, in the same way they were used to. The good thing was that once they changed their looks they no longer attacked, so Fiore could let go of the vines and turn her focus to the liberation spell. Chris kept an eye on the situation until he was sure Flower had everything under control, then he ran to his partner, who was beginning to wake up.

Fiore smiled to herself when the last souls disappeared in a haze of light, satisfied to have given them the peace they'd so been lacking for more years that she could safely count. She turned in time to see Chris helping Lily stand, but before being able to give a single step, she lost consciousness.

Lily blinked several times, trying to remember where she was and why, especially once she noticed that she was half-sprawled against a column. The attack of vertigo she got when she sat up abruptly almost made her throw up, and when she brought a hand to her head she felt dampness there. She looked at her hand and found it bloodied, the blood was in her hair; the strange part was that when she pressed her head, even searching with her fingers, she couldn't find any wound.

The worry increased when she noticed Rosie beside her, curled up with her head in Lily's lap, seemingly asleep. Before the amber-eyed girl could say a single word, Chris was kneeling by her side, hands extended; he didn't seem to know what to do.

"Elena!" he cried out, relieved and worried to see her so bloody.

"I'm alright," she assured him softly.

"You have blood on your head," Chris pointed out, fear evident in his eyes.

Lily couldn't help it, she turned to look over her shoulder, searching for the blood, all she managed to see was a slight reddish stain on the back of her arm, but could find nothing else. She didn't feel any pain beyond the normal after exhausting all her energy in such a difficult battle, either.

"But I'm fine," she insisted, not quite understanding everything that was going on.

Was she now healing even faster than before? She'd had time to get used to her abilities, and she knew that beyond her energy attacks, she was also faster, stronger and more agile than the average person her age, Chris too. Suddenly healing of her injuries, however, to the point of there being no trace left, was something new. Could it have something to do with Flower's presence or...?

Lily's thoughts were abruptly interrupted when she felt the presences that had just invaded the area. She and Chris raised their heads at the same time... but it was already too late.

They saw six individuals moving away in a hurry, the same six they'd seen before, and one of them had the unconscious Flower in his arms.

"No!!" Lily cried out in despair. "Flower!"

She couldn't even jump to her feet, not with Rose on her lap. Even if she'd been able to, the other six were fresh, not exhausted like her and Chris, they would never catch up to them.

Chris was about to say something, horrified by the fact that those six had been able to get so close without him noticing them. They had taken his friend... and he'd done nothing to stop it. The young man hadn't noticed his hands were balled up so tight his nails were carving into his palms until Lily took hold of one, opening it carefully.

In the distance several sirens broke the silence.

"We need to get out of here," the Lily stated seriously.

"Flower..." Chris began.

"We'll get her back, but we're not going to be able to do that if the police find us here and detain us," Lily pointed out. "We need to get out of here, make sure Rose is safe. Flower will never forgive us if something happens to her. And once we're sure she'll be alright; you and I will get Flower back."

Chris knew she was right, he didn't like not going to save his friend right now, but he understood that Rose needed to be their priority and getting out of the station before the police found them. So, he gathered the child into his arms and stood.

Lily rose to her feet slowly to avoid another vertigo attack; she was exhausted due to the battle, but felt no pain, despite the blood she'd already noticed on her clothes. In the end she chose to ignore that detail and after recovering Fiore's bag from where she'd dropped it during the battle, she followed after Chris.

They both had experience avoiding authorities, and it was relatively easy for them to leave the station without the onlookers noticing them. They avoided public transport and the crowded streets, the last thing they needed was people asking questions about the blood on them or the unconscious kid. They needed to get back to the apartment, make sure Rose would be alright and then plan how they were going to find Flower exactly and get her back. There simply was no other option.

It took them two days to find Flower. The remainder of Saturday, the day of the incident, Chris and Lily had spent it in their apartment; eating, sleeping and making sure Rose would not worry over the absence of 'Mommy Flower'. On Sunday they'd managed to convince her to stay with one of their neighbors, who had three children. The neighbor in question, Rita, had accepted it, believing Rose's mother was in the hospital due to the 'horrible accident' in the subway station the day before. The authorities had no idea what had happened and while some insisted on calling it a criminal strike from one of the gangs, most did believe it had been an accident; after all the station was somewhat old. Other people had ended up in hospitals, nothing serious fortunately, but it was enough for the neighbors to buy their story and not ask too many questions.

After spending the whole day going through several neighborhoods in the capital, the couple still hadn't the slightest idea of where their friend might be. And they couldn't even track her effectively. Not when there were traces of Fiore's energy in many different parts of the city, and it wasn't even just where they'd fought before, but in a variety of parks, gardens, coffee-shops. Lily had no idea what the connection between all the spots were supposed to be, aside from the fact that Flower had been there at some point.

By the end of the day they couldn't help but conclude that if Flower didn't use her powers, they had no way to track her. Chris doubted even that, as they'd no idea how the energy from the other six might interfere with Lily's ability to track Flower, and while they'd tried it before, they couldn't follow their tracks. He didn't say that to his partner though, he didn't want to seem negative and a part of him still believed that, one way or another, they'd find Fiore.

Neither of them counted on Rose being the key.

It started that Monday morning, when the little girl declared she wanted to see her 'mom.' Lily tried to dissuade her, without admitting that they hadn't the slightest idea where her mom was. They even tried to distract her with a visit to the new rose garden that had just been opened to the public a few blocks from the apartment. Neither her nor Chris expected it when the little girl, instead of walking in the direction they had indicated, turned around and began walking the opposite direction.

"But baby, the garden is this way." Lily tried to convince her.

"I don't want flowers, I want Mommy Flower," Rose insisted in a tone that could almost be called imperious, and absolutely cute on someone her age, *"and she's this way."*

It took the two young adults several seconds to comprehend the implications. Chris was the first to recover, running to the girl and offering her his hand.

"Very well," he announced with a smile. *"Let's go then, why don't you lead us?"*

Rose gave a big smile, probably feeling pride that her friends wanted her to guide them.

It was Chris's decision to take the bikes. They were old but quite good, as he and his best friend had restored them. That had been before meeting Lily, the girl so affected by everything that had happened to her until that moment. Meeting had changed their lives, and not only because of the magic and the way it connected them, but also because they'd managed to heal each other. Lily had helped Chris finish the bikes and he had insisted on her taking the one meant for Jerry; he himself being the one to teach her how to ride it.

Chris, being the most experienced, was the one to take Rose with him, securing her against him to make sure the little one wouldn't fall off. Then they were on their way.

In an old restored house in the State of Mexico, the tension was such it could almost be cut with a knife. Belladonna and her companions had done everything to try and make Fiore 'listen to reason', but the young woman refused to give in. She hadn't said a single word since waking up in a bed of a big bedroom that seemed to have been restored in a colonial style, though it was decorated with clearly pre-Hispanic artistic pieces, or at least replicas of such.

It wasn't like Fiore was torturing herself, she ate what she was offered, walked when she got tired of sitting down, she hadn't even tried to lock herself in the room she'd been assigned, or run away; though she could have done it once she recovered her energy. She knew her friends would be worried, but she couldn't just take off, not until they'd settled matters. If she just left they'd never be able to talk things out seriously. Besides, Fiore had no doubt they would find her.

Her only sign of rebellion was her silence, no matter how many times anyone went to her, tried to convince her that they were right, she'd stay quiet, neither agreeing nor denying their declarations. The last time Belladonna had told her off for her attitude, her insistence to refuse to accept the inevitable. The woman truly believed Fiore was being childish, was fighting against the impossible… She had no idea, Fiore hadn't begun to fight just yet.

And then the bell rang.

The surprise was absolute, all seven inhabitants of the house were in the main sitting room in that moment, and they all seemed completely surprised… All except Fiore, who just observed them.

"Nobody move," Belladonna ordered after a beat of silence, "We were not expecting anybody."

"If they get no response they'll leave," Eduardo agreed with her idea.

But the bell kept ringing, for a whole minute, and then it stopped. For a moment no one said a single word, as if they were all expecting something more.

Fiore was the first who sensed it, the essence beginning to force entry. She noticed the exact moment when the others became aware of it: Hyacinth and Julian straightened abruptly, while David jumped to his feet, no doubt with the intent to investigate what was going on. Fiore knew it was the time to act, and she did.

It took a couple of seconds for the six young individuals to become aware of the fact that they couldn't move, a few more to discover why exactly. At the same time the front door was forcefully opened, the slam of the doorknob against the wall echoing throughout the house.

There was a murmur, a female voice that seemed to be giving instructions, which were promptly ignored by the little missile that shot into the room.

"Mommy Flower!" Cried out the little girl, running towards her.

"*Rosie, honey,*" Fiore dropped to her knees just in time to catch the little one in a hug. "*How have you been with Lils and Chris this whole time?*"

"*Good,*" Rose answered eagerly. "*But I missed you.*"

"*I missed you too darling,*" Fiore assured her, getting on her feet with the girl still in her arms; she switched to English when adding: "Everything OK Lily, Chris?"

Lily nodded, apparently without words as she observed the other six individuals in the sitting-room.

"And what happened here?" Chris finally asked, watching everyone up and down.

And it was that there was a very good reason why none of the other six had tried to close the door, or at least stop Lily, Chris and Rose from entering, they were all immobilized... by plants.

Fifteen minutes later they were all sitting in the living room, Lily couldn't help but let out a giggle every so often, and while Chris rolled his eyes every time she did, neither he nor Fiore tried to stop her. It was quite funny. The way Belladonna and the others had given her so much freedom, as long as it was limited to the inside of the house, never imagining she would be able to use that against them. That she could turn the plants against them... which was absolutely ridiculous, weren't they the ones who called her enchantress? The Flower Enchantress?!

"It's good to see you can defend yourself if necessary," Chris declared with satisfaction.

They were all calm, Fiore had made it quite clear how fast she could contain them all if they so much as thought about starting another fight. Though it was hard to know if that warning was what kept them settled, or the fact that Belladonna and her people were still baffled about who the girl curled up into Fiore was exactly.

"I could have gotten out of here, had it been absolutely necessary," the black-haired young woman admitted with a slight shrug. "But we need to talk, all of us, and this place is as good as any to do it."

"Talk?" Lily arched a brow at the serious tone her friend had taken. "About what?"

"About what we're doing and what we'll be doing in the future to avoid something like what happened two days ago from happening again," Fiore explained calmly.

The effect was immediate, they all began talking at the same time, each defending their actions, then condemning those of others. In little time Chris and Lily were involved in the argument too. Fiore let it go on for a couple of minutes, until Rose's little hand began clutching at her side, she could almost feel the little one's emotions in that moment, the argument was making her nervous, perhaps even afraid. It was then that she decided it had been enough.

"Silence."

There was no need for yelling or harsh hand motions. A single word, said in a solid tone, full of authority was more than enough. Silence fell.

"I'm going to ask a few questions, want you to answer them with yes or no, and only that, am I clear?" Fiore announced, still in the same tone.

"Yes." The answer was unanimous.

Strictly speaking, the questions were for all of them, but Fiore focused on Belladonna, knowing she was the leader of the group.

"You claim to be priestesses and guardians?"

"Yes."

"You claim to be followers and protectors of the Enchantress Xochiquetzal, the presumed goddess of flowers."

"Yes."

"You also claim that I'm the reincarnation of this Enchantress."

"Yes."

"That means you owe me fealty and respect. You're my subjects."

"That's right, mistress."

Fiore decided not to point out that they'd already gone against her instructions. It didn't matter...

"If so what makes you think you have the right to kidnap me? Separate me from my friends by force, while I was unconscious and them injured and exhausted after a hard battle? Not counting the fact that it was at least partly your fault that the battle got so complicated."

They looked at each other, shocked in silence, having no easy yes or no answer to give. Instead David sputtered before demanding, "And why would it be our fault?!" Clearly, he was annoyed by the accusation.

"Because it was your freaking idea to go after the shades even knowing you cannot free them," Lily spat. "You should have left the matter to Flower and us."

"Why should we care about freeing those monsters?" Magnolia inquired. "They ought to be destroyed."

"Because they're not monsters, they're innocents, trapped souls," Chris pointed out with a roll of his eyes.

"You cannot kill someone who's already dead, and you cannot destroy a soul," Fiore added. "But leaving theological matters aside. That doesn't answer why you felt you had the authority to get me out of there without my permission or my knowledge."

"Our duty is to protect you," Eduardo tried to explain.

"And my friends?" Fiore interrupted him. "The ones that were with me? The ones who understand and respect what I do? Did they not deserve help? Weren't you the ones who said you're all the same?"

"You love them more than us..." Julian said through gritted teeth.

Fiore almost laughed at that, he really sounded like a kid. Lily could barely swallow her own chuckle, probably with help from Chris nudging her.

"They're with me," Fiore pointed out. "They support me, respect me. What have you done except try and force me to be someone else, to be a symbol? You need to decide. Forget about ancient legends, about reincarnations and sacred duties. Choose for yourselves. If you want to be by my side, that means no more harassing or pressuring me; support me, respect me, be my equal. If not, then this is where we part ways. I need to know who I can count on because we cannot have something like what happened two days ago happening again. Next time it could cost someone their life."

"Why do you sometimes speak like you know who and what you are and others like you don't believe a word of what we've told you?" Hyacinth asked, curious.

"I don't know," Fiore admitted with a slight exhalation. <*Maybe it's that sometimes I've no idea who I am exactly...*> She shook her head, choosing not to reveal that part. "You don't need to decide now, take some time to think it, discuss it among yourselves."

"We're leaving," Lily added suddenly, a serious look on her face.

Fiore nodded. She'd said all that she needed to say, the next step was up to Belladonna and her people.

They were almost at the door when Eduardo called to them:

"Who's the kid?" he inquired, curious.

Fiore really wasn't in the mood to explain the whole story about Rose and how she'd ended with her; so, she gave the shorter answer:

"She's my daughter," she said simply.

She could have never imagined the revolution those words would cause.

Chapter 14
Violet

Things went well enough the following weeks. Fiore and Rose were still living in Jess's penthouse for the time being, though Fiore knew they needed to move out sooner rather than later. The problem was, she had no idea where to. Few places were even available in the area, and even the few that were, were simply too expensive for her to afford. She'd been so lucky when Jess offered for them to live together, somehow Fiore hadn't realized that before.

There had been a couple of fights against the shades, though they weren't hard at all, at some point she had become used to it all. Also, while they'd met Belladonna and her group again, there still was no reply regarding Fiore's ultimatum.

Another thing that kept happening were the animal sounds that terrified Rose. Fiore hadn't the slightest idea how to help her and the situation was stressing her out even more than the shades themselves. Those she knew how to fight, the animals... She had no idea.

It was early January now and Fiore had made a habit of taking Rose to the closest park or garden in whatever neighborhood they'd gone to check-out apartments, once they were done with that. The little girl loved that part of their outings, it didn't even matter if most parks had little more than dried grass and half-wilted flowers here and there. It didn't matter because, as they'd discovered at one point, Rose had the same gift Fiore did for restoring plants, making them bloom again. In some ways it was even greater than Fiore's own gift, as she needed there to be some kind of sprout or offshoot to make plants grow again, like she was pushing them forward. Rose, on the other hand, could fully undo any damage plants may have received. As long as there was the slightest hint of life, she could make them fully perfect again, and took great delight in doing so.

A part of Fiore wondered what others might think of what they were doing. And not just those like Chris and Lily, who knew what Fiore and Rose got up to in their free time and saw it as a simple game to keep the little girl busy. The young woman wondered what those with no ability, no magic, thought as they saw the dried-out parks and gardens in their respective communities suddenly in full bloom. It was the middle of winter and yet every blade of grass had turned green and every flower open, bright and colorful as if it were spring.

And it wasn't even just the season, most of those gardens hadn't been truly green for much longer than that, and now they were. Fiore liked to imagine that people liked it, that they might enjoy the beauty she and Rose got to share with them. Though a part of her did wonder if it might be too much, if some might find it too off-putting. Not everyone liked there to be sudden changes to their lives, even when those changes might be good.

It was probably easier in ancient times, she told herself, back when people believed in powers and those with them, when people believed in gods. Xochiquetzal, the princess Belladonna and her group were so convinced she had to be a reincarnation of, had been considered a goddess herself in ancient times, as well as a priestess and an enchantress, she'd also secretly been the intended of none other than Ce Acatl Topiltzin Quetzalcoatl. Who, himself, was a warrior, priest, king, god; all depending on the sources she chose to look up. At times it seemed completely insane to her, beyond that even. Yet there were times when a corner of her mind told her it wasn't that crazy, she had the power, after all, as did the others. So, what if there was some King out there whom she was supposed to aid? What if her own soulmate was somewhere out there, waiting, perhaps even looking, for her? Fiore wasn't sure which of those prospects terrified her the most.

It wasn't quite seven just yet, but between the smog and the clouds remaining from an earlier light rain, no sun could be seen. Fiore decided to cut their little excursion short, as they were currently in a neighborhood with few street lamps, and she just had a bad feeling about it all.

Regretfully, she didn't act on that feeling in time. She and Rose had just left the small park when the sounds began, the mix of barking and meowing and something that sounded even worse. Rose practically shrieked in fright, and while a part of Fiore wanted to stop, to go down on one knee and explain to her little charge that there was nothing to fear, that everything would be alright her gut told her it would have been a mistake, because things would not be alright. She'd no idea where that thought came from, but she was as sure of that, as she'd been the first time she'd pronounced the words of the prayer that freed the tortured souls behind the shades. So, with that in mind, she picked up Rose and began running.

She ran almost three full blocks before she accepted that running wouldn't be enough. Whatever was after them, and she knew something was, she could sense the darkness approaching, less encroaching than the shades, but no less dangerous; she couldn't outrun them. She was about to begin pounding on the closest door, hoping for someone to take pity on her and her little girl before whatever was following her caught on, when she heard a buzz, an electric door being unlocked.

At first all she could see was the front of some big office building, already closed for the day, and a couple of buildings of what looked like apartments, with the kind of doors that required special keys. And then she noticed, at the very end of one of those buildings, there was a second door, and it was just the slightest bit open. The sound of growling approaching pushed Fiore into making a split decision as she held Rose tighter, opened the door and stepped in, making sure to close it behind her.

Stairs, that was the first thing Fiore saw, at least two floors worth of them. Still, she did not move from the first step for a little while. She heard something slam against the iron door, at the same time Rose whimpered quietly into her neck. Then came the sound of something, nails? Claws? Scratching at that same door without effect. It went on for quite a while, until Fiore was quite sure there was more than one animal out there… and then came the music.

It sounded like a flute, not quite like the normal flutes she sometimes heard students in junior-high practicing with, or those that could be found in orchestras, like the one that had given a concert in the University's Auditorium once; but a flute nonetheless. Fiore found herself so entranced by the melody, that it took her almost half a minute to realize she couldn't hear any scratching or growling any more. The animals were gone. She was beginning to debate with herself whether she should try getting out, or chancing going up, when there was a slight buzz sound, and the voice of a woman came from the tiny intercom she hadn't noticed until that very moment:

"You may come up... If you wish."

Fiore would never be able to tell for sure what made her do it, but up she went.

She wasn't expecting what she found up there. The place looked so empty, not a chair in sight and barely a couple of tables, one which held a laptop computer and a vase made of beveled glass that held about half a dozen pink and white flowers. There were two doors, one was open and lead to a small kitchen with every surface lower than what was standard; the second door was closed, though Fiore assumed it lead to a bedroom or perhaps a bathroom. What was most evident though, was the lack of any person there.

It was the music that called her attention to the third door. One not made of wood, but of glass, a sliding door, fully open, leading to an open balcony lined with flowers in various pots. In the center of the balcony sat a woman in her late forties or early fifties, her hair was a very dark brown and went to her shoulders, she was wearing a wide raw manta skirt with what loosely looked like pink flowers painted here and there, her blouse was of raw manta as well, except for the pink thread edging the sleeves, neckline and bottom. She was playing what looked like a little flute made of some old wood. A haunting, almost enchanting tune.

The tune certainly seemed to have settled Rose, enough that the girl allowed Fiore to put her down rather than holding onto her as she'd been doing since the growling had begun chasing them.

Fiore took advantage of that to satisfy her curiosity, approaching the edge of the balcony, just enough to look down. They were straight above the door she had gone through, and right before it, there were four animals, moving in close circles; they were no longer scratching the door, but neither were they leaving. She noticed something else too:

"Those aren't dogs… or cats..." she muttered out-loud.

She got no answer, but there was a slight shift in tune, the animals seemed to react to it; they crouched low, as if waiting for an attack that wasn't coming. Then the music came to an end, a moment before a fistful of a red and green plant along with white flowers fell from beside Fiore and right onto the animals waiting down below. There was some more of that sound from earlier, the mix of a growl and a mewl, and then they left.

Fiore followed them with her eyes for several blocks, until they vanished in the shadows of a big office building. Then she turned, meeting the white hand that had let the assorted plants fall, it wasn't the white from foreigners, like she saw many times in the university, but more like a pale tan, like someone who's skin color is supposed to be dark, yet has spent so much time out of the sun, the color has lightened somewhat. She then followed that hand, up the arm, and to the owner. The woman's other hand was on her lap, she was still holding the flute she'd been playing, and she was looking at Fiore with an odd mix of contentment, curiosity and something very close to sadness.

"What's going on?" the questions began falling from Fiore's mouth instantly. "What were those things? What did you throw at them? Why were they after us anyway? Why did you help us? … And who are you?"

"Easy..." the woman murmured in a soft, soothing voice. "Answering your questions in order. You were being hunted; those animals weren't dogs, though I suppose you could call them cats, in a way… they're jaguars; I threw wintergreen and lemon flowers at them, to cover your scents so they might leave; I helped you because you needed help and I was in a position to give it; and my name is Camellia."

"Jaguars?!" Fiore's voice went through an octave or two as she cried out that word, it was the part that had shocked her the most. "Did they escape a zoo or..."

"No, them going after you wasn't an accident, you were being hunted," Camellia pointed out calmly.

Fiore knew all about being hunted. Except it was one thing to be hunted by shades that turned out to be tortured souls needing her help to be free... she'd no idea how she was supposed to handle being hunted by actual wild animals, jaguars... and then her mind caught something else their savior had just said:

"Camellia..." It couldn't be a coincidence that this woman had the name of a flower, not with her life being what it was, there were no coincidences for her.

"I was wondering if you'd notice," the older woman pointed out with a small smile.

"You're not going to begin calling me Mistress or anything, are you?" Fiore asked with a hint of hysteria coloring her voice. "Because my evening is freaky enough already."

"No, I will not call you that," Camellia assured her with a small chuckle. "I'd rather call you cousin."

That should have been better... it really wasn't.

"Cousin...?" Fiore had no idea what else to say to that.

"Third or maybe fourth cousin once removed, but yes, we're family to some degree," Camellia nodded. "Then again, our family was always very close, all cousins seeing one another as siblings..."

"If that is so, why am I alone? Why did I grow up with no one but my grandmother ever since the death of my parents?"

"That... is a very long story. One I'm not sure you're ready to hear."

"I wouldn't know, though something tells me that whether I'm ready or not, this is something I need to know."

"Perhaps you do," Camellia nodded, mostly to herself. "Let's go inside, shall we?"

It was until that very moment, as the brunette turned to do exactly that, that Fiore noticed she hadn't been sitting on a bench of some kind; no, she was on a wheel-chair.

Soon enough Fiore found herself sitting in one of the scant seating spots in the main room she'd arrived to first: a wooden rocking chair. Rose curled up in her lap and promptly fell asleep while Fiore carded her fingers through the little girl's hair in a rhythmic and soothing manner. Camellia disappeared into the kitchen briefly, eventually returning with a tray on her lap that held a couple of mugs with what was evidently chamomile tea, as well as some milk, lemon and honey.

"I know that most people in the village prefer to drink their tea as is, but I've always preferred mine with a splash of milk, and I've no idea of your preferences," Camellia muttered as she placed the tray on the empty coffee table, gesturing to the contents.

"I prefer it with some honey, please." Fiore inclined her head slightly.

With Rose in her lap she couldn't move enough to prepare her own tea, or even grab the mug, but Camellia seemed to have noticed that, taking care of the preparations and then handing over the cup with a cloth handkerchief so they wouldn't risk burning either of them.

"Thank you," Fiore murmured softly as she tasted the tea.

It wasn't quite as good as the one her grandmother used to prepare, but good enough nonetheless. Certainly, much better than the commercial teas she'd found in the stores; back when she first decided to go back to teas, but realized she'd need to buy the flowers and dry them herself if she wanted things to be right.

"So… family…" she breathed out eventually, not quite knowing what else to say.

"Our bloodline, young one, is very old," Camellia explained thoughtfully. "It goes back all the way to the Toltecs, a culture that preceded the Aztecs, the better known pre-Hispanic culture in our country. Their main city once stood where it's now Tula, Hidalgo. Though their territory extended around. Most of them were normal people, with no special gifts, no magic… but there were a few who were different. Women most of them, they were Lady Xochiquetzal, High Priestess of the Flower Temple, and her charges. Four girls raised by Xochiquetzal herself to be priestesses; they could influence the effectiveness of plants in healing and other less-known uses. Lord Quetzalcoatl, the King of the Toltecs, was said to have power all his own, and he also assigned four of his best warriors to serve Xochiquetzal, protecting her temple, and especially her girls. It's said that it was she, with intervention of Higher Powers, that granted them the ability to influence the elements."

As interesting as the whole thing was, Belladonna and the others had told her she was supposed to be Xochiquetzal, priestess, quasi-goddess and whatever-else, but no one before had explained who Xochiquetzal was supposed to be, or have been, exactly. Still, she had no idea what any of that had to do with their family, and Camellia seemed to be able to read that in her expression.

"It is said that when the Flower Temple and everyone in it were gone, there was one survivor, a little girl," Camellia went on. "Sometimes orphan girls would stay in the temple for a time, when no one would come forward to claim them. Most of them acted as servants in exchange for food, lodgings, clothes, and an education, eventually leaving the temple to have a life of their own. There was only one girl in the Temple at the time of its fall, and she was sent away before the battle truly began. She was taken in by some couple or another, with no children of their own; they passed her as theirs. She eventually grew and had children of her own, all daughters, all who were gifted. It was believed that Xochiquetzal herself blessed her, tasked with carrying on her power, so there would still be flower priestesses and, some believe, so one day she herself might return..."

"And this is supposed to be our bloodline?" Fiore didn't quite believe it.

"Haven't you ever wondered why we can do the things we do?" Camellia inquired. "I can hypnotize animals through my music; Cattleya can predict what's coming, not quite visions, she just knows; Calendula could heal bruises, cuts and other minor wounds."

"Cal... my mother...?" Fiore didn't know quite what to do with that information.

"The little nameless town where you and I grew up… it stands where the Flower Temple once stood. Some of us believe that's why it's not in any maps, why only those of us who've lived there can even find the place…"

"Because Xochiquetzal's magic still protects the place…"

"Exactly. The little girl… no one remembers her name anymore… her descendants and their families founded the village, after the fall of the Toltecs. They wanted a place where their gifted girls could be safe. And enough time had passed since the fall that they thought it'd be safe enough there, they were right. For over a millennium our bloodline was safe there. There were never that many of us, but that didn't matter, every generation we saw each other as sisters, regardless of how far removed we might have been. We were part of matriarchal lines, so different from the way the world around us had evolved… Most never left the town, and we were happy enough like that. Especially with the wars, of Independence, and the Revolution, it was risky to be out and about during those times." She shook her head and let out a sigh. "But anyway. There were five of us in our generation: Cattleya, Calendula, Ivy, Vervain and me. Only Cattleya and Calendula were sisters by birth. But still, we all saw each other as sisters, as family…"

"If so, why did I grow up alone with my grandmother?"

"I… I don't quite know how to explain it, except to say that something happened years ago. It began almost twenty years ago. Every few years one or two people would leave the village to travel around the country, find out more about it, and the world as a whole; so, they might bring the news back to the others still home. So, we could keep up with the changes outside our little haven. Vervain insisted on being the one to go that year… She never returned. Several more went looking for her, only one returned, with stories about beasts and monsters and being hunted. It was then that the Elders of our village decided to close it, that we were safer inside. It worked for a few years and then… then we got visitors. Vera… she was technically part of our bloodline, though she had never lived in our village. She was born overseas, and she took a European husband, had a child with him: a boy, the first boy to ever be born into our bloodline. She technically wasn't one of us, but she was coming to us, to introduce her family, she wanted to be part of the family, but she never made it. I was the one who retrieved the child from their hotel in the capital, it was so fortunate he hadn't been with them in their car when that horrible accident happened, the very same that took Calendula's life, and her husband's..."

The shock was so great Fiore couldn't speak, she could hardly breathe as images ran through her mind in quick succession. The old woman who'd informed Nana and her about the loss of her parents, the funeral, and the boy... The boy who'd stood by her as the bodies were lowered into the graves, as they were covered with dirt, as she grieved... The boy who was later taken away, leaving her all alone...

"It didn't end there," Camellia went on, either not noticing Fiore's shock or paying no mind to it. "In the following years, whenever one of us had to leave the village for whatever the reason, we'd be hunted down. It came to the point where we did not leave the borders of the village unless it was absolutely necessary, but sometimes it just couldn't be helped. Sometimes things were needed that the town just did not have... Ivy was lost to us, Cattleya lost her husband, and then decided to leave with her infant daughter. I think she found a good man, married him and took his name, hoping that would allow her and her child to escape our hunter's notice. And for my part... I was lucky enough to survive, but then again, I didn't do so whole." She was obviously referring to her paralyzed legs. "By the time you were seven Cattleya and I were the only ones left from our generation, and I was the only one in the town; though I too left eventually. Hoping to set down roots in some other place, where I might be more helpful when the time came to fight back. And from the elder generation, there was only my mother: Gardenia."

"What about Nana? Azalea?"

"She wasn't part of the bloodline, not really. She changed her name, chose a flower for herself, when Calendula married her son, but she wasn't truly of our blood. A descendant of one of the believers instead."

Fiore herself had pointed out to her Nana that she wasn't really a flower; though back then the young woman hadn't understood what that meant. The true weight of that statement, that truth. There was still so much that she didn't comprehend, like why someone, anyone had been hunting her family in the past twenty years, why then and not before, why at all. Was it the same people who were hunting her down in that moment? The shades... the jaguars... did they come just because, or was someone behind them all? She had no idea what the answer to those questions might be and had no idea how to ask them either. Camellia was exhausted, Fiore could see that much; perhaps some other day, the questions would be asked. But not that night, not yet. Enough information had been shared for the time being...

Chapter 15
Wallflower

Fiore and Rose spent a considerable amount of time visiting Camellia in the following weeks. Fiore liked learning about her family, especially her mom, all the things she didn't get to see and never dared ask her nana. Surprisingly enough, Camellia never asked about Rose; Fiore told her about looking after the girl for the time being, and the older woman just nodded, never questioning Fiore or her choices.

It was also Camellia who helped Fiore find a solution for her apartment situation. There was a building not too far from the university, where single or widowed parents all lived with their children; they were a very tight knit group and had even developed a system among themselves that allowed them to take care of the kids while keeping up with their jobs and/or school. Camellia knew a few of the families there, from either her time in college, as well as her years as first flute in the Orchestra. One of the apartments had been emptied recently, as the single father and two children had moved to Monterrey due to his job, leaving a two-bedroom apartment in the third floor empty.

It took very little time for the other families to welcome Fiore and Rose into their midst. Only one of them knew Nahuatl, and even then, she only knew the basics, but the others were willing to learn enough to communicate with the little girl. Soon enough the pair had moved in, Fiore leaving behind a letter for Jess, thanking her for everything, keys on top. It wasn't like she wouldn't see the redhead again; chances were, she would, more than once, but things were changing so much and so quickly, and Fiore knew more was coming her way. It was her last semester, and then there was Rose, and the situation with the shades, and the jaguars, and whoever might be behind them… it was insane.

Camellia had told her as much as she knew on that front, though that could mostly be summarized to the contents of some old myths and one name: Tezcatlipoca. Truth was, no one knew for sure what had happened, back in the first half of the tenth century, when first King Quetzalcoatl and later Lady Xochiquetzal had disappeared, right before the Flower Temple was razed to the ground, everyone inside lost. Legend told so many versions of the story… and most made no mention of Xochiquetzal, her temple or her followers!

So, best case scenario: some crazy psycho who had something against her bloodline, gifted people in general, or maybe just believed way too much in certain myths wanted to kill her and possibly everyone in her family. Worst case scenario: there was an actual man-god somewhere in the country, quite possibly the city, who wanted her dead, had been hunting her family in general, and herself for at least twenty years!

The only thing Camellia seemed to know nothing about, were the priestesses, Belladonna and the others, and quite possibly Lily as well. She agreed with the chance of reincarnation, though the exact individual Fiore was supposed to be reincarnation of was left unspoken; but had no idea where they'd come from exactly, in either life. Gardenia, Camellia's mother, had confirmed over the phone that there were no records of girls being born in the town with any of those names; and not just that, from all the children born in the village in the past twenty-five years, Xochitl and her cousin were the only ones to have been born to the bloodline… and if anyone remembered the name of Cattleya's daughter no one was saying, and all records seemed to have been burnt, probably for their own safety.

So many questions, not enough answers, and Fiore had no idea where she was supposed to find them.

Fiore was so distracted with everything going on in her life, she forgot completely about having to go to the university to sign up for her classes. It was probably a good thing that her tutor had called her to remind her, gave her the chance to go in on Friday. She had few classes left, as it was her last semester. She noticed that she didn't have many options with professors, unlike other terms, where she had signed up on the first day, but she didn't pay much attention to such things, it just didn't seem important, not with everything else going on; with her, Rose, Camellia, Lily, Chris, the shades, the jaguars, Belladonna and her group, legends and myths and destiny… There were things far more important for her to worry about than who would be her Foreign Relations Professor.

Things went well enough. Fiore signed up for classes, got her schedule that same afternoon, and then on Saturday she was back on the Campus's Bookstore, acquiring her books. One thing she did not expect was to meet Professor Solis there; and he wasn't alone either. He was with Professor Magdalena Lopez Nayal, she was a woman somewhere in her late forties or early fifties, with darkly tanned skin, dark eyes, long black, straight hair in a thick braid she kept pinned in a crown around her head; she usually wore a loose blouse with flowers embroidered, dress pants and low-heeled open-toed shoes. Like an odd mix of Pre-Colombian and Modern; a mixed heritage. And Fiore knew how true that was, while she'd never met the woman, she'd seen her before, during her year in Yucatan; back then the woman had been one of those teaching Mayans.

Fiore had just run her student ID card which, with her scholarship, allowed her to take the books without having to pay. She was on her way out when Professor Solis noticed her and called her over; she really didn't want to go over to him, but she didn't want to antagonize the man either, so she went.

"Miss Fiore!"

It occurred to Fiore to wonder for a moment if the man even knew her surname. He'd always referred to her as Miss Fiore. When he referred to all other students by their last name, he used her first; somehow, she'd never stopped to ponder about it before.

"Professor Solis," Fiore greeted him stiffly, before turning to greet the woman. "Professor Lopez."

"Miss… Fiore, is it?" The woman offered her hand to shake.

"That's correct," The young woman nodded, shaking the hand, before turning back to the man. "Did you need me for something sir?"

"Yes, you can help me explain to Lopez that Mexico has defeat and surrender in its blood," the man stated. "The country has it, everyone born in it has it. It's our curse… terrible and unavoidable. But Lopez refuses to accept it."

"Because it isn't true." Lopez's tone of voice showed the argument had been going for a good while, and she was growing tired of it.

For a moment Fiore considered giving a generic answer, maybe even something one of her classmates had said the last time the professor decided to bring the matter up; perhaps even a non-answer, the kind the man used to hang onto when he wanted to believe everyone agreed with him. And then Rose's image slipped into her mind, crying in terror whenever they heard the jaguars on the prowl, curling into her, knowing she was safe with Fiore… Lily, and Chris, fighting the shades, even when they were hit, and injured, and slammed against a wall, the ground, even when they were bleeding and in pain, they never gave up… she thought of Camellia in her wheelchair, moving around her floor, telling Fiore about her family, and little Rose stories of her youth, and legends of times long past… they all refused to give up. So where did Solis get the idea that they had surrender in their veins?!

"No." The black-haired woman didn't quite notice when the word slipped through her lips, not until the other two turned to look at her, both equally surprised.

"Fiore…" Solis began, and there was a hint of warning in his tone.

"I don't agree with you sir," Fiore said evenly. "I understand where you're coming from, but I do not agree."

"Everyone knows I'm right," Solis insisted. "If our country weren't cursed with defeat we wouldn't be so dependent on others to survive. Just look at the numbers, the exports vs. imports, the national debt, the number of young people who choose to go live and work in other countries rather than here; because they know there's no hope for them here!"

"That's their choice," Fiore pointed out, more serene than she expected herself to be. "If they refuse to believe in their own chances here, to go elsewhere, that's their choice. Just like it's your choice to believe as you do, and to teach others to do the same, instead of challenging them to do better, to fight for themselves and for this country. We all make our choices sir, and that's not our country's fault, or our parents' or anyone else's fault; it's no one's responsibility but our own."

"It's our culture!" Solis snapped. "The very way we have been raised!"

"Huh?" Fiore had no idea what he was talking about right then.

The student turned to look at Professor Lopez, who was rolling her eyes at Solis right then, she apparently had some idea what he was talking about; however, before she could explain, Solis was talking again.

"You just need to think about it a little, all the things we're taught in our youth," he elaborated. "Like calling adults 'mister', being supposedly respectful, saying 'excuse me' when first calling someone, instead of just saying what you need. And the whole 'at your service'... those are all crutches designed to make us less!"

"Those are just ways of being polite!" Lopez intervened, obviously annoyed. "And it's not like we're the only country who can be polite. If others choose not to be that's not on us."

"I don't understand," Fiore admitted softly, head canted to a side in contemplation. "I mean, being polite is not the same as being submissive. Just like being helpful doesn't mean being a servant. I can refer to you as sir, can ask you or another Professor, or anyone else, what you need, how I may be able to help you but that doesn't mean I'm your servant or your slave. It just means I'm nice, that I'm the kind of person who likes to help, and while that may have something to do with how I was raised, I would be the same had I been raised in this country or in any other. And it still wouldn't make me any better, or worse, than any other person, in this country, or, again, any other." She let out a breath. "It may be nice, to be able to blame something or someone for what goes wrong, but that doesn't make it right, or even true. It's just petty. It's not Mexico's fault if things don't go right, it's all our faults. Mine, and yours, everyone else's. I recognize my fault, in the things I could have done better and didn't; and you should be able to do the same. Because blaming others, or blaming everyone, for what's wrong, won't solve anything."

"You have no idea what you're talking about," Solis retorted.

"Maybe I don't… maybe I do." Fiore shrugged a bit at him; she was about to take her leave when something else occurred to her. "You've spent years giving all your classes the same spiel. Has it changed anything? Has it made things any better? I don't think so. But I wonder, what might happen if instead of making us all, yourself included, feel like we're lesser, if you tried challenging them to do better, to be better… who knows? You might even surprise yourself."

Solis didn't reply. Fiore wasn't looking at him anymore, but Lopez was, and she couldn't quite believe the expression of absolute shock in the man's face in that moment.

Magdalena Lopez had heard of Fiore before; had heard the stories, about the unofficial leader of the little clique of popular girls in the university; of the way she dressed and walked, how she lived with a rich student…She had also noticed other facts, like how no one seemed to know that she was a scholarship student, not even what her surname was, everyone knew her simply as Fiore, even the teachers. Professor Lopez had known all that, and a picture had formed in her head, of who Fiore was: the poor, popular girl who hid her past, her family, because she wanted to fit in. And with a surname like hers, Yolotl, there were at least some things that girl was keeping under wraps. It made her seem like the kind of girl who would do anything to be accepted, the kind who never stood for herself out of fear of being rejected, and yet that wasn't the kind of girl, the kind of woman, that had stood before her just seconds before. Who'd disagreed with Francisco Solis in the middle of the university's bookstore, before dozens of people, who'd countered every single one of his arguments, and then even went as far as challenging him to change. Lopez wondered if she had really judged Fiore Yolotl so wrongly, if everyone in the school had, or if something had changed recently. She had no idea…

Fiore had no idea what made her say all the things she did in the bookstore, it was insane, just a few months earlier she couldn't have imagined thinking something like that, much less doing it, but she just couldn't hold herself back. It was as if she had been honest, everything she'd said to Professor Solis, she truly believed it; and yet before she would have never had the courage to do so. It had been easier, to go with the flow, to do what others expected of her but she couldn't do it anymore, not when the mere thought of it felt like an attack on Chris, and Lily, and Camellia… and Rose. People she respected, that she loved, she just couldn't stand it.

There was no way of knowing what the consequences of her actions might be, and Fiore just knew there would be consequences. But, they couldn't be any worse than what she was already going through, with the shades, and the jaguars. That thought, insane as it might be, comforted her some.

The rest of Saturday and even Sunday passed by quickly, leaving the young woman in a sort of daze. She was anxious, like a part of her was waiting for something, even if she hadn't the slightest idea of what that was exactly. Something was coming, she just knew it, and her instincts were never wrong.

When Monday came Fiore walked Rose to Alondra's apartment on the fourth floor, it was the day for the widower mother of two to look after the children. There was no school just yet, not until the next day, but the parents in the building had convinced Fiore to take the day to herself, especially when learning it was her birthday on Tuesday, and she wouldn't be celebrating it then as it was the first day of classes and she was expecting there would be a lot to do. Alondra had even insisted on keeping Rose for the night. So, Fiore took the day, went on a long walk through a beautiful garden that had just opened five blocks away, had a perfect lunch in her favorite restaurant, treated herself to a massage with someone Simon on the sixth floor had recommended, and a long bath with an oil mix Camellia had prepared just for her.

After her bath Fiore was sitting on the edge of her bed, towel-drying her hair, when she noticed the cardboard box in the corner of her bedroom. She thought she'd finished unpacking everything, but apparently not. So, putting aside her towel, she walked to the corner, to find a single thing inside the box: a small, wooden chest inlaid with semi-precious stones… her Nana's chest. Half-instinctively Fiore brought a hand to the pendant hanging around her neck. She never took it off, even if she sometimes forgot she had it, she never took it off.

Without a thought, Fiore pulled the chest out of the box and went back to the bed, placing it on her lap. She opened it, breathing in the scent of all the tiny flowers and petals, a corner of her mind wondering how they could still look and smell so good when they'd obviously been there for a very long time. And then she noticed something, something she'd somehow missed the first time she opened the chest: there was a paper bag half-hidden beneath the flowers, somewhat darkened and stiffened with age. It crackled as she opened it, pulling out, first a piece of yellowed paper; though the shock came when next she pulled out a light-yellow tea rose, perfectly fresh, as if it had been cut off its bush not even five minutes earlier… it was impossible.

She unfolded the piece of paper then, and that made the shock three-fold, there was a single phrase written there: *When you're ready to remember, you'll know what to do.* The staggering part: it was her handwriting, only she didn't remember ever writing that note at all…

Fiore sat in that bed chest moved beside her, with the tea rose in one hand and the note on the other for what seemed like forever. No matter how much she turned it around in her head, she had no idea how she could have possibly written that note, much less done anything else, and not remember… Except the note seemed to imply not only that, but that there was a way for her to remember it, and who knew what else, when she was ready.

Was she ready? She didn't even know what it was she was supposed to remember! How could she know if she was ready?!

And then she thought of her conversation with Solis and Lopez on Saturday, of everything that had been running through her mind when she decided to open her mouth and go against something the man had said for the first time ever. She thought of everything going on... Could her 'lost' memories have something to do with that? With the shades and the jaguars and Xochiquetzal...? And if they did, was she truly ready for it? Could she risk not knowing the answer either way?

She hadn't the slightest idea of what she should do, all she knew was what she could do, and so she did it. Without allowing herself to think too much about it, to risk not daring to do it, Fiore closed her fist around the tea rose, crushing it between her fingers. A part of her expected to end with a fistful of petals and perhaps some sap and pollen in her fingers... instead the rose seemed to turn to ash and slip between them. She didn't even get the chance to wonder about that, as a moment later she felt a current run through her whole body, and then she collapsed onto the bed unconscious.

Chapter 16
Rosemary

They were sitting, face to face, in what could be considered her private sitting room, right beside a window aimed towards the garden, and there was just enough shrubbery right outside it that they could observe those waiting outside without them knowing they were being watched. There were cups half-filled with tea, her own special mix of several different flowers and herbs, in front of them, half-forgotten as they argued. Their voices weren't loud or harsh, but they were most definitely arguing.

"They are just children," she stated in a nearly horrified tone.

"They are offerings of their peoples," he pointed out evenly.

"Political hostages? Or an intent for future alliances?" she asked, cocking her head to a side as she appeared to consider implications.

"Neither." He shook his head, lowering his eyes as he added. "I believe they expect them to become sacrifices..."

"But they are just children!" Her voice went through an octave or two as her emotions got away from her. "Little girls, nothing more..."

"And you know I do not condone human sacrifice," he pointed out for good measure. "Whatever my predecessors' ways might have been, they are not my own. Of course, I know they are children. I wish them no more harm than you do... which is why I brought them here."

"I do not understand."

"The girls were not the only ones sent, there were boys as well. But they are older, I have sent them to be trained along with

the youngest recruits, to be future warriors, as has always been my choice to do with orphaned boys. The girls are different. No family in the capital is interested in taking them, not as daughters, not even as wives for their sons; and even if they were, with the situation as it has been I cannot be sure they would treat those girls as anything more than unwanted guests at best and prisoners at worst. Whatever the reasons their people's rulers might have had for sending them, they deserve better."

"And so, you brought them here, to me."

"I trust you to do right by them. You know I trust you above all others, I..."

"I know." She cut him off, turning her eyes away to avoid his own, at the same time she fought down her blush. "Have you any plans for them?"

"None at all. I guess time will tell."

"That it will."

Having agreed, the two finished their tea before walking out of the room, and then the temple, returning to where a couple of guards awaited, as well as three young girls, with tanned skin, brunette hair and brown eyes, they seemed to be about seven years of age, give or take a year, and were dressed in plain sand-colored dresses, their feet bare.

After directing a last look at the man, who seemed to have chosen to stand back so as to allow her to take charge of the situation, the woman approached the girls. She was in her twenties, of average height, slim built, soft factions, golden-tanned skin, with eyes the color of cacao seeds and long, straight, thick hair as dark as ebony, mostly covered with a delicately knitted white veil, she wore a short-sleeved, floor-length tunic made of white manta and her feet were as bare as the girls'.

"Hello," she greeted the three young girls with her kindest smile. "I welcome you into my home. This is the Flower Temple, and I am Xochiquetzal."

Xochiquetzal woke up in the middle of the night to the whispered warning from a murmur only she could hear. Her girls were getting better every day, but they were still young, and they did not have the connection with the plants, with the earth itself, that she did. They never would. She could make them priestesses, could intercede with the Higher Powers to grant them wonderful gifts, but they still would never be her, and that was alright.

The Enchantress slipped off her bed, pulling an off-white rebozo over her night-clothes and with her feet still bare, as she only wore sandals when leaving the temple grounds, she walked quietly out of her bedroom and down the hall. She made sure not to wake up her charges as she finally stepped out of the temple and down the twisting path, walking by an incredible variety of flowers. She didn't stop until reaching the very end of the path, where the forest began. The woods weren't technically part of the Temple or its grounds, but her power was enough that it extended to some of them too; the trees responded to her, and she to them.

"I know you are there," she murmured softly. "You do not need to say a word. My name is Xochiquetzal and this is the Flower Temple, my temple. I do not know what has brought you here in the middle of the night, but I can tell you are afraid. And you need not be. Whatever may have brought you here, I promise you, you will be safe here. All you need to do, is trust me."

There was no response, but Xochiquetzal wasn't really expecting one. She just turned around and returned to the temple. She walked to the kitchen, where she pulled out a couple of slices from the bread that had just been delivered that morning, along with some atole. All the food in the Temple they got either trading flowers, herbs, or from things people she helped, or the rich donated. The King had some things sent to them every week with the excuse that she was providing a service by raising and teaching the three girls he'd left in her care seven years earlier.

She left the food on the counter and walked away. She was just stepping back into her quarters when she heard the quiet sound of steps as a small figure slipped into the temple. She didn't turn back, didn't stop; she'd done what she could to help, the rest would be up to their little visitor.

The next morning, the child was still there.

She wasn't quite a child, older than Iris, Carnation and Acacia had been when first arriving to the Temple, about eleven or twelve years old; a girl on the cusp of womanhood. She was also a would-be sacrifice.

It hadn't been easy to piece it all together. The girl was understandably nervous and nearly hysterical, she also kept talking in a mix of tongues, not all of which Xochiquetzal was familiar with. She'd had a privileged enough education, and a gift with languages, but at least one of the tongues was from one of the tribes in the far North, beyond the desert, she wasn't familiar with that one. Even then, they managed to make out that she was the youngest daughter of a working family, her parents had pretty much sold her to be a sacrifice; only her brother had intervened, he'd rescued her and sent her away. He'd saved her, and it had cost him his life. The girl had been running for the past few weeks, avoiding villages as much as possible, afraid of someone finding her and sending her back, or just killing her outright, when she'd accidentally ended close enough to the Flower Temple that Xochiquetzal detected her presence.

It was easy enough for Xochiquetzal to convince Quetzalcoatl that the girl should stay in the temple, and for them to create a cover story for her, to make sure she'd never be found by those who'd want her dead. As far as the King was concerned, the girl deserved a new life, she certainly had fought for it, and managing to cross the desert on her own and with no supplies at all was nothing short of a miracle. She never gave them her name, claimed it was no longer hers, but was happy enough to choose a new one when given the chance; she decided to be called Lily.

The miracle part of all of this became even more evident when they discovered the girl was gifted, and not with the kind of gift Xochiquetzal could pray for. Iris, Carnation and Acacia were each blessed in a different way, abilities they'd earned after Xochiquetzal had prayed for them. The new girl... she was different, her gift was strong and, in a way, with more potential for violence than any of the others'.

It wasn't easy, to have a new girl join them, but they adapted to her. In the end Xochiquetzal loved them all equally, and they knew it.

Xochiquetzal pulled back, sitting on her heels and blinking slowly, as her mind tried to comprehend what had just happened. She didn't quite notice when she brought two fingers to her lips, her mind seemingly in a loop. Quetzalcoatl for his part said not a word; he just sat on the dirt-ground, waiting patiently for her reaction.

Quetzalcoatl had dropped by for a visit, like he did at least every other week, sometimes more often. They would always take a walk around the temple grounds, talk about whatever was going on. They trusted each other absolutely, would tell one another everything. It was how she'd told him about worrying that someone might try to take one of her girls by force; which prompted him to send four of his best guards to stay permanently in the temple. Sometimes he'd ask for her advice when a problem came up and she did her best to help him, either by giving him ideas, or simply being his sounding board. It had gotten to the point where everyone in the territory knew that they were each other's confidante and she was officially acknowledged as one of the King's advisers.

That day Xochiquetzal decided to show him some of her newest flowers. They were roses, but with some careful gardening and a tiny nudge from her gift she'd managed to create some beautiful new colors, one was even two colors at the same time. He'd been very interested in the flowers and had eventually called attention to the single pure white bush that remained. The one only she didn't try to change. The bush was important to her, and he could see it, white flowers had always been meaningful to her... that still didn't explain how they'd gone from talking about white roses to him kissing her!

"Sacnite..." he began.

"Topiltzin..." she replied automatically.

They never did that, or almost never at least; saying each other's first names. It made things complicated. They were friends, had been friends for a very long time, most of their lives in fact; since before they'd been Quetzalcoatl and Xochiquetzal, King and Enchantress. They were connected, in ways even they couldn't understand sometimes. Ways that made them afraid, though perhaps not for the same reason.

"I cannot be your bride," Xochiquetzal blurted out.

Quetzalcoatl opened his mouth, about to say something, but Xochiquetzal didn't let him as she went on.

"I am too old, and too independent, and too opinionated..." she said, pretty much in a rush. "The Council can barely stand me being one of your advisers, your confidante... they will never stand for me being your bride, your queen..."

"It is still my choice... and yours," he finally got the chance to weigh in. "I care not for your age, I like that you are independent and unafraid to voice your opinion; you would not be the woman I knew if you did not do such things. The Council can complain as much as they wish, but they cannot force their choices on me, or on you, not if we do not allow it." He made a pause, extending both hands, palm up, in offering. "I love you Sacnite, my beautiful flower, with every breath in my lungs and every beat of my heart, every inch of my soul... The question is, do you feel the same for me?"

In the end, she didn't really have to think that hard about it. The doubts were still there, yes, but they weren't about him, they'd never been. If there was one thing she was sure of, it was what was in her heart.

"I do," she breathed out. "I love you too..."

Days passed, and weeks, months, years; at first the love between the two was such that every day seemed to be tinted by a palette of perfect colors, like seeing the world through something that made everything look brighter. Eventually that sensation passed; it wasn't that the two loved each other any less, more like they were beginning to understand things weren't as simple as they'd wish. Much as they might love each other, they just weren't ready to deal with everything they knew would come if they were to announce their love, to marry before the eyes of their nation. And it wasn't just the council, or the nobles, it was the people, who might just not be ready for a queen like Xochiquetzal. Also, she didn't believe her girls were ready to be on their own, and it didn't feel right to leave the Temple until then.

Thus, time kept passing, and ever so slowly the relationship lost its intensity, its passion. The love was still there, it would always be, but the two no longer idealized the future, they were all too aware that things both good and bad would come once they fully became a match, and while they were still completely in love with each other, and willing to face whatever the future might bring, they were not so eager not to do everything in their power to make sure things would be as smooth as they could make them, and especially that those they loved would be well.

The visits continued, and the walks, and the talks. The couple would hold hands and even kiss sometimes, always making sure no one would see them. It wasn't that they didn't trust those in the Temple, the girls were as good as Xochiquetzal's daughters, after all, and Quetzalcoatl himself had hand-picked the Atlantes. Other girls had come and gone as wards of Xochiquetzal and her temple, but only the first four stayed after becoming of age, by their own choice.

Their favorite part of the garden was the rose-patch, it was around a bend and far enough from the temple to have them out of sight. It allowed them privacy they so lacked most of the time. Still, it would be improper, if someone were to ever discover them, or even suspect that there was more between them than friendship. They couldn't risk something like that, not when they so wanted to make things right, not when he still loved her, wanted her to be his bride, his queen...

One day the couple was in a spot with particularly colorful flowers. It was the spot that their most recent ward: young Daisy, tended to. The flowers weren't as carefully groomed as the ones the four priestesses looked after, and they certainly lacked the near-otherworldly aura that the ones that had Xochiquetzal's touch possessed; but they were still beautiful, and a sign of what that little girl represented for everyone in the temple. The hope of a young life, all the things that could and should be nurtured...

Xochiquetzal was kneeling among the flowers, with her King and lover standing but a couple of feet from her. The Toltec King chose that very moment to pull out something he'd been carrying in between the folds of his clothes, placing it in Xochiquetzal's hands; who'd moved to receive it without being quite aware of it.

"It's beautiful..." she whispered, looking at the object in admiration.

"It's for you," he informed her.

"For me?" The Enchantress seemed very surprised. "I'm not sure I deserve something of such great value."

"You deserve that and so much more," he assured her, going down on one knee before her. "No gift is too much for the 'most beautiful flower'."

"Oh, my lord..."

"I've told you many times, Xochiquetzal, not to call me that."

"But that's exactly what you are sire, my lord, my king."

"I don't think you could be ignorant of the fact that my interest in you goes beyond that of a king with his adviser."

Of course, she couldn't be, they'd talked about it before, even if, in the last year, the talk of marriage had lessened, they were both so busy. Her trying to make sure her girls could be without her, him seeking to ensure his people would give her the respect, admiration and loyalty he fully believed she deserved. Not only because she was his chosen, but because of everything she had done, for him and for their nation, for years. It seemed to have been a silent pact, that they wouldn't mention marriage again, until they were finally ready for it.

"I know," she sighed. "Though I'm still not convinced that I may be worthy of your affections, or the post you offer me."

It was only natural. It wasn't even that she doubted his love, because she certainly didn't. But there were still days, dark days, when it seemed like the time for them to truly be together would never come. Those days made her, made them both despair. However, then there were the good days, when hope came back, when they believed again that their time would come, for them to be together, for the world to know they loved one another and always would. Yes, that day would come.

"There's nothing you're not worthy of. Whether they be feelings, a crown or a whole kingdom. You are worthy of everything your heart desires. That's why I've brought you this gift, so it might serve as token of my promise."

"Promise?"

"You well know that much as I might wish to announce right now what is in my heart, the current situation does not allow it."

"The closeness of that encampment of nomad warriors seems to have everyone in the town quite tense."

Yes, that was the latest problem, the latest reason for them not to announce their relationship; and it was something that worried them both, not just for the whole nation, but also for the Temple. After all, even with all their gifts and blessings, how could nine people and one child ever hope to survive an all-out attack, if the nomads were ever to decide on doing such a thing?

"But that shall not last forever. That's why I give you this gift now, with the promise that the day will come when I shall come for you; and you will enter Tula on my arm, as the queen you've always been in heart, and shall be for my people. That is, if you will have me."

"It'd be my honor."

The young woman then took the gift and put it on, with the resolve never to take it off again, sealing the promise made on that day.

She had no idea what was yet to come, neither of them did...

That was the last day Xochiquetzal saw her lover. There were still messages, short ones, sent with a messenger every week. Even if he couldn't visit, he wanted to make sure his beloved would know she was in his thoughts. And then one day no message came.

Two days later a messenger arrived, he carried no written message, but instead was there to inform Xochiquetzal about the King's disappearance.

The shock caused by this news was such that the Enchantress couldn't hold back her wail, filled with agony at the prospect of what the messenger before her what suggesting; her knees folded beneath her and she curled upon herself, lost for a while as her mind tried to comprehend what her heart refused to accept.

"It is said that a man arrived seeking him out two nights ago, claimed his name was Tezcatlipoca." She vaguely heard the messenger explain the situation to her charges. "Lord Quetzalcoatl agreed to walk with him, talk in private, neither of them has been seen since. There are rumors that perhaps our King might be dead."

"No!!!" The new choked cry that left the enchantress's lips seemed to squeeze the hearts of everyone present.

"My Lady!" Priestesses and Guardians cried out in unison, alarmed.

He couldn't be dead! He just couldn't! And she would know if he were truly gone, wouldn't she? She would know inside, in her heart... in her soul, she would know! So, he couldn't be gone, he couldn't have left her, not then, not after everything they'd gone through already, the future they had always dreamed of... He promised her a future!!!

"He broke his promise..." Xochiquetzal whispered in between sobs. "He said he'd come to me once it was all over, that we'd be together; that he'd he my king and I his queen. But now that shall never be, he shall never come back. He's broken his promise!"

When she moved, she didn't even think about it, in moments she was on her feet and running, fleeing the temple. She didn't even notice when the delicate chain and pendant she'd been clutching tightly in her hand through her denial, the very gift her beloved had placed on her hands when she'd seen him last, slipped through her fingers to lay forgotten on the ground.

"My lady!" all those present cried out again.

She heard none of them, she was already too far away, in body, but especially in mind, to hear any voice at all. She didn't know it then, but she would never step, or lay eyes on the Flower Temple again... not in that lifetime at least.

When her eyes opened again she didn't know how long they'd been closed, neither did she know how she'd ended up in such a place, wherever it might be. When she'd left the Flower Temple there had been no plan at all in her mind. After an hour or two running almost non-stop, uncaring about the bruises and minor cuts on the bare soles of her feet. Eventually it occurred to her to try and track down her beloved, but while she could find traces of his energy, they were obscured by something... smoky. She was beginning to go insane with her inability to find him when something happened. She'd no idea what exactly, she just knew something had knocked her out and she woke up to find herself somewhere strange.

The ground was stone, rather than dirt, hard and cold and beyond her ability to either sense or influence. Which was probably the very reason why she was there. Whoever had gone after her, had taken her, knew the power she had, what she was capable of, beyond force-blooming plants and mixing teas. Considering that the only person who was supposed to know that was her missing lover... that was not a good thing.

There were no windows, no doors, everything around her was stone, except for a wall which seemed to be made of something like glass, except it was much hardier and she couldn't see whatever might be on the other side. Xochiquetzal had no illusions about what might be in store for her, and spent the following hour or so meditating, mentally preparing herself for whatever might come. When she finally picked up on movement on the other side of the glass wall and realized the time had come, she thought she was ready, that she could handle whatever might come. She was so wrong...

Xochiquetzal didn't realize at first what was going on. There was a man on the other side of the transparent wall, covered head to toe in black, and she couldn't make out his face, couldn't make out much of him in fact; as if something made him blurry to her eyes. He waved his hand and suddenly the glass began showing colors, which solidified into images... it was the Flower Temple... at night... and they were being attacked.

The Enchantress knew not how long she screamed, though it certainly was for a long time, enough for her throat to hurt, her voice to become hoarse... and still it was useless, nothing she did or said changed anything. They were still right there, fighting... dying... her people... her children!

"No!!!" she practically screeched, uselessly pounding at the floor with her fists, her legs had long since stopped holding her up. "Don't you dare hurt them! Leave them alone! Leave them! My children!! Don't you hurt my children!!!"

There was nothing she could do, and that hurt her more than anything the bastard on the other side of the glass could have ever done to her.

Xochiquetzal didn't notice when exactly she began to bleed. With everything going on it just didn't seem that important. She'd already lost everything...

Everything seemed to come to an end in the hour before dawn. The fight at the Flower Temple had ended, the subsequent fire razing all that was left to the ground, only a few flowers remained, valiantly trying to rise among the ashes and blood. It was a gruesome image to everyone, but especially to the woman who had been forced to bear witness as every single person she called family, her girls and their protectors, were slaughtered. Only one hope remained, the single figure she hadn't seen throughout the fight... yet she said not a word about it. If such a miracle was possible... she wouldn't be giving her away. She was their one and only hope... or perhaps not the only one.

"It is done." a dark, hissing, male voice announced with a terrible sort of glee.

"Done...?" The Enchantress was so horrified that she didn't seem to quite grasp what he meant exactly.

"Your Kingdom is at my feet now." There was obvious satisfaction in the shadowed-figure's words. "And it is just the beginning. In due time all the tribes will kneel before me."

"They will not." She refused to believe it. *"Someone will fight back. Always."*

"Who do you suppose will do that? Who will even know they need to do it? Your dear King is gone, the brats are dead... and soon enough you will be as well. I've won."

"No... No!" It couldn't end like that. All the losses, so much death... it couldn't be all for nothing! It couldn't!

"Accept it already. You've lost."

"No!!" She wouldn't accept it, she wouldn't. Even if she hadn't the slightest idea of what could be done... she refused to believe it was over.

"What can you possibly do? Your brats are dead, your King might as well be, you too will be gone soon enough, and no one will be left to defy me. No one will know I existed... History will forget you all..."

"I will not forget. I will never forget!"

"You will be dead."

He said it with finality, as if that were the end of the argument, and it should have been except... except death did not have to be the end, and she knew that.

Xochiquetzal knew not how long she had been playing with the little rounded nut she held in her hand in that moment. It had been a gift from a merchant from the West. He'd traveled from his village to her temple, seeking her aid with a sickness that plagued his wife, she'd given what help she could, and it was good. He didn't have much to pay her with, but she didn't mind. In the end he'd given her some wares, including that little nut, a seed from a foreign flower... she'd been planning where to plant it, the man claimed it was a water-blossom... the Enchantress had no idea why the nut had been on her when she left the temple, but perhaps that wasn't too important in the grand scheme of things. That tiny seed was the only plant at her disposal, and it wasn't much but maybe, maybe it would be enough.

There was already a blade inside her cell, one made completely of stone, hard and cold. And the reason was simple enough: Tezcatlipoca, for she knew that hiding behind the smoke, it was him, the same individual who'd called on her King, who was *responsible for his disappearance, and for his death... She'd felt him die, shortly before the attack on the Temple had ended, it had been as if something inside her snapped; her heart, already bleeding with all the horror and grief and tragedy she'd been forced to witnessed, shattered into pieces. She had no idea what could have possibly broken her lover, but it couldn't have been good. And something must have broken him, there was no other way he could be dead. It was the same reason why the blade had been left there...*

Those like her love and she, and she suspected Tezcatlipoca as well, they couldn't just die, because they weren't quite human, not completely. It took a great power to truly kill them, and even then, they could come back from most things; unless they died by their own hand. That was the purpose of the blade, and of the whole show, Tezcatlipoca was pushing and waiting for her to fall deep enough into despair that she'd choose death over her current existence. She was beyond that point already, yet, she still refused to give up.

She was playing with dangerous forces; the Enchantress knew that much. Whatever some people chose to believe, Quetzalcoatl had been no god, and neither was she. Much as they might not be fully human, they weren't divine either. Still, they had access to power, and she was going to make use of it, in the hopes that it might be enough to, someday, make things right. Someday, there would be justice for all the lives that had been lost that night, and would be lost in the days, months, years to come, in Tezcatlipoca's mad desire for power.

Once she acted, she moved fast, knowing Tezcatlipoca would try to stop her, if he so much as suspected what she was doing, but she wouldn't allow that, she couldn't. Even exhausted and weary as she was, there was enough power in her for one spell.

Taking a deep breath Xochiquetzal slashed open her left palm, waited for the blood to pool in the center of her slightly cupped palm and then placed the seed there. Another deep breath and then she called on every spark of power that was in her and made the flower bloom.

It was a beautiful blossom. About the size of her open palm, with many big petals curving up and out, almost like a star... it was obvious the flower was supposed to be white, but with the touch of her blood, it came out looking an almost haunting mix of white and red... Xochiquetzal didn't stop to admire it, instead she began chanting, calling for something that was meant to be beyond her power, and yet she still hoped... for her proteges, for her child, for her love, for their people... she hoped.

All too soon, Tezcatlipoca became aware of what she was doing, but by then it was too late already. She only vaguely heard his roar of fury at the same time the glass wall seemed to explode into pieces. Knowing time was running out Xochiquetzal finished her chant, even as she flipped the blade around in her free hand and then used it to stab herself in the heart. The last thing she saw was the flower in her left hand seemingly liquefying and slipping through her limp fingers, even as she sensed the power take hold.

It was done.

Chapter 17
Anemone

The first thing Xochitl was aware of when she woke up, were the fresh tears slipping down the corners of her closed eyes to get lost into her hair. Those were real enough. She could feel wetness on her fingers, even though she knew they were dry. She could also vaguely feel a phantom pain in her chest even though she was quite certain there was no stab wound there... a part of her really wanted to turn on her side, curl into as tight a ball as she could and forget the world around her existed, but she couldn't. She wasn't six years old anymore, she was an adult, and she had responsibilities.

And the very first of which presented itself a moment later, as she heard the doorbell ringing. The young woman didn't even think about it, she wiped her face with the back of her hands and rushed to the door, opening it immediately. As she thought, it was Alondra on the other side, with Rosie beside her. Rosie... her dear Rosie...

Fiore had no idea what the widower must have thought of the younger woman's red eyes or her lack of small talk. Chances were she believed Fiore to be hungover or something like that. It didn't matter. The reincarnated enchantress managed to keep herself in check just long enough for goodbyes to be said, the door to be closed, and hopefully enough seconds for Alondra to be out of hearing range... then Xochitl dropped to her knees, enveloped the little girl in her arms and broke into tears all over again.

Rose never asked why her Mommy was crying, or why she held her so tightly; the little girl just held her back. Only two words would leave Xochitl's lips every so often:

"My baby..."

Fiore still had to attend classes in the afternoon. Thankfully by that point she'd managed to pull herself together enough. She left Rose with Will, the young single father of a four-year-old boy living in the same floor as her; it was his day off, and his turn to look over the children that afternoon.

The first couple of classes went alright, she kept to herself. No one approached her. Not until she was at the end of her break and on the way to her third and last class of the day.

"Fi...? Fiore?!"

It took the young woman a couple of seconds to realize she was the one being addressed. With her recently recovered memories, and before that the weeks she'd spent in the company of people who'd rather call her Xochitl, or Flower... people who knew her in ways her teachers and classmates never would. Once she stopped she found it was Jessica calling her, and she wasn't alone; there was also Ximena, Marlene, and at least half of their clique. And they were all looking at her like she'd grown another head.

"Is that really you Fi?" Keiko, the petite half-Mexican, half-Japanese girl asked in a somewhat shrill tone of voice.

It hadn't occurred to the young woman until then, how different all her classmates probably found her. Maybe the reason no one talked to her that afternoon wasn't because they suddenly disliked her, but until then no one had realized it was, indeed, her. And it was that Xochitl wasn't wearing her contacts anymore, she hadn't been wearing them since the start of the winter break; her hair was in a messy French twist, yet a few rebel locks of her had managed to escape, enough for others to notice her hair wasn't curly at all. Then there were her flats, she'd stopped wearing heels entirely; while the rest of her clothes were the same she'd been using before, everything else made the overall image different enough.

"It is me," she answered simply.

"I didn't recognize you!" Keiko cried out in a somewhat obnoxious tone. "You look so... different."

"I've changed," Fiore said easily with a slight shrug.

"You moved out," Jessica commented, more quietly than she usually did. It was as if she didn't quite know how to react to Fiore's changes.

"It was necessary," the older girl responded, not wanting to mention Rose and risk someone saying something disparaging about her.

She didn't wait to see what else one of them might say, having decided they just weren't her problem. She already had enough of those, and no space for any more.

That evening Lily and Chris visited with dinner. They'd insisted on doing so as a small celebration for Xochitl's birthday. It took everything the older girl had not to throw her arms around Lily, holding her tight, never wanting to let go… It'd have been next to impossible for her to explain it, without also telling them about her recently recovered memories, and that was something Xochitl was not doing.

She'd made up her mind earlier. Remembering that life, especially the end… it was a heavy burden to bear, all the blood, the tears, the grief, the pain… There was no way she was putting that kind of weight on anyone, especially not one of her girls. So, she held her tongue, received the two like they were just friends, exactly as they'd been two days before; all the while praying to the Higher Powers for the strength to do what needed to be done.

By the time the next battle took place, on Thursday, Fiore was better able to keep herself in check; make sure nothing she did would end up calling attention, not Lily's, or Chris's, and certainly not from Belladonna or any of the others.

By Saturday though, Xochitl had come to accept the fact that she couldn't just ignore the fact that things had changed, and she couldn't handle it on her own. She needed someone she could trust, someone she could vent to, and who was able to be her sounding board, if she ever needed one. She chose Camellia.

"I remember."

Those were the first words out of Fiore's mouth the moment the two women were alone, with Rose taking a nap on a small mat after Camellia played a few melodies for her.

The older woman didn't say a thing, just waited patiently until Xochitl was ready to elaborate on those two words.

"My life… as Xochiquetzal… I remember."

That was certainly clearer, though Camellia really had no idea what to say. She'd known something was bothering her niece from the moment the girls arrived and yet, from all the things she imagined could be in her mind, that one had never occurred to her. She hadn't even known it was possible!

"Did you… did you want to remember?" Camellia wasn't even sure how to word that question. Was it an accident or on purpose?

"I… I suppose so, yeah." Fiore let out a breath.

She hadn't known what would come of it, but she'd certainly broken that spell consciously. And truth be told, as stressed out as the whole thing had left her, and even with all the dreams and the nerves she couldn't help but feel, she didn't regret her choice. Not only because she knew she would need those memories sooner or later, but because she was coming to realize she really was Xochiquetzal as much as she was Xochitl, or even Fiore.

"I didn't expect things to be… to have been… like that," Xochitl elaborated a bit more. "But yes, I chose to remember."

She explained some of it to Camellia. Not everything, certainly none of the more personal parts, but enough for the woman to at least begin to understand why gaining those memories was affecting the gal so much.

"There's something I've wondered," Camellia commented after a while. "Have you always known for certain that you are Xochiquetzal or did you learn that with these memories? Or at some other point?"

"That's a complicated question, and an even more complicated answer," The younger woman replied quietly. "I didn't know, not for sure. When the shades began pursuing me, and I met Lily and Chris, I realized I had power. Some things I've always been able to do, like mixing teas, making plants grow… I just never paid attention to it. Then I discovered my magic, and it just… it felt natural, effortless. Then Belladonna and her group appeared, they were the first to call me Mistress, and Xochiquetzal and… it was like a part of me knew they were right, but there was an even bigger part of me that was just… afraid to embrace that truth. So, while I didn't deny it, I didn't acknowledge it either. I did began changing though, from the persona I created when I came to live in the capital to… not quite my old self, but perhaps a healthier version of myself. After Rose came into my life, and the appearance of the jaguars, meeting you… I think I was slowly accepting the truth about myself, even before regaining my memories. That was just the final piece of the puzzle. Like everything coming together, finally."

"What about the others? Your priestesses and their protectors?" Camellia inquired. "Will you tell them what you've remembered? Will you try and bring back their own memories?"

"No!!" the reincarnated Enchantress's response was stronger than even she expected. "No, I would never do that to them." She shuddered at the mere thought of it. "I shall acknowledge who I am, and who they are, but that's all. If they ask questions, I will consider giving them answers, but there are things they just don't need to know. As for their own memories… no, if it's up to me, I shall not do that. That's one burden they deserve to be free of."

Camellia didn't fully understand, but then again, she wasn't a reincarnation, so there was no way for her to; and she respected Xochitl enough, both as who she was in her current life, and who she'd been, not to insist.

It was until the following Monday that Fiore came across Draco for the first time since their ill-fated near-kiss back before winter break. A part of her might have noticed the details in her memories, but she hadn't been aware of it; not until she saw him walking by, then it hit her, hard enough she became breathless. Her hand closed convulsively around her pendant as she spun around and walked away as fast as she could without calling undue attention.

It was him… It was Him! Draco Yao Tamay was the reincarnation of Ce Acatl Topiltzin Quetzalcoatl. Her King… her lover… hers…

Suddenly some things made a lot of sense. The feelings and instincts she'd gotten in relation to him from the very start; their mutual attraction… Even his rejection of her! She wasn't sure if she should feel honored that after so long, centuries and lifetimes even, he was keeping his promise to her; or aghast that he allowed a thousand-year-old promise to keep him from making his own choices. Then again, she was wearing his pendant, hadn't taken it off even for a moment since finding it in that wooden box. And after finding out the truth it had only become even more precious to her.

So, no, maybe she wasn't aghast, maybe she was honored… she still had no idea how she was supposed to handle it all. He hadn't recognized her! Was she that different from who she'd once been? Her children seemed to be able to see through her facade just fine, and yet the man who was supposed to be her soulmate had looked her in the eyes, had almost kissed her, and then walked away. What was she supposed to take from that?

Days passed, one by one, and Xochitl could sense to her very core the changing of the seasons, the way the ice and snow of winter melted away to give way to the spring blossoms. She felt it with both her human and magical senses and it was a precious gift to be allowed to rediscover them and herself in such a way. While the Flower Temple possessed enough magic, both of herself and the Higher Powers, that it was always spring there, and the plants always bloomed true, Xochiquetzal had always had great appreciation for the passing of the seasons. She loved the way the world changed and, especially, the way the earth around her sung about those changes.

Time kept moving on and, somehow, the reincarnated Enchantress managed to adapt to her changes without calling too much attention upon herself. Lily and Chris at least had obviously noticed something was going on; but just like they'd respected her secrets in the past, they did the same then.

At some point Fiore took Chris and Lily to meet Camellia and they all got along great. No mention was made of Xochiquetzal, though since they all shared gifts, there was a lot for them to talk about. Also, Chris managed to convince Camellia to go out with them, rather than always stay in her apartment. He would carry her down the stairs, while the girls carried her wheelchair and bag, then they'd seat her again and go on a walk through a park, or a greenhouse, or even a couple of galleries. They didn't even limit themselves to the neighborhood. Camellia had told them the first couple of times not to bother, but eventually the younger adults managed to convince her it was no bother, they loved going out with her, seeing new places, hearing her stories…

One such day some time mid-March, they were all visiting a petting zoo near Xochimilco. Rosie was absolutely delighted, taking turns to feed and pet every animal she laid eyes on. Camellia didn't even mind how hard it was to maneuver her wheelchair on the gravel, just seeing the joy in that little girl's eyes was enough to make any trouble worth it.

It took them almost two hours to make it to the opposite end of the zoo, where they stayed for a while, sharing a picnic lunch and then watching the ducks for a while. Little Rose kept giggling as she watched two ducks fight for a piece of her cookie that she'd thrown at them. Even the adults were laughing some; either at the ducks, or the girl's childish delight at the whole thing.

And then came the roar.

No one said a thing for one or two seconds.

"There are no wildcats in this zoo," Lily eventually blurted out. "I checked!"

Of course, she had. She knew Rosie was absolutely terrified of jaguars, and with good reason. Yet there was that roaring… and even the animals in the zoo were beginning to look more than a little nervous. The ducks took flight, other small creatures scattering in their fright and the world seemed to go deathly silent except for the roaring. It could only mean one thing.

Xochitl didn't wait for anyone to say a thing, in an instant she scooped Rose into her arms and turned to the others.

"Run!" she yelled to them.

They weren't the only ones running. The roaring had grown and multiplied. No one knew quite what was happening, aside from perhaps them, but everyone understood it was nothing good. And so, they all ran.

Soon enough it was absolute pandemonium. Knowing that the wheelchair was a liability Camellia didn't hesitate the moment Chris approached her, she just threw her arms around his neck, allowing him to take her into his arms, and then they were running as fast as they could.

Then came the real problem. There were so many people running, things being thrown around, and then there were those who fell, who were trampled on. In an attempt not to step on a poor man who had fallen before them, Chris ended losing his balance completely, he barely managed to turn in midair so as not to crush Camellia underneath him; which had the side effect of him slamming his head against a rock, knocking himself out.

"Cristobal!" Lily practically screeched in panic.

The roaring kept getting both louder and closer.

Lily stood there, frozen, seemingly not knowing what to do. Fiore and Rose were ahead of them, hadn't noticed what had happened just yet, and probably wouldn't for a while. Rosie was Xochitl's priority, and there was nothing wrong with that, but it still left Lily in a quandary she despised.

Camellia took a deep breath, focusing, before staring straight at Lily.

"Don't think too hard about it," She ordered with an odd mix of serenity and deep authority. "Take him and run."

"What?!" the young woman couldn't believe the older one had just said that.

"I said, take him and go!" Camellia insisted.

"But Cam..." Lily began.

"It's quite simple girl!" the paralyzed woman stated. "You cannot carry us both, and you need him. More importantly, Xochitl needs you both."

"She needs you too. You're her aunt!" Lily snapped.

<And you're her children... she cannot lose you, not again,> Camellia thought to herself but did not say.

"She needs you more," she said instead. "Now take him and go. Hurry! There's no time to lose!"

Lily hated it, almost hated herself even, in that very moment, but in the end, she did as told. She pulled her partner over her shoulder in a fireman carry and got on her feet. She was about to say something else, when movement from the corner of her eye called her attention. She turned her head and saw him then, a man standing in dark, muddy, slightly torn jeans, thick tanned leather boots and a brown leather jacket over a white wife-beater; there seemed to be no hair on his head, and his eyes were like solid amber. Lily completely lost her breath at the sight of him.

"Run!!!" Camellia practically screamed at the girl, having no idea what made her freeze like that so suddenly.

The woman's scream woke her up and, forcing herself to turn away, Lily did exactly as she was told: she ran.

Camellia for her part took a deep breath and settled herself to wait. She took a moment to arranger her legs and her skirt somewhat; a pointless endeavor perhaps, but it gave her something to do while she waited... not that she believed she would be waiting long.

And yet, when the moment finally came it wasn't quite how she was expecting.

Lily caught up with Fiore in the area being used as parking lot, people were hurrying to their cars, buses, any transport they could get to. In fact, the young mother was waiting for them at a bus's door, apparently having managed to convince the driver to wait for them. Her dark eyes widened when she realized Lily was carrying an unconscious Chris, and Camellia wasn't with them. So many questions came to mind, and yet she couldn't find the words to voice one; especially when Lily looked at her, amber eyes filled with tears as she shook her head once.

Xochitl pressed a hand to her mouth. For one wild, insane second she honestly considered jumping off the bus and straight back into the zoo in search of Camellia. She wanted to believe she might still make it to her in time, but then what? Even if she did, her chances of outrunning the jaguars weren't that great, and she seriously doubted the bus would wait for them. Also, if she got herself killed in the attempt everyone would be angry, and worse, disappointed in her, Camellia especially. However, the most important reason for her not to do something like that, became obvious in the form of the tiny hand holding onto her clothes tightly. She had sat Rose down, but the girl refused to let go completely; as if a part of her feared her Mommy might go away... and so the young woman knew she couldn't do it, she couldn't leave Rose. So instead she just looked at Lily as she ran the last few yards to the bus, trying to convey so much in a single look: her understanding, her acceptance, resignation, pride... and even relief. Because Lily was alright, Chris would be alright, they survived... and one day they'd do justice for Camellia.

One day the Enchantress would do justice for them all. She so swore.

Chapter 18
Chrysanthemum

"I saw Esteban… in the zoo… he was there…"

It wasn't the first time Lily had said those words since the group had returned from Xochimilco; at least after they managed to put aside the shock over the loss of Camellia. Fiore still didn't quite understand the significance of that development; but then again, that's what they were there for.

They were in Chris's apartment, and Xochitl had prepared one of her special blends of tea, at their insistence; one meant to help keep them calm. That at least was enough to tell her that what was coming would be grueling.

"There are secrets we don't share, we're all aware of that, we all respect that," Lily began, emptying her voice of all emotion, doing her best to distance herself from things. "I'm not saying this to pressure you Flower, but because one of my secrets, perhaps my biggest secret of all, has now become relevant. More than I ever expected it to be."

"I see," Fiore nodded quietly. "I won't judge you Lils, I hope you know that."

"I know." The amber-eyed girl nodded with a small smile. "I don't know if you're aware of it this but, Lily isn't my real-name… or not my birth-name at least. I was born Elena Susanne Norwood Valle, only daughter of a rich man's mistress. He lived in some ranch in south New Mexico. All things told, his family probably still lives there. He'd cross into Chihuahua every other week for work, and to see my mother." Lily shook her head. "She died when I was little, five years old or so. My mom's family did not want me, illegitimate daughter that I was, they saw me as nothing more than the fruits of a sin…" She let out a sigh. "I'm not sure how it was that I ended living with my father, I just did. Mrs. Norwood hated me, as did her two daughters; but her eldest, her son... he liked me, he loved me. Esteban was... wonderful, everything an older brother is supposed to be. He was seven years older than me and absolutely perfect. He would serve me breakfast and then walk me to school every morning, then pick me up in the afternoon. Some days we'd even go for a milkshake on the way back. Then he'd help me with my homework, he was always so patient when I didn't understand something, or when the language gave me trouble. He always defended me from his sisters whenever they were mean, and even from his mom. Then at night we'd read a new chapter of some book before he tucked me into bed."

Yes, the best big brother one could hope for. Xochitl could tell she loved him; that did not explain what was going on in that moment though...

"Around the time I graduated from middle-school, Mrs. Norwood finally grew tired of me," Lily went on, "She wanted to send me off to boarding-school. She'd been wanting to do that since I arrived... and then father died... He was the only one stopping her, and with him gone she decided to get rid of me outright. Her daughters told me all sort of things, and I never truly knew what she was planning on doing. They would say she was going to throw me out of the house, send me to an orphanage, sell me... In the end I decided I'd rather not find out. I packed a bag and ran away." She shook her head almost ruefully. "Of course, I hadn't the slightest idea where to go or how to live on my own. Esteban found me two days later, trying to sleep on a park-bench. He told me he'd spoken to his mother, that he'd never forgive her for being so cruel to me, and he'd chosen me... he chose me, above his mother and sisters!"

Tears began falling down the priestess's cheeks, and her friend really wanted to hold her; but she knew that wasn't a good idea. Lily, no Elena, needed to get it all off her chest, Chris for his part just rubbed his partner's back, conveying all his support, then and always.

"It was his idea to come to Mexico," the amber-eyed went on. "He thought it was the perfect place for a new beginning. He bought both of us tickets to Ciudad Juarez, Chihuahua, where my mother was from. We crossed the border alright, and then made our way to a hotel. Wanted to wait a few days to decide where we would go, as I didn't actually want to stay in Juarez permanently. We never expected for someone to try and kidnap me the very next day." She shivered involuntarily. "I'd heard the stories, of course. Who hasn't? But I never imagined being a target. Esteban got there just in time, he saved me, but we knew the hotel wasn't safe, so we ran. The idea was to find a bus or something and get at least to Chihuahua... but something went wrong. We got mugged, a man tried to rape me, when Esteban defended me they beat him up and before I quite knew what was happening I was in the middle of the desert, running, without the slightest idea of where to go! The last thing I heard from Esteban he was yelling at me to run."

"Don't look back, just run! Run Lily!!!"

"He called me Lily, because my favorite flower is the lily of the valley," the copper haired girl murmured quietly. "I eventually made it out of the desert. Somehow managed to bypass the whole state of Chihuahua too and made it to some small town in Coahuila, lived on the streets for a few weeks, and then I met Chris. It was also in that desert that I discovered my gifts, they're probably the only reason I survived."

For a moment Fiore couldn't quite believe what she was hearing. The similarities of Lily's story with... well, the other Lily's, were uncanny. She wasn't sure if it was coincidence, irony or fate, and she didn't want to know. Reincarnation was already a delicate matter, the possibility of history repeating itself. The mere thought of it filled her with fear and the most terrible despair.

"I met Lily several weeks after she got to Coahuila." Chris took over the story. "At first I didn't want her to get too close. The shades had been appearing recently, always coming after me, and I didn't want to put her at risk. And then I saw her shooting lightning from her hands!" He chuckled to himself at the memory. "We became good friends after that and, eventually, somehow, we found ourselves here, where we met you Flower."

"Did you know, before coming here, did you know about… Xochiquetzal and all this reincarnation thing?" Xochitl asked quietly.

"No," They both shook their heads.

"Though," Lily added after a moment. "I've been having dreams. About me, except with long hair, and the other girls, and guys, and… and you in a white dress and a veil over your hair, walking with a man in linen and leather clothes…"

While dress was probably not the best way to describe her past life's attire, the reincarnated Enchantress had no doubt that they were, indeed, talking about her, and about everyone else. Lily definitely remembered.

"Didn't begin having the dreams until after we met you, though," the reincarnated priestess added for good measure.

None of them mentioned that, for the first time, Fiore was talking openly about things, about who she was. Even if she hadn't said it outright, who she was, they all understood.

There was no talking for several minutes, the three of them just sat there drinking their tea. Fiore's mind just kept turning Lily's story around; she wanted to help her friend so much yet knew they couldn't do so in that moment, not with everything going on, but perhaps once they'd dealt with Tezcatlipoca.

"Wait a second." Something occurred to the Enchantress right then. "Didn't you say you saw your brother in Xochimilco? How…?"

"Yes… I saw him," the Priestess nodded stiffly. "Flower…" she swallowed. "He was the one controlling the jaguars…"

Of all the things Xochitl had been expecting to hear, she didn't see that one coming.

Elsewhere, Camellia opened her eyes. From the start she realized something was very odd, she hadn't exactly expected to be alive, and yet… then she remembered.

Camellia had been sitting there, on dirt and rocks, skirt muddy and slightly ripped, one of her shoes was missing, though she hadn't noticed until that moment. Not that it mattered much, she could hear the jaguars approaching, they were on the hunt...

And then another sound, louder than the growling... It was a bike, it did a half loop around her before stopping less than five feet away from her. The man on it didn't even take off his helmet, he jumped off the bike, scooped her up and sat her on the back of the bike, before climbing on again and kicking it into gear.

"Hold on!" he yelled at her sharply.

She did so instinctively, throwing both arms around the man's waist a second before they were off, rocks and dirt flying behind them.

Camellia wasn't sure when exactly she lost consciousness, or when she got to... wherever it was she was in that moment. She wasn't alone. In the following hours she saw girls in casual clothes and rebozos come and go, sometimes they'd enter the room to check on her; if they saw her awake they'd ask how she was feeling, if anything hurt, if she was hungry, thirsty, or anything at all. They never tried to chat with her or explain who they were and where she was. Eventually Camellia just snapped.

"When is anyone going to explain to me what by the Earth is going on here?!" she demanded in her sharpest tone.

"That's what I'm here for," a new voice called from the door.

Looking at her, Camellia immediately knew she was different from all the other girls she'd been seeing all day. Chocolate eyes and mostly straight light-brown hair pulled up messily with a clip; she was wearing skinny jeans and a gray long-sleeved top, she was also wearing a wide off-white rebozo with blue and violet stitching on the hem. Camellia knew, instantly, that she was different, more, than any of the other girls; and it wasn't just that her rebozo, which she used as a shawl, was wider than any of the others'. There was something about the young woman, about the way she held herself, her very aura gave her away… the older woman got it then.

"Hello, my niece…"

The following week was more than a little hectic. All the classes, and Fiore did her best to meet with Chris and Lily at least every other day. They heard jaguars in the distance every night, but hadn't seen them, or Lily's brother again. There had been no more attacks from the shades either, but they all could feel the tension, something was brewing.

By Friday Fiore was beyond exhausted. Her only comfort was knowing she no longer had classes on Saturday. Since she'd already gotten all her language credits, her Saturdays were completely free; which compensated somewhat for her having a late class on Friday and being unable to have dinner with Rose.

She was on her way to that last class when, unexpectedly, Draco caught up with her:

"Miss Fiore…" he greeted her in a quiet tone.

"Just Fiore is fine," she murmured, not quiet looking at him.

"Have you been avoiding me?" he asked her rather bluntly.

"Wha…?" she wasn't expecting that question. "No! Why would you think that?"

"I mean… I know I was very rude back before winter break..." he began, rubbing the back of his neck, looking apologetic.

"No m-, Q-, T-… Draco." It took everything she had for Xochitl not to blurt out the wrong name.

So maybe she had been avoiding him, but not for the reason he thought! Truth was she was afraid of doing something wrong, and it wasn't just about the name. What if he truly didn't remember her? Even if she knew he remembered the promise, or at least seemed to, that didn't mean he remembered everything. He'd remember her if that were the case, right?

"I have just been very busy this semester," she added for good measure. "I promise you it's nothing against you, and it certainly has nothing to do with our talk in the park before winter break."

At least worded like that she wasn't really lying.

"I see." She might have been wrong, but his tone sounded like he didn't quite believe her. "I suppose with it being your last semester it can probably get insane."

"Definitely," she agreed, and then there was everything else she was not going to tell him about!

A part of her knew he had a right to know. He was as much a part of it as she was, after all; Tezcatlipoca hadn't just been after her before, but him as well. And yet if he didn't remember... how could she be expected to explain the situation to him? Their history... their love... he'd believe her to be insane for sure!

"Have dinner with me."

Fiore almost tripped then.

"What...?!" Where the hell had that come from?!

"OK, so that may not be the best way to ask you out," he admitted ruefully; then, taking advantage of the fact that they'd finally stopped, he stood before her and in a very formal tone said. "Would the beautiful lady do me the honor of accompanying me to dinner on this fine night?"

The Enchantress's mouth felt dry, as a memory rushed through her head; those were the exact same words her beloved would use to invite her to dinner every time... even before he kissed her for the first time.

"Miss Fiore...?" he asked, puzzled.

The young woman blinked once, twice, and then finally allowed her dark cacao-colored eyes to meet his own dark-as-night ones. She could feel inside her, her soul shiver and something, like a piece of her heart and soul, tendrils coming from her very core, reaching out... then he blinked, and it was over.

He was still staring at her, waiting, and all she could do was nod. That moment, those few seconds had been enough to rob her of her speech completely. And she'd no idea how she was going to survive having dinner with him!

Surprisingly enough, the senior student had yet another unexpected meeting right after the end of class. Draco had been in the classroom for most of the time, until a secretary called him; apparently someone was looking for him. He'd slipped Fiore a note asking her to meet him in the parking-lot after class ended. With the teacher taking way too long explaining the paper he expected the students to write for their next class, the young woman was already a tad late; which made her less than willing to stay and chat with anyone. Only the identity of the person approaching her made her stop at all, and that was mainly because she never expected her: it was Veronica Resendiz.

"I need to talk to you," the Publicity major stated without so much as a greeting.

"I'm afraid I can't stay and chat right now," Fiore stated as she shouldered her bag. "Someone's waiting on me and I'm already late."

A part of her wondered what made the younger woman approach her, if it was important at all; but most of her mind was occupied with thoughts of Draco, and how to handle the upcoming dinner without saying more than she should and giving herself away.

"I really need to talk to you," Veronica insisted. "It's a serious matter."

"You can tell me on the way," Xochitl decided as she lead the other girl out of the classroom. "I need to get to the parking-lot and like I told you before, I'm already late."

"What I need to talk to you about will take a lot longer than two minutes." It was obvious the younger girl did not like being paid so little attention. "It's complicated, and we must talk in private."

"I really don't have time right now," Fiore insisted. "Why don't I meet you before my first class on Monday and then we can talk?"

Veronica was going to refuse, to insist that the older girl stay and talk to her; but she knew already it was useless, perhaps the whole endeavor had been pointless from the start. At least she tried…

"Sure," she finally said, a part of her wondering if Fiore had yet thought of the fact that there were no classes on Monday, they had the whole week off for spring break.

"See you then!" the older student called back before rushing down the hall.

Veronica didn't reply to the farewell right away, silently watching the black-haired girl walk away; it was only as she crossed the doors, that three words crossed her lips:

"Good luck princess..."

Xochitl reached the parking lot in a rush. She hadn't even gone by her locker to leave what books she could spare, not wanting to be any later. And yet Draco wasn't there. She could see some other students getting on their vehicles and leaving for the night, but none of them were Draco. Fearing the worst, she looked for his car, but it was right there, where he always parked it, and he wasn't in it, or anywhere nearby.

Eventually Fiore decided that whatever it was he'd been called for earlier must have him running late himself, so she elected to wait for him. She sat on a bench near his car and settled down for doing exactly that.

Almost an hour passed before she finally admitted that maybe he'd just stood her up. Accidentally or on purpose. There might have been an emergency of some kind, some unavoidable meeting and he just didn't get the chance to tell her he couldn't make it; perhaps he simply forgot about her. Unlikely as the last one might seem, she just wasn't sure how well she knew her old lover anymore. She kept discovering new things about her children, so why not him as well?

In any case, she couldn't wait all night for him. It was late, and while Lulu had promised to make dinner for Rosie and put her to bed, Fiore couldn't in good conscience leave them on their own for much longer. Rose was her daughter after all.

The reincarnated Enchantress tripped over her own feet as she was getting off the bench, half falling against Draco's car, she barely managed to use her left hand to stop herself from hitting her head against the edge of the door. Cursing her klutziness Fiore picked up her bag and began the trek through the parking-lot and to the closest gate out of campus.

Once home she found Lulu almost falling asleep while a romantic comedy was playing on the tv, low enough not to bother Rose as she slept. She thanked the girl, the eldest child of the oldest father living in the building, paid her for babysitting and then decided to go to sleep. The plan was for her to rest a bit, then get changed, eat something and go to sleep; but it was late, and she was so tired that the young woman ended up falling asleep in her clothes the moment her head touched the pillow.

Chapter 19
Garlic Flower

Xochitl felt on odd tension when she woke up; she had trouble breathing, like the air around her was thick somehow, and she'd no idea why. She rubbed under her eyes with her hands and on the bridge of her nose, trying to relieve the tension somehow, nothing worked. She was about to go to the bathroom, hoping some water on her face might do the trick, when her door opened, and a tiny torpedo rushed in, jumping onto the bed and practically into her lap:

"Mommy, Mommy, Mommy!" the child cried out with delighted giggles.

"Rosie, Rosie, Rosie!" the young woman replied in a sing-song tone.

The girl blinked right then, before breaking into louder laughter.

"Sweety…?" Fiore was confused as to what was going on.

"Half your face is all black Mommy!" the girl explained, giggling even more.

Confused, the black-haired gal slipped off the bed, padding barefoot to the bathroom. Looking at herself into the mirror she could see Rose was right, the left side of her face looked black in places, lines and smudges, as if she'd rubbed something on it. Immediately she turned her eyes to her left hand, and there it was, the lower half of her palm was black, and she couldn't for the life of her begin to guess why.

"This looks like…" she murmured to herself, twisting her wrist this way and that to try and get a better look at the smudge. "Is this soot?"

It came to her then, the memory of the previous night, the moment when she'd tripped, raising her hand to stop her head from smashing against the door… she'd used her left hand to hold herself, the very hand that was smudged with black!

The Enchantress swore. It was completely unlike her, but she truly believed the situation warranted it. At least Rose didn't understand that much Spanish yet, so she was unlikely to understand what Xochitl had just said.

The black-haired woman took a handful of seconds to look at herself in the mirror, watching realization fill her eyes, as her hands tightened into fists and she began almost vibrating with what was probably the beginning of a panic attack. She didn't allow it to take hold though. She gave herself those five seconds to embrace her feelings, the mix of unease, growing horror and near despair; then she took hold of them all and pushed them as deep down as she could, forcing herself to focus on what needed to be done.

Almost without thinking about it the Enchantress let out a sharp pulse of magic, she knew it would be enough to get the ball rolling.

One more look into the mirror was enough for her to decide washing her face wouldn't do, so she jumped into the shower for a quick wash and then returned to her bedroom to get dressed. Rose was still waiting for her, sitting on the bed; she either hadn't sensed the pulse or simply didn't see a reason for questioning it. Fiore just smiled and told her it was time for breakfast. She wasn't about to explain the hell of a mess they were about to go into, that they were technically already in, to the little girl unless she had to.

Xochitl was putting away the just-dried breakfast dishes when her doorbell rang. Rose brightened up, as she always did when they got visits, and rushed to open the door. The black-haired young woman let her, knowing that the security in the building was such that only people she'd invited were let in; also, she could sense the people just outside the door, they were all there.

"*Hello!*" Rosie greeted them all brightly.

"*Hello Rosie!*" Lily smiled brightly at her.

Chris said his own greeting, while the others just waved at the child; it seemed like Belladonna and the others still didn't know quite what to say or do about the girl. Hyacinth had mentioned at one point her inability to 'see' anything about the child, she was invisible to her gift of foresight; something that seemed to upset not just her, but everyone in their little group.

Still inside the kitchen, standing just out of sight of the newcomers, the reincarnated Enchantress took a moment to watch them in silence. While it wasn't the first time she saw them since regaining her memories, she hadn't had the chance before to just look at them. Her chest hurt; as if some invisible force had punched her in the lungs, leaving her breathless, and were trying to squeeze her heart completely, all at the same time. Those people in the other room, they weren't just priestesses and warriors, they weren't just her subordinates. Matter of fact, she'd never seen them like that; they were hers... her children. Finally, after so long, her children were back with her and yet again they were in danger. In that moment the young woman wanted nothing more than to go to them, embrace them tightly, kiss each of their brows, tell them how much she loved them, how much she always had but she couldn't, she couldn't do it, it was too risky. This time, in this life, she would protect them, she wouldn't fail them again.

The moment Fiore stepped into the sitting room everyone straightened up abruptly, as if some kind of force had just called them to attention. They were all staring at her, and it took Xochitl a moment to realize that it was the first time all of them except Chris and Lily saw her without any kind of makeup or hairdo. Right then, with her cocoa-brown eyes and long, straight, jet-black hair cascading down her back, if any of them had any memories of their past lives they were probably shocked at the realization of how much she truly looked like her old-self.

"What's going on?" Chris wanted to know, curious.

"We were summoned here," Julian pointed out, cocking his head to a side in contemplation. "Why?"

"There's no easy way to say this, so I'll be blunt:" The Enchantress stated, taking a deep breath before saying it: "Quetzalcoatl has been taken."

She had probably been a tad blunter than entirely necessary, but there really was no easy way of explaining things, and they didn't have the time for long explanations.

"What?!" Still, it would seem that some explanation would be needed, as the shock was just too great.

"The King is... he was taken?!"

"You know where he is... was...?!"

It was hard to tell which of those two the young adults before her were truly more fixated upon, Xochiquetzal's reincarnation still focused on being succinct in her explanation.

"Yes, I know who he is in this life, have known for several weeks." And she'd suspected beforehand... or at least the part of her that hadn't been focused on her lack of conclusive evidence of her being Xochiquetzal had. "I didn't mention it before because it wasn't relevant."

"And now it is?" Lily arched a brow.

"Evidently," Fiore nodded. "He was taken some time last night, before ten, from the Mater University Campus. I know because he was supposed to meet me after my last class was over. I waited for him for an hour to no avail."

"If this all happened last night why are we only learning about it now?" David wanted to know.

"Because last night I was too tired, didn't realize the wrongness of it all." She hadn't noticed the soot stain on her hand, didn't know what it meant. "This morning I understood. He's been taken."

"By whom?" Eduardo demanded.

"The same person as last time," Xochitl answered grimly. "Tezcatlipoca. I have no idea who he might be in this life, what he even looks like though..." A sudden realization came to her, along with the memory of a lawyer she'd met once, months earlier. "I know he's here, that he has money and influence."

"How do you know that?" Belladonna asked in a suspicious tone.

Xochitl did not want to even imagine what they might say if they were to know that she'd effectively sold the grounds of their old temple to Tezcatlipoca, so she chose to keep that to herself. It's not like the man could ever set foot on the place anyway, there was a reason why he'd sent a minion. Even after more than a thousand years the magic in that place was too strong for him to violate it; it was the same reason why back in their other life humans had been the ones to attack. Also, he was quite fond of manipulating others to do his dirty work... except where it came to Quetzalcoatl and her. He knew if he wanted to truly destroy them, he had to see to it himself. Not that she planned on allowing it. She might not have been able to do much in her old life, nothing more than guarantee they would have a chance someday in any case, but she was no longer the person she'd been then. She was... more, in some ways. More willing to get her hands dirty, in any case. She was also far more aware of the dangers those she cared for were in. The thing in Xochimilco had taken her by surprise, there was nothing she could do for Camellia, but she'd be damned if she let her children die, again.

"That's not important," she finally answered Belladonna. "What's important is finding Quetzalcoatl."

"Can you do that?" Chris wanted to know, taking a quick look at the other group he added. "When they took you, we had trouble finding you."

"Because our auras are similar enough for theirs to mask mine with some effort, and the traces of me all around the city did not make things any easier for you," the reincarnated Enchantress pointed out kindly. "This is different, on all accounts. While Tezcatlipoca certainly has the power to mask other auras, just doing that would show his own aura strongly enough for me to pick up on that instead. And if he doesn't mask... that will only make it easier for me to track the King. Unlike me, he hasn't been here for long, not even six months, his aura won't have seeped into the earth as much. I can find him."

"Very well, when are we leaving?" Lily wanted to know.

"Don't get me wrong." Fiore shook her head. "I didn't call you here, didn't tell you this, so you would come with me. Only so you would know the situation, so you'd be aware of the danger. Tezcatlipoca is in this time, this city even, and he will very likely come after you."

"Are you not going after the King?" Belladonna demanded in an accusatory tone.

"Of course, I am!" Xochitl practically snapped at her. "Doesn't mean I'm going to take you with me."

"Why not?" Eduardo demanded in turn.

"Because I don't want you to die again!" The reincarnated Enchantress finally cried out, just for one second losing all composure.

"What...?" They certainly weren't expecting that.

"*Mommy!*" Rose cried out, reacting to Fiore's own distress.

The black-haired woman's own reaction was instinctive, as she enveloped the little girl in a one-armed hug, doing her best to send quiet reassurance to her, even as she kept her eyes on her children. She needed to make them understand...

"I failed to protect you once, failed to understand the danger you were in all those years ago, the fact that Tezcatlipoca would go after you." She tried her best to explain to them. "I had to watch you die..." Her voice broke at the mere hint of the memory. "I won't do it again. I won't... I..."

"Mistress..." Hyacinth began, extending a hand hesitantly.

It was obvious none of them were expecting that.

"You told me, when we first met... you mentioned all of you, and you called Lily my favorite... but you were wrong," Fiore said quietly. "So very, very wrong. I don't know exactly how much you might or might not remember of your past lives but... you were mine, my children. I loved you as my own flesh and blood, and I was forced to watch you die when the temple was attacked, I was forced... I saw you fall, one by one, and that broke me, almost as much as feeling my own beloved die himself. I lost it, I did something... I called on powers that aren't meant to be messed with. It's the whole reason we're here in the first place!" She shook her head. "But I didn't do it so you'd end up dying all over again. So, no, I won't allow it. I am going after Tezcatlipoca and Quetzalcoatl. And you are going to take yourselves to a safe place, and that's that."

She would not risk them again, no way.

What Xochiquetzal didn't know, was that it simply wasn't her choice to make…

Somehow Fiore managed to convince Lily and Chris to take Rosie with them when the group split, minutes later. She didn't want to leave her without someone who might be able to protect her, in case Tezcatlipoca found out about her, and tried going after her to hurt Xochitl. The reincarnated Enchantress had no idea that her former wards were planning on leaving the child with someone else and then going after her, unwilling to leave her alone with the very being that had already been responsible for all their deaths before.

In the end both plans were pointless. The moment Fiore opened the building's door to the street there was a car waiting on them. The car was a non-descriptive black sedan, nothing special about it, the black-haired young woman would have thought nothing of it at all if the door hadn't opened right then, a man in a dark-gray suit stepping out and turning straight towards her stoically.

"Miss Yolotl," he called in a completely emotionless tone.

"Mr. Ahumada," she replied, just as evenly. This was the man who had come to her grandmother's home to buy it off her.

She did not ask him what he was doing there right then, it was obvious enough. Behind her back she made a simple sign, hoping Chris would see it, would choose that moment not to fight her, to take Lily and Rose and walk away. And he did try to do that, whatever he might think about her choices, at least he valued Rosie enough to try and save her, but it was not to be. Before he could give a single step, Ahumada was in his way.

"You will be riding in the van," he informed them, in a tone that left it very clear it wasn't a question.

"Oh, will we…?" Belladonna began, a hint of challenge in her voice.

"Stop," Chris took charge then. "We can't risk a fight here. We can't risk innocent lives like that. That's not what we do…"

No, it was what Tezcatlipoca did, which explained why he'd sent his minion, it made Xochitl curse for never considering such a possibility before. They had always been the ones to care about innocents, not Tezcatlipoca... he would care very little about killing the passersby, and everyone in the building behind them: Alondra, Lulu, Miguel, everyone... parents and children, innocents. They couldn't allow that.

"Get in the van," She said simply, as emotionless as she could.

Inside she was hurting. She hurt because she knew the danger she was putting them all in by giving that order. The fact that they all may very well die... and yet, not doing so would only put more people in danger. If doing so then and there didn't work, Tezcatlipoca wouldn't hesitate to attack others, houses, businesses, a school? He cared very little for the lives of others. And as much as she might love her children, none of them, and not even Xochiquetzal herself, were worth innocent lives.

And so, they went.

Thankfully Lily thought to keep Rosie with her. Somehow managing to keep her from calling to her Mommy as the group boarded the big van. Fiore herself waiting until they were all on it to climb into the black car. Then they were off.

Chapter 20
Rhododendron

They were on the road for around seven hours. Xochitl had been able to half-sense when they passed several miles away from the grounds of her old temple, and then past Tula; and very little afterwards. She noticed when they entered the Reservation, nature calling to her; it was once she sensed her own, very old trace in the land, that she realized exactly where they were. The Mines…

The Enchantress couldn't help the violent shudder than went through her whole body as the vehicle drove straight into one of the tunnels. She could feel it, the moment her bond to the Earth became strained, almost to the breaking point. Almost, but not quite.

She was still shivering when the door opened and Ahumada bid her to step out. The van had stopped behind them and she could see her girls stumbling somewhat, their partners doing their best to help them without making it too obvious that something was wrong. Lily was the one who seemed the least affected; then again, they were in the North, they were in her land, which probably helped her some. Also, she was busy enough holding a sobbing Rosie; the child was feeling the same as Xochitl, probably worse even because she didn't understand why it was happening at all. It took every drop of Xochitl's will not to rush to the little girl and try to comfort her. But she couldn't do that, she couldn't risk revealing their connection to Tezcatlipoca or his minions, for both of their sakes… for all their sakes.

They were all led down several tunnels, deep into the mines, until they eventually ended in an open space, some sort of chamber. Parts of the wall seemed to have been purposefully carved in such a way as to form benches. Also, in the middle of the room rose a rocky formation shaped like a throne. It was huge, made of some odd-looking stone, in mixed shades of gray, like those of silver and mercury. They were all led to one of the side walls, except for Fiore, who was made to take a seat right before the empty throne. For a moment it looked like Belladonna, or perhaps David might challenge the decision, but the reincarnated Enchantress shook her head calmly, signaling for them to settle. Things were complicated enough already, they did not need to make matters worse. Besides, she knew that it would be pointless to challenge; the others might not have fully realized it just yet, but their gifts were next to useless that deep inside the mine. It was Tezcatlipoca's mine after all, and while Xochiquetzal might be able to call on some power if she tried hard enough… she'd rather leave that as a last resource… she hoped it wouldn't come to that. Not again.

They were offered food and drink at one point, but Fiore declined it, and the others followed her lead silently. Lily for her part pulled an energy bar from the inside pocket of her jacket and gave it to Rosie. She was in the habit of carrying them and decided the girl should probably eat something. Xochitl mouthed a silent 'thank you' at her the next time the girl's amber eyes turned in her direction.

It would be impossible to tell how long they all sat there. Hours. But eventually she sensed him before she saw him; his aura was like encroaching darkness to her senses, like some thick, viscous… thing slithering towards her, suffocating her without even touching her. It was sickening. She vaguely realized that never before had his presence affected her so badly; she knew the reason of course and could only hope that would end up being a good thing. At least Rosie had fallen asleep at some point in the last hour, and Lily and Chris were doing their best to keep her out of sight, hopefully Tezcatlipoca would have no reason to turn his attention to her. Xochitl would die, again, before he let that monster lay a single finger on her baby.

"I heard you refused my kind hospitality, princess..." a smooth, silky, almost inhuman voice called.

Everyone turned in the direction of the voice instantly, watching as a man entered. He was tall, with broad-shoulders, extremely short black hair, nearly cropped to the scalp, and eyes the same color as the purest obsidian. He was wearing a perfectly pressed bespoke suit, completely black, and shoes polished to a mirror-like finish. There was also a hand-made cigarette held carefully, almost elegantly, between his fingers.

Fiore chose not to respond to the provocation, and he did not insist. Instead the man walked straight across the room before sitting slowly, gracefully on the throne. All his moves were slow, sleek, perfectly measured, well-practiced; the kind of motions one expected of those born as royalty. It was a facade Tezcatlipoca had cultivated a very long time prior, back when he'd been next to nothing, yet liked to pretend he was everything, back then he'd needed to get certain individuals out of the way to get what he wanted. In the current day and time, it was impossible to tell if he really believed Xochiquetzal and Quetzalcoatl to be that much of a threat to him at all, or if he simply wanted to destroy them for the sake of it, for his own satisfaction, a sense of victory. It didn't change things any in the long run, though the reincarnated Enchantress did wonder why he couldn't just let it go.

"I have to admit, I didn't see this coming, didn't see you coming," he revealed, looking straight at Xochitl as he spoke. "Not as you are now. I was so sure we were done with you, finally. After you signed those papers, gave away your own birthright like it was nothing... you didn't care, I know that much. So why then? Why didn't you just walk away?"

Fiore could hear muttering from the side, as Belladonna and the others tried to understand if Tezcatlipoca was telling the truth, what he meant exactly, the implications... but Xochitl paid them no heed. It wasn't important right then.

"Because you were hurting innocents, again," she told him simply. "Though, now that you mention that, I want to know too. Why don't you walk away? Truth be told, if you hadn't come after me, that would have been it. I had no reason to seek you out, to provoke a confrontation, so why send the shades after me?"

She knew the answer already of course, or at least had a very good idea of what it was: while for her, living was enough of a victory, would have been enough to make her happy, satisfied; Tezcatlipoca would allow for nothing less than the total destruction of his enemies. It simply wasn't in his nature to settle for anything less.

"It's time to end this little war of ours, princess," he said instead. "After a thousand years. The time has come, wouldn't you say?"

"I couldn't agree more," she nodded serenely.

Of course, they each had different ideas of how their war was supposed to end.

"Break your enchantment," he ordered, in the tone of one who expects to be obeyed without delay or hesitation.

"You know I cannot do that," she answered with absolute serenity.

Tezcatlipoca snapped his fingers and in the next instant there were two men pulling a struggling Magnolia from the group, struggles that ceased abruptly when a stone blade was pressed tight to the side of her neck.

It took everything in Xochiquetzal's reincarnation not to scream her denial. But she knew she couldn't do that, for Lia's safety, for all their safeties. She needed to stay focused, calm, to keep control…

"You know if you kill one of them you'll have to kill us all, and then we'll have to do this awkward dance all over again," she reminded him in her most even voice. "You should know by now Tezcatlipoca, killing my children will not make me bend to your will, nothing ever will. Whether in this life, or the next, or a dozen from now, one day I will succeed, we will succeed, there will be justice."

"What the hell is going on?!" David snarled.

The other men were barely able to hold him back.

"Oh… you mean your princess hasn't told you yet?" the evil mage stated in a provocative manner. "This isn't the first time we all do this dance."

"What…?" The confusion was evident in them all.

"What does that mean?" Eduardo demanded.

"It means this isn't our first reincarnation," Hyacinth stated serenely.

"You knew?!" Her companions all turned towards her.

"I suspected, didn't know for sure." Hyacinth shrugged slightly.

"Did you really believe that it would take us a thousand years to come back?" Lily asked with a snort. "Like, what? The planets aligned and that allowed us to come back precisely now?"

It was ludicrous, once seen like that, Lily was right. There was no reason to believe that anything was different in that moment than it had been in the previous thousand years. Any reason for them to have been reincarnated then and not at some other point in time... except they had, and more than once. Only they didn't remember, or at least most of them didn't, they weren't supposed to.

"You knew?!" Belladonna demanded of the youngest priestess.

"I have vague recollections, nothing concrete." Lily shrugged slightly. "Didn't seem that important. It doesn't change anything. Besides, this is my life now, why should I care about the ones I've left behind?"

Even her original life. It wasn't that she didn't believe it to be important, but truth was that even if she'd never had those dreams about Xochiquetzal, that wouldn't have stopped her from seeing Flower as a friend, from loving her almost like an older sister. She was who she was, and while it was nice knowing that she could always count on someone like Flower, and of course on Chris; even if they hadn't been a part of her past, they were a part of her present, and that was what really mattered to her. Just like with Rosie! Rose had never been a part of any of her, of their past lives, far as the amber-eyed girl knew, that didn't mean Lily loved her any less in the current one.

"How many times?" Belladonna wanted to know. "And why don't we remember?"

"About half a dozen for you, more for me," the Enchantress revealed with as little emotion as she could. "And you never remember because you're not supposed to. Because that's a burden I never wanted you, any of you to carry."

"Yet you remember..." Hyacinth murmured quietly.

"I never forget," Fiore nodded. "It comes with being the one who cast the enchantment that allows us to live again, and one of the only two people still alive at that point; the other being him." She waved her hand in Tezcatlipoca's direction. "As long as the conditions of the enchantment aren't met, we'll keep doing this over and over again."

"Unless you break the enchantment," Tezcatlipoca insisted in a near hiss.

"I cannot do that," Xochitl told him.

"Cannot or will not?" A whimper from Magnolia added vehemence to his demand.

"Cannot." The reincarnated Enchantress radiated honesty as she explained. "I did it in such a way it couldn't just be broken. Powered it by the spilling of more than just my blood, my life, my very soul went into that spell. It cannot be broken, not by you and not by me. I made sure of it. One day there will be justice."

"I will destroy you all!" Tezcatlipoca practically roared.

"And we will be back here, in this world, doing this same dance all over again in a century or so," Fiore almost drawled.

It was insane, to take things like life and death, her own and that of others, of people she cared greatly for, with such disregard... but she had died and been reborn so many times, she was tired. A part of her believed that if she could actually break the enchantment she might do it, if only to be able to rest, finally. When she cast that spell it'd never occurred to her how wrong things might go. How hard Tezcatlipoca would fight back, how much he might be willing to destroy.

"I was supposed to win this time!" the evil mage snarled. "Destroy you, your line, raze your filthy temple to the ground, end this little dance of ours once and for all!"

"I know," Xochitl nodded. "You've been hunting my line down for what feels like an eternity, but you see, that was your problem this time. You came after us too early; either that or we were born too late..." She hadn't thought of that before. "We were born late..."

"What...?" None of the others got it either.

"I told you before," Fiore stated, not quite looking at her people. "In our first life, you were my girls, my children, all of you. I raised you girls since you were young, when Quetzalcoatl brought you to me. And then he sent the Atlantes to guard us all. You were mine, my family, and Tezcatlipoca dared take you all from me. And not just you but..." Her voice broke off at the memory. "That's why I cast that enchantment. Powered by blood, and life and soul, I sacrificed all I was, all I had left for a chance. For justice... for us to have a chance to live the lives we deserved, the lives we were denied. That's why we were reborn, and why we'll keep reincarnating until we get to live those lives."

"Or until I finally destroy your line," Tezcatlipoca deadpanned. "I came so close this time... so close..."

The Enchantress shook her head. While the former warrior was, indeed, right, regarding how close he'd come to destroying their line... it simply couldn't be done. As long as one girl lived the line could be rebuilt... and what Tezcatlipoca failed to realize was that it didn't even have to be someone from her blood. After all, the one to begin the line in the first place: Daisy, had been nothing of hers, not by flesh and blood; she'd been her daughter in her heart and soul and that was enough. Even if things had been terrible enough for all her blood family to have died, Xochiquetzal could have easily enough chosen someone else, grant her blessing, and the line would start anew.

"Why can't you just let us be?" she was tired, so very tired. "Why do you insist on continuing this endless war? Haven't you had enough?"

"Never." Tezcatlipoca snarled. "Not until this world is mine."

"Ha!" Fiore could have laughed, for real. "This world will never be yours, but that's due to more than just us. Humanity will never allow you to win Tezcatlipoca. They didn't allow it a thousand years ago, and they won't do it now." She let out a breath. "We no longer live in a time when people worship those like you and me, like Quetzalcoatl; we're no longer gods to them. We're just people. Gifted people, yes, but as mortal as the rest of them."

"I am no mere mortal!" the man roared. "I will never be! I'm a god!"

"We might have been more once," Xochitl shrugged slightly. "And you certainly managed to hold onto that which made us different for a few centuries longer than either the King or I did, but you're just like us now. Reborn in a mortal body, confined to human limitations. We may have power, but it's not absolute. It was never supposed to be. And while in the past our gifts might have granted us power as well as a responsibility, the people still alive who would accept us, what our presence here means, they're few and far between. You must also know they'd never accept you."

"I could make them," Tezcatlipoca sneered. "I can be very… persuasive… and they don't remember you."

"I know," she nodded again. "You managed that much, erased me and my children from history, like we never existed. But you could never erase our King. And you must know that the same people who would know your name will also know his. And they will always choose him…"

"I am meant to be King! I will be King!"

Fiore did not insist. A part of her wondered at the point of even arguing; it's not like she ever expected to be able to reason with a man like Tezcatlipoca. He hadn't been exactly an honorable man a thousand years earlier; much less in the present.

All thoughts were erased from her mind in an instant though, as another figure was suddenly in the room. Prostrated before Tezcatlipoca, who stood before his throne, hand raised before him. Xochitl was the only one who could truly recognize the curled-up figure in dusty, slightly tattered clothes, covered in bruises, cuts and with dried blood on the side of his face.

"Quetzalcoatl!" Xochiquetzal shrieked, unable to hold herself back.

She threw herself towards him instantly, or at least tried to. However, before she could give more than two steps Tezcatlipoca turned his attention towards her. The black-haired young woman suddenly found herself being slammed against the stone wall; and unceremoniously dropped to the ground but a second later.

"Xochi... quetzal..." The reincarnated King's voice was low, hoarse and somewhat broken, but everyone could sense the underlying power in it.

Yes, Quetzalcoatl was well and truly awake, in every sense of the word; he knew himself, and he knew her...

"I grow tired of this state of affairs," Tezcatlipoca announced right then and there. "I think it's about time we finish this little dance of ours, once and for all."

Yes, talks were over, the fight was about to start... again.

Chapter 21
Apple Blossom

Draco Yao Tamay always knew he wasn't exactly normal. Growing up his mother kept an herb garden, and he was sure he knew more about natural teas and remedies than the local herbalist. Also, as a child his mom would always tell him old stories, legends, about a great warrior king that would one day return to save his people. At first, he'd confused the story with that of King Arthur, thought his mom had just chosen to change his name for whatever the reason. And then he learned the truth about Quetzalcoatl...

Neither of his parents ever told him about his fate, they didn't have to, Draco just knew. The moment he found that book about Quetzalcoatl, read the man's full name: Ce Acatl Topiltzin Quetzalcoatl, he just knew. He didn't quite remember, not everything, but enough. When his parents announced the trip to Mexico he was both nervous and excited, he knew she would be waiting for him there and he could hardly wait... And then the accident happened, his parents died, and so did hers.

Over a decade later he still remembered how she looked that day, in the long tunic, knitted veil covering her dark locks of hair. No one would approach her, either of them, as if there was a barrier between the two of them and the rest of the world. Draco wanted to stay with her forever, to protect her, like he'd failed to do so before; he'd no idea what had happened, exactly, but the sense of failure was there, deep inside, like an itch he just couldn't get rid of.

It wasn't in his hands, though, he knew that, as did she. And so, he walked away, leaving her alone. He promised her he'd come back... it took him eighteen years to do so, and by then it was too late already. She was long gone. His Enchantress, his princess, was gone, and he'd no idea how to go about finding her.

There were times when Draco wondered why he accepted fate so easily, why he didn't fight back. He never liked the idea of having his life written before he was even born, it wasn't fair, didn't he deserve to make his own decisions? And yet, wasn't it his choice to travel to Mexico the second time? He could have finished his doctorate at a distance, the internet was a wonderful tool; it would have been enough. It was also a perfect excuse, a reason to go back, to try and find her. He didn't expect her not to be in the village; the whole family had vanished, and he hadn't the slightest idea of where to even begin looking for her.

She was alive, that much he was sure of. He knew that if she'd died, he'd have felt it, because they were connected. Even after more than eighteen years since their last meeting, the bond between their souls was just too strong. So, he decided to finish his studies and take the time to try and find her. Mexico City was the perfect place, not too far from the village, and he could sense the traces of the Enchantress's power that had seeped deep into the earth.

The jaguars were a surprise; not only because they were in a city, and attacking him, but because he understood it wasn't just a coincidence or a freak accident, they were hunting him, undoubtedly. That realization brought another with it: the possibility that he might not be the only one that was being hunted. And if they were after his princess as well, then maybe it was a good thing that she couldn't be so easily found.

If there was one thing, person, Draco never saw coming it was Fiore Yolotl. That girl... she was like nothing he could have ever imagined. So many contradictions... a mystery wrapped in an enigma. Talking to her was so easy, so natural; he was somehow sure that no matter what he did or said she'd never judge him. Even though she seemed to be part of the clique of popular and conceited girls, she was nothing like the rest of them. She was kind, and clever, and witty; with an aura that seemed to mix humility and serenity in a way he hadn't seen in a lifetime. She was simply... fascinating.

He'd almost kissed her once, back in December. It wasn't planned, and he wasn't sure which he regretted more, almost doing it, or not doing it in the end. He knew it was wrong, he'd made a promise, twice, to a girl, and he couldn't go back on that promise; he was an honorable man and would keep his word. Still, he'd never forget her expression, her eyes, that moment, right as their lips were about to touch… and when he pulled back.

It wasn't exactly a surprise when Fiore began avoiding him once they returned to school in February. Not a surprise, but still, he didn't like it. A part of him told him it was better to leave things as they were, focus on finding Xochiquetzal, his princess, the one he made the two most important promises ever too and yet he just couldn't let go of Fiore. A tiny voice in the back of his mind even began asking if his Enchantress could possibly be anything like Fiore, because the girl was just so amazing. And it was insane, the way the curly-haired gal was so deeply entrenched in his mind, when he'd already promised his hand, his heart, to another. Someone he'd loved for a thousand years…

Also, the way she changed, it intrigued and confused him at the same time. It was obvious enough he wasn't the only one who noticed, but while to most her changes seemed to be a reason to pull away, he only felt his fascination grow. Also, he was quite sure that Fiore's eyes used to be a dark turquoise and yet, when he finally managed to get close enough to her to really look into her eyes after months… they were brown, like the earth after a rainstorm or… no, a warm brown, like chocolate.

When he invited her to dinner, pretty much insisted that they have dinner together, he'd no idea what he was doing exactly. Regardless of how hard he tried to stay away, to leave her alone, to focus on keeping his promises, there was a part of him that just couldn't let it go. So, he told himself it was just one dinner, he'd talk to her, make sure there were no hard feelings between them, and then he'd walk away. That was the plan. A plan that became pretty much pointless when he never even made it to dinner.

Draco did not know he'd been knocked out until he woke up. Which, he knew, was a sign that something was very, very wrong. The fact that the first thing he saw upon waking up was the maw of a jaguar, so close he could practically smell its putrid breath, only made things worse. He was also in pain, the kind of pain that told him he hadn't just been manhandled but beaten up some while unconscious.

"You alright man?" A voice with a bit of an American accent asked him.

Draco turned his eyes some in the direction of the voice, not quite daring to turn around, to so much as move a muscle with the beast so close.

"Ah, right..." The man chuckled some, before adding something in a language that sounded a bit like Nahuatl, but not quite.

The effect was immediate as the jaguar sniffed him once more before padding away. Still, Draco waited a handful of seconds longer before rolling onto his back and sitting up. He found himself in what looked like some kind of underground chamber, perhaps a mine, and he certainly wasn't alone. The place was quite big, though the dozen or so jaguars stalking around made the place feel almost claustrophobically small. Then there was the man who'd spoken before: he looked to be in his mid-twenties, tall, broad-shouldered, muscled, his skin darkly tanned, there hardly seemed to be any hair on his head, though there was some on his face, showing he hadn't shaved in a few days at least and his amber eyes held odd shadows in them that looked more than a little unnatural.

"So, you alright?" the man repeated the question.

"I'm... I will be fine," Draco corrected after a little thought move pulled on a muscle and he felt his back screaming in pain.

"Yeah, they gave you quite the beating man," the amber-eyed nodded. "The boss did not like that, at all."

"Who is this boss?" Quetzalcoatl's reincarnation wanted to know, though truth was he suspected the answer. "Who are you anyway?"

"Oh right, my name is Steve, Steve Norwood," he introduced himself. "I would say it's a pleasure to meet you... but I think I'll save us the trouble and say nothing of the like."

"Good." Draco really didn't feel like lying for politeness sake, even though, as far as wardens went, Steve wasn't anything like he was expecting. "My name is Draco Yao Tamay." He looked around him and then began asking questions. "What is this place? Why are we here exactly?"

"We're in the White Smoke mine, a few miles from Arroyo Seco, in Queretaro," Steve explained to him. "I've no idea why you're here, exactly. Though you were brought very early this morning. As for why I'm here, I'm in charge of these guys."

He waved a hand around vaguely, encompassing the beasts prowling all around them, letting out a guttural word, to which the jaguars responded with low noises before going back to whatever they were doing.

"Wait, so you are the one who controls them?" Draco was in absolute shock. "You're the one who's been sending those things after me for months?!"

Several of the cats let out a sort-of hissing noise, as if they perceived a threat towards their master. Steve pronounced another word, which calmed them down just as fast; pretty much confirming that he was in control of the animals.

"It wasn't my choice," he admitted after what seemed like forever. "I was following orders." He cringed slightly at his own words. "And I know how bad that sounds, but I didn't have a choice."

"There's always a choice," Draco muttered between clenched teeth.

"Not for me," Steve shook his head, and there was a hint of some very profound sadness as he explained: "You see, this I am... I did not choose to become this. It was chosen for me, and I cannot turn away. He won't allow it." He waved vaguely at his own eyes, as if trying to explain something without quite saying it. "I wouldn't do it anyway, disobey him, I mean, because if I do it, if I even think of going against what the boss commands, he will kill my little sister. My Lily..."

Draco had no idea what he was supposed to say to that, so for the longest time he said nothing at all. And what could he have said anyway? What would he have done in Steve's place? If Tezcatlipoca had found him, had forced him into service by threatening his princess's life... The dark-eyed man could only be thankful that such had never happened, he really didn't want to have to seriously contemplate the answer to that question. Still, that did not change the current situation, and a part of him really wanted to believe he could do something to help the other man.

"Would you...?" He shook his head and revised. "If I could make sure your sister would be safe, would you help me?"

"How could you possibly do that?" Steve began, then scoffed to himself and shook his head. "You have no idea the power the boss has. It's not... it's not human."

No, it wouldn't be; and while Quetzalcoatl's power might not be quite as flashy as Tezcatlipoca's, or Xochiquetzal's, that did not mean his was any less; the three of them were the same in the end, the last of their kind... and even reincarnated into human bodies, their power was a part of their souls, it'd always be there.

"No, it's not," Draco confirmed. "But I promise you, I can help you. I will, but I need you to help me as well."

"How?" Steve didn't understand. "What can you possibly do against such a monster?"

"It's my destiny to fight him." And this time... this time he'd win.

Steve had been and done a lot of things in his lifetime, and there were more than a few he wasn't exactly proud of. The one he'd never doubted was that he was a good brother to Lily, she was the reason he did so many things, to ensure her safety, her chance at happiness... and yet, because of those same choices he couldn't be with her, hadn't seen her in years. If there was any possibility of him being free and her staying safe... but, how could he trust the word of a man he didn't know? Whom he'd never met... the only reason he didn't dismiss the thought out of hand was: the man was there because the boss had ordered he be brought in, which meant he was, in fact, someone of importance...

"Who are you, really?" Steve blurted out. "Why did the boss want you brought here?"

Draco opened his mouth, but he never got the chance to explain, as right then a cloud of dark smoke seemed to appear out of nowhere, enveloping the dark-eyed man; a handful of seconds later it was gone, the reincarnated King along with it, leaving Steve with no company but his jaguars.

Chapter 22
Black-eyed Susan

The dizziness and vertigo the teleportation spell caused him was so strong that for several seconds Draco could do nothing except lay on his side, slightly curled up, eyes tightly closed as he fought against his body's instinctive reactions to get back control. It wasn't easy, being displaced like that, his human body did not agree with it; and his warrior instincts did not make it any better.

"Quetzalcoatl!"

The first thing he was aware of, beyond the feeling of nausea and the pounding of his own head, was his name, his old name, from a lifetime ago, being called, by a voice he recognized instinctively.

A second later there was the sound of a body being slammed, once, twice, followed by a very quiet whimper, in the same voice. The reincarnated King felt himself break, just a little, understanding that his princess was hurt.

"Xochi... quetzal..." his reply, the call of her name, was completely instinctive, coming from deep inside his core.

She didn't answer and the thought of why she might not be able to only hurt him even more. Then came a voice that explained that, and made him cold inside, all at the same time.

"I grow tired of this state of affairs." The once King knew that voice, of course he did, it belonged to the old nomad warrior-sorcerer, his nemesis: Tezcatlipoca. "I think it's about time we finish this little dance of ours, once and for all."

An instant later a shockwave threw everyone against the nearest wall. Lily barely had a moment to curl her own body protectively around Rose as best she could; Chris taking a stand before them both and using his power to anchor himself to the earth beneath his feet, so he might serve as a shield. The rest were thrown against walls haphazardly, though only Magnolia had been far enough for the impact to truly hurt her. On the positive side, the throw forced the men keeping her hostage to release her, as they too were thrown away. Once given the chance David made sure to pull her towards him and the others, they wouldn't be letting anyone be threatened again.

"Stop it!" Xochitl yelled, forcing herself onto her knees. "Leave my children alone!"

In any other circumstances it might have been ludicrous, in their current life she was hardly older than any of them; and yet the feeling behind her words was so intense, none of them doubted her sincerity.

Belladonna used her own gift against Tezcatlipoca in an attempt to hurt him in turn, but she was no rival for him. Regardless of how much she might have trained, she was still a mortal, even being tied to the others in a cycle of reincarnations, she was still very much human, Tezcatlipoca has no trouble brushing her effort aside.

"Julian..." Hyacinth called quietly. "Do you trust me?"

"Always," the man replied without hesitation.

How could he not? Hyacinth was the dearest person to him, as good as his sister, even if they hadn't been born as siblings. He'd always do his best for her, and he'd always trust her, with his life.

"Find the nearest source of running water and pull on it as hard as you can," she instructed him.

Julian didn't question her on it. There was no doubt in him that she must have a good reason to request him to do such a thing. So instead he closed his eyes, held his hands, palms splayed open, at his sides, and focused on finding the nearest source of his element. It took almost half a minute, but eventually he did it, there was a river somewhere nearby. He didn't even stop to ask her partner if she was sure, he just focused as much of his power as he could on that river, and then he pulled.

Several seconds passed, with Eduardo and David trying and failing to use their gifts over air and fire against Tezcatlipoca, same as Belladonna had failed. At least they managed to take down his men, which was good. Fiore did all she could to pull Draco as far away from Tezcatlipoca as possible, while Chris did his best to cover her and Lily stood back, focusing on keeping Rosie safe.

Loud noises came, announcing the arrival of about a dozen jaguars and a single man in slightly torn jeans, a wife-beater, thick-soled boots and a brown leather jacket.

Everyone turned in his direction at the same time and at least two pairs of eyes widened at his arrival, whatever came out of their mouths drowned a midst the growls from the jaguars, the near-hysterical shrieking from the newly woken Rose and a rumbling that no one could quite place. Not until a few seconds later, when one of the walls abruptly fell into pieces and water began pouring in at vertiginous speeds.

"Run!" Fiore, Draco and Belladonna screamed at the same time.

It was insane. With the water, and the beasts, and everyone else. Tezcatlipoca kept yelling and cursing at Xochiquetzal and the others, but the water and his own jaguars made it harder for him to aim his own attacks properly. Something everyone realized, as they took the opportunity to attempt an escape. It wasn't too complicated to get out of the chamber and yet, making it out of the mines was another matter entirely, since they hadn't the slightest idea how deep in they were at all. Still, they ran.

Draco had a hard time believing what he was seeing. The Priestesses and Atlantes had been enough of a shock, not to mention the little girl in one of the men's arms. However, most of his attention had been instantly captured by the woman running right beside him, in a brown top with a torn sleeve, pale blue skinny jeans with marks of dust and a rip on her left knee, and brown ballet flats. It was her, there was no doubt about it, he could see it in her long jet-black hair, her cocoa-brown eyes and her inhuman aura, it was his Xochiquetzal running by his side… it was Fiore.

They ran for very long minutes, tunnels spiraling in every direction, the water seemingly always at their feet. And then, the worst that could possibly happened: they reached a dead-end. A chamber with a single entrance, the one they'd entered through, and yet they couldn't go back, not with all the water rushing in behind them.

"Get us out of here!" Belladonna yelled.

She probably expected either Julian or Chris to answer her demands; to use their powers over either water or earth to somehow save them; but truth was that, gifted as they might be, they simply didn't have enough power for something like that. The Atlantes could influence the elements but couldn't truly control them.

"Gather close!" Hyacinth ordered abruptly.

No one really knew what was going on, but they followed her instructions nonetheless. The moment when they closed ranks was the first time Fiore and Draco truly came face to face. A thousand questions running through their minds, yet neither of them said a word, there was no time, not with the water so high already. So Xochiquetzal simply nodded once at him, extending one hand to him, and the other behind her, taking hold of the closest person. Prompting them to do the same.

The reincarnated King waited until everyone was connected one way or another, and then he turned his head up, yelling something in Nahuatl that no one except maybe his Enchantress could quite catch. There was a bright flash of off-white light and in the next second, the chamber was empty of anything except water.

There were sounds of retching as the reincarnated Toltecs fought to get their bodies under control; followed by violent shivers as the cold night-air hit their wet clothes.

"Julian!" Belladonna barked, being the first to force her body to settle.

It took a few seconds more but eventually Julian managed to wave his hand once, pulling as much of the water off their clothes as he could. It wasn't perfect, he was still exhausted after pulling at the river and the run through the mines, but at least they'd made it out.

Draco blinked a few times. Since he'd been the one calling for the teleportation it affected him less than when Tezcatlipoca had used it on him. At the same time, he hadn't called on so much power in centuries, whole lifetimes, and it left him feeling more than a little weakened. The first thing he was aware of once the light stopped blinking behind his eyelids, was a smooth, tanned hand extended before him; he took it without quite stopping to think about it. There was a rush of energy from her to him, and he realized what was going on at the same time he caught up to the fact that it was his beloved's hand he was holding.

"Xochi... quetzal," he breathed out, half in disbelief still.

He looked up then, their eyes meeting, for the first time without any secrets on either part. He could see it then, the little details he'd always missed, the explanation behind all the inconsistencies, the apparent contradictions; it seemed so obvious considering current events.

"My lord Quetzalcoatl," she greeted him politely with a ceremonial bow.

He wanted to tell her there still was no need to call him that, she was his intended after all; while at the same time he wanted to demand explanations, to know how long she'd known the truth, remembered their past, and why she hadn't said anything about it. Then he caught sight of something silver sparkling, reflecting the starlight, half-hidden beneath the neckline of her blouse.

In the end he got the chance to say nothing, none of them did, as the loud crash of a tree splintering and slamming into the forest ground interrupted them; closely followed by growling... the jaguars were approaching.

"Run!" Someone yelled yet again.

And just like that, they were all on the move once again.

The pursuit lasted for a while, possibly hours, none of them could be sure of anything other than it was the middle of the night and they were in some kind of forested hills. The last one at least was an advantage, as they all had ready access to their respective abilities, which helped in defending themselves against the jaguars pursuing them, and even the men that would pop up every so often.

Quetzalcoatl was, doubtlessly, the most powerful of them, but he was exhausted still after teleporting eleven people, himself included, out of the mines, through meters of rock and dirt, all the way to the surface, to the forest. Even with Xochiquetzal giving him a boost before they were initially found, it just wasn't enough; and she couldn't give him more, busy as she was using her own abilities wildly to make sure they stayed ahead of their enemies at all times.

Something went wrong eventually, because something always has to go wrong at some point. There was shooting from behind them, the west, men using the trees as vantage point just like they were; one of the bullets grazed Belladonna's arm when she failed to deflect them properly. Her cry distracted Eduardo, who ended picking her up and pulling her away from the line of fire. Lily for her part stopped running completely, spinning around and throwing as much lightning as she could at the upcoming bullets, as well as the shooters themselves to make sure her companions would be safe, or as safe as possible in their situation. No one was expecting the jaguars that came from the south. Lily spun around again, to find her path blocked by four very big jaguars growling at her.

"Lily!" At least three voices cried out in unison.

The amber-eyed girl snapped her fingers, calculating her odds of taking on the beasts, even as they prepared to leap at her. No one was expecting the interruption that came then, in the form of a single word, practically roared.

The jaguars dropped onto their bellies abruptly, almost whining; leaving Lily standing in place, hand raised and fingers sparkling.

All eyes turned towards the speaker.

"Steve..." Draco murmured, having already expected who it'd be, even if he didn't understand why he'd suddenly stopped the animals, and then he caught on to the name that the others had called the girl...

Two sets of amber eyes met in that exact moment.

"Esteban?!" the youngest priestess practically shrieked in disbelief.

The older man said not a word, just stood there, watching the young girl he knew to be his sister in absolute shock.

For several seconds no one moved, or spoke, it was as if time had frozen completely; until someone else intruded on the moment.

"Tamer." Tezcatlipoca's hissing voice announced his arrival. "You have a duty to me... Why aren't you performing it?"

"Did you know?" Steve, no Esteban, demanded hotly, turning towards his would-be master. "Did you know my little sister was one of them? That you were sending me after my own sister and her friends?!"

Tezcatlipoca's smile, with too many teeth, was all the answer that was needed.

"No!" Steve roared. "I agreed to serve you to protect my sister, not to hurt her! This wasn't what I agreed to!!"

"You serve me," Tezcatlipoca reminded him, the weight of his power in every word.

For an instant his amber eyes darkened, as if some power were trying to take him over. But in the end Esteban's love for his little sister would always be stronger than Tezcatlipoca's power; no magic could ever surpass love...

"No!!!" Steve snapped, snarling an order and waving his hands wildly, as if fighting off an invisible force, even as he ordered the jaguars to attack Tezcatlipoca.

Tezcatlipoca's reaction was immediate, flashes of dark power jumped from his hands, hitting the jaguars, which fell to the ground, one by one, whining pitifully, at least half of them dead before landing. One of those same attacks hit Esteban on his raised arm. It was as if he'd been hit by flash-fire, sending him flying several feet, until slamming against the trunk of a tree, breaking branches as he slid down.

"Esteban!" Lily shrieked in horror as she hurried to him.

Tezcatlipoca tried to attack her, causing Chris to yell in panic as he summoned walls of dirt and mud to protect her. It made it necessary for him to let go of Rose, who instead of hiding away, ran towards Lily and her brother and then... then there was a white light coming off her hands and Esteban's wounds began healing before their eyes.

"Well, well, well... what have we here...?" Tezcatlipoca drawled.

He suddenly was too fast, throwing several attacks in quick succession which collapsed Chris's walls, threw him to a side, and then the last one was going straight for not just Steve and his sister, but Xochitl's sweet little girl. She couldn't stand it.

There was a wordless wail, and Tezcatlipoca's attack never managed to reach its mark, as it was blocked by the unexpected appearance of a silvery shield. A shield created by the reincarnated Enchantress suddenly standing in the way.

"I told you to leave my children alone!" she yelled at him, redirecting the power of her shield in such a way it became a wave of energy which impacted on Tezcatlipoca, throwing him back several yards.

"Don't you get it, little princess?" Tezcatlipoca called to her in a drawl, as he got back on his feet and practically stalked towards her. "This will never end. Not until you, and all your dear little children are dead..."

Except, once she died, the enchantment would be reset, and then it would start all over again. On and on until they got justice, until they finally got to live their lives, as they deserved to.

"I will not allow it." Fiore stated, with a fierceness never shown before, in any of her previous incarnations, it was enough to make even Tezcatlipoca hesitate.

Seconds, it was all the Enchantress needed. She pulled a handful of seeds from one of the pockets in her jeans and, with a flick of her wrist, threw them to the ground, having them land spread around Tezcatlipoca. After that she needed but a thought and the seeds burst, turning into vines, which took hold of Tezcatlipoca.

"What do you think you're doing?!" the warrior-mage demanded trying, and failing, to get free of the vines.

"Making sure you will never hurt anyone else," Xochitl stated quietly.

"You cannot kill me princess," Tezcatlipoca hissed. "It's not in your nature."

He was right, of course; but what he didn't realize was that she had planned for that. She pulled a new seed from a different pocket; though instead of throwing it she held it in the open palm of her hand.

"I need a blade," she murmured quietly.

One was being offered to her but a moment later. It took her a second, but she recognized it as a very old dagger, beautifully conserved. The one offering it was none other than Draco. It was Quetzalcoatl's favorite dagger, and not just that, but one Xochiquetzal herself had commissioned from the best blacksmiths of the time and gifted him, for his coronation, so very long ago; just like he'd commissioned a certain jewelry box he'd given her the same day he named her his adviser. The Enchantress wondered briefly if his family had guarded the dagger, much as her own had kept guard over her pendant; or if he'd somehow found it…

"Thank you," she nodded at him, taking the blade.

"What are you planning?" he wanted to know.

"He's right that I cannot kill him," she admitted. "And not only because it goes against my nature, but also because killing him, even in mortal bodies as we all are now, wouldn't be an easy thing."

"What then?" he knew she was right, but still had no idea what the enchantress might be planning to do then.

"I'll take away that which makes him a threat to us." she answered simply.

That which made him Tezcatlipoca… the warrior mage was the first to understand what she meant and began fighting the vines with more vehemence than before. And she could do it, that night more than at any other point; because it was the eve of the Spring Equinox, the very day when her powers were the strongest. Truth was that if Xochitl had ever actually planned on going against Tezcatlipoca that would probably have been the best moment for it; not that she ever wanted to fight him, to fight anyone. For her it had never been about war, but about peace, about having a chance to live in peace.

Something like black smoke began oozing from his pores, ever so slowly rotting the plants holding him; Tezcatlipoca knew that his time was running out, and he wouldn't give up so easily. It wasn't in his nature, it wasn't in any of their natures.

"I need you to hold him in place," Fiore stated to the King, completely serious.

He nodded, even as he signaled for the Atlantes to join him; and it wasn't even just them, Lily responded to the summons as well, and after a moment's hesitation so did the other three girls.

Xochitl did her best to block the confrontation as she focused completely on the enchantment she was working. It was easy enough for her to use the dagger to cut open her palm. The spell was so important, there was no room for mistakes, and so she'd tie it to her blood to ensure success. Her blood, her very life would power the enchantment, her life but not her death; and so, as long as she lived the magic would hold.

She sensed the moment the last vines rotted away, almost at the same time she began chanting her own spell. It was long, and very specific, she couldn't make a single mistake, too much depended on it working right...

Cocoa-brown eyes snapped open as the last word of the enchantment passed her lips, right in time to watch the dark-eyed reincarnated King call on a sword, his sword and use it to run Tezcatlipoca through his flank, while at the same time spearing him into the ground. It wouldn't hold him long, and the wound was nowhere near lethal, but it was enough for what they needed.

The flaring of Xochiquetzal's aura was enough for everyone to understand it was time and, in unison, they all moved, allowing the Enchantress to approach unimpeded. They all watched as she did, holding in her bleeding left hand a single white flower with eight big petals that overlapped just enough to make it look like an almost perfect circle. The center was dark, and the stem a pale green, no leaves. All priestesses recognized it easily enough as a white poppy, though they'd no idea what it was supposed to be for.

Tezcatlipoca didn't either, plants had never been his thing, but he recognized the confidence in Xochiquetzal's steps, the power in her aura; he knew he would be defeated, for good, unless... he had a single card left to play.

"You cannot do this!" he yelled, fighting against the sword keeping him down, though he failed to free himself. "You cannot take me out."

"She can, and she will," Lily stated, obvious satisfaction in her voice.

"Justice will be served," several of the others added quietly.

"If you destroy my power you will destroy her!" Tezcatlipoca yelled.

No one said a word to that, it seemed like none of them could fathom what they could say at all, perhaps not even what Tezcatlipoca meant.

"Think I didn't notice her?" The mage's voice gained a wicked, almost proud tone as he kept talking. "That I couldn't see who she is? What she is? I can see. And you know I am right, if you do anything to erase my power, she will be gone too..."

No one understood what he meant... except the one those words were meant for.

"I know," Xochitl whispered after what seemed like forever.

It was all she said, it was all she needed to, in the end. Tezcatlipoca was already roaring his disbelief when she dropped to her knees beside him, pressing the white flower and her still bleeding palm to his forehead as a string of words passed her lips. He twisted and cursed at her through it all, but nothing made her stop. She kept going.

"Curse you Enchantress!" he roared as he began to feel the magic take hold. "Curse you! You will regret this!"

"I know," she whispered very softly, once she had finished her chanting. "Goodbye Tezcatlipoca." Then she turned over her shoulder, her warm brown eyes meeting the dark-as-night ones of the little girl who'd been so important to her for what seemed like so short and so long a while at the same time... "*Love you sweetheart...*"

"*Love you Mommy...*" the girl replied with her brightest smile, a hint of something in her eyes that seemed to show someone far beyond her years.

Fiore blinked a couple of times, doing her best to keep the tears from falling; then she took a deep breath and turned all her attention back to the fallen mage. He was no longer moving, and when she pulled back her hand, everyone could see that the poppy was no longer white but red. Also, her hand was no longer bleeding.

Seconds passed, one by one, and nobody moved.

"Is it done...?" Lily asked eventually.

"What just happened?" Magnolia inquired, almost at the same time.

"It's done," Xochiquetzal stated quietly, vanishing the poppy completely with a flick of her hand.

"What, exactly, is done?" Belladonna and Eduardo wanted to know.

"Is he dead?" David nudged the unresponsive man with a foot, doubtful.

"No," Quetzalcoatl's reincarnation, probably the only one capable to understand what the Enchantress had just done, replied. "He's just unconscious for the time being. He will wake up."

"Shouldn't we kill him while we have the chance?" Eduardo wanted to know.

"You cannot kill him," Xochiquetzal stated.

Truth be told, she wasn't sure even she or Quetzalcoatl could. Not even with all the power of the Equinox to back them up. But that was alright; she'd known that, it was the whole reason why she'd made that plan.

"I took away what made him a threat to us," Fiore stated yet again, before elaborating. "His memories, and with them most of his power. I don't know who he might be in this life, but he's not Tezcatlipoca anymore."

"How long will the spell last?" Lily wanted to be sure.

"For as long as my blood lives," Fiore answered serenely.

That was the important part, her blood, not strictly herself. And if they'd finally gotten it right, if they finally got their justice and the lives they deserved, then once their current lives ended, that would be it. No more reincarnations, no more endless war, it would be over… finally.

"We won..." Chris breathed out, not quite believing it yet.

"We won!" Lily and Magnolia cried out at the same time.

They all began celebrating, embracing each other, some even kissing; like Chris and Lily, and even Eduardo had the guts to kiss Bella, just for an instant, before running away, just in case she tried to hit him.

Xochitl paid them no mind, she just got on her feet as gracefully as she could, walking away from them, past Lily, who'd stopped making out with Chris to go make sure her brother would be alright. The cocoa-eyed young woman walked a few steps further, before going down on one knee and extending a trembling hand to touch the single white rose that seemed to have come out of nowhere.

Behind the young enchantress the celebration of their victory went on and yet all she could do was cry, cry for the loss only she would ever mourn…

Chapter 23
Zinnia

It took them some time to get down the hill, exhausted and injured as most of them were. Chris and Lily were holding Esteban up in between them, while Draco was pretty much carrying an only half-awake Fiore, who was carefully cradling a white rosebud in her cupped hands, like it was the most precious treasure ever. Even after getting down the hill, it took them some more time to make it to the closest road.

The true surprise was when they finally found the road, and it wasn't empty. There were several cars and even an SUV. The moment they became visible under the cars' headlights the passenger door of one of them, a dark gray hybrid one by the look of things, opened and a figure stepped out. A young woman, early twenties, in pale-blue skinny jeans, an azure long-sleeved top, ivory-colored zipped up vest and off-white ankle boots; she was also wearing a wide off-white rebozo with blue and purple stitching on the hem, which covered her head and shoulders, only vaguely allowing some locks of light-brown hair to be seen.

The reaction from those who'd just survived a battle against the warrior-mage was automatic; as they took formation around their leaders, all while trying to be as discreet as possible. They weren't at their best, if there happened to be another battle, but neither would they just give up.

"*We're here to serve,*" the woman in the rebozo announced in an almost ceremonial tone with a deep bow of her head. "*My lady...*"

There was something about her, about her voice, her very aura, that sparkled recognition in Fiore's mind. With some gestures she managed to convince Draco to let her stand, though he refused to leave her side. She agreed to that, and then pushed forth, past the loose circle formed by her over-protective children.

"I've heard your voice before, haven't I?" she asked, tilting her head to a side in consideration.

"You have," the newcomer nodded, and then, without further ceremony, rearranged her rebozo just enough to uncover her head.

The reincarnated Enchantress recognized her instantly.

"Veronica..." she breathed out in realization. "You're the Keeper, the one who holds the bloodline."

The one on whom the continuation of the line would have depended, had they all lost their lives that night.

"That I am, my lady," Veronica nodded deferentially, yet with an undercurrent of pride as she added: "I'm also the leader of the group you see before you. We're here to aid you in any way we can."

Soon enough arrangements were made, and they were all in vehicles and on their way back to Mexico City. Xochitl and Draco were the ones on the same car as Veronica, which was being driven by a blonde, green-eyed man she introduced as Ken.

"You never told me," Fiore murmured quietly, she was still so tired...

"No," Veronica agreed. "When we first met you had no idea, and for the longest time you weren't ready. Not until recently." A rueful smile appeared on her face as she added: "I tried to warn you on Friday night..."

"... but I refused to listen," Xochitl finished for her, having realized what the younger girl had been trying to do. "I'm sorry."

"It's alright," Veronica shrugged. "I suppose things are as they're meant to be."

Fiore said nothing, just held the white rose close to her heart, brushing her lips against the half-closed petals.

"I'm sorry for your loss..." Veronica whispered to her, very quietly.

The Enchantress let out a quiet sob, tears falling on the white petals.

"Fiore…" Draco wasn't quite sure what it was that prompted him to use that name, rather than the one he had known her by first, he just did. "Why… what happened to that little girl? Why hasn't anyone else asked after her since w… you defeated Tezcatlipoca? And who was she?"

"Rose was my daughter," she reminded him, before elaborating. "She's gone. No one has asked after her because, as far as they're concerned, she never existed… because she shouldn't have."

"I don't understand," Draco admitted quietly. "I remember her…"

"Your nature allows you to, just like I'm sure Veronica remains aware of her due to her own gift," the enchantress pointed out.

"I can see the truth, even when its veiled, even when its kept secret, I can see it all," Veronica offered softly.

"Rose wasn't human, not really," Xochitl admitted. "She… I guess you could say she was a part of me." She took a deep breath before explaining. "She was a part of my soul for… a very long time, lifetimes. She protected me through it all, from Tezcatlipoca and his followers, she would shield me whenever I was at my most vulnerable, and even in my sleep. It was until this lifetime that Tezcatlipoca became aware of her. I don't think he knew who or what she was exactly, but he realized she was the reason he couldn't get to me, he tried to destroy her. Instead he ended throwing her into the real world, gave her a form, a life…" She drowned a sob, continuing with her tale. "I didn't know any of that when I met her, of course. All I saw was a little girl, all alone, with no one to protect her. And I felt connected to her, somehow. So, I took her in, told myself it was only until I could track down her family. Then I discovered she was gifted… and I didn't understand, who could ever abandon such a beautiful, gifted little girl? So, I kept her with me, looked after her, I… I loved her." She drew in a sharp breath. "Eventually all the pieces fit together, I understood why I felt so deep an attachment to her. I also understood she couldn't remain here forever."

"Because she wasn't real?" the reincarnated King still wasn't getting it.

"Yes," Fiore nodded, closing her eyes. "Her body was created from magic, her own and Tezcatlipoca's, and perhaps even some of mine, since she'd been a part of me for so long. But it still wasn't a real body, not truly flesh and blood. She'd have never grown, never aged... it wasn't right. But I kept telling myself I'd find a way to make it right, someday, once we were finally safe... then Tezcatlipoca came after us."

"He knew..." Draco realized. "What he said to you..."

"Yes, it was about her." The Enchantress confirmed.

"You knew what would happen, and you still did it..."

"It's..." Her voice broke very briefly. "It's the hardest decision I've ever made. I came so close to never making it... but it wouldn't have been right. Rose couldn't have stayed as she was forever, and even we don't have the power to create life, not like that. Also, we both know that if we hadn't defeated Tezcatlipoca then he'd have killed us all."

Rose included, really, nothing could have saved the little girl, and the enchantress knew that very well. Didn't make things any easier though...

"Xochiquetzal... who was she really?" The seriousness of his voice, the choice of name, it all showed that he knew already the answer to that question, he just didn't want to accept it yet.

The cocoa-eyed young woman kept her eyes closed, tears slipping through the corners, even as she nuzzled her face carefully against the white rose in her hands, all that was left of the little girl she'd loved so much. She took a deep, ragged breath before finally saying the truth that needed to be acknowledged:

"Our unborn daughter."

Fiore had no idea when exactly she fell asleep, she just knew she had when she woke up in a bed that wasn't her own. Though that wasn't the first thing she noticed, no, it was the fact that her hands were empty. Thankfully whoever had gotten her into that bed must have known the white rose was important, for she found it placed in a simple but nice glass vase on the night table, directly in her line of sight.

A look out the window told her it was past noon, and that she wasn't anywhere she was familiar with. It wasn't too different from most neighborhoods in Mexico City, but she knew for sure she wasn't in the capital, as she didn't feel surrounded by the traces of her power. She could also sense Draco and her children in the same building, nearby; and two other gifted individuals, she could feel the bond of shared blood.

It was easy enough to put her clothes and shoes back on, they'd clearly been washed at some point, no longer damp and muddy, though the tears remained. She ran her fingers through her long hair to take out the knots. Then, after considering things for several seconds, she took the vase with the white rose in her hands and carried it with her as she left the bedroom. She found herself on the second floor of a nice town-house. There were three other doors on that same level, inside one she could sense traces of Veronica's aura, the others held the auras of her children.

Downstairs she found a woman buttering some toast, two mugs of tea beside her. She was of average height and built, with brunette hair that was beginning to gray, age-lines on her tanned skin, and her eyes were the same chocolate brown as Veronica... Xochitl need not ask who she was, in that moment it was so obvious...

"Cattleya..." the enchantress murmured quietly.

"My lady..." the woman greeted her in turn, bowing her head respectfully.

Fiore need not ask, she knew one of the mugs of tea was meant for her, as well as some of the toast, so she took both as they were offered and ate silently. She hadn't focused on her hunger before that moment, but once she did she realized she was starving, as she hadn't eaten anything since breakfast the previous morning... or what she imagined was the previous morning.

"It's Sunday the 20th of March, 1:30 pm," Cattleya answered the unasked question. "Everyone is safe, you're in my house, here in Coacalco. My daughter and her friends brought you some time before dawn. You were asleep, as were most of the girls.

I fixed the two guest-bedrooms for your children, Veronica insisted on you sleeping in her bedroom, while the King spent the night in the sofa bed in my husband's study. My husband, Sergio, is out of the country until Wednesday, so you need not worry about anyone learning your secrets."

"How much does he know?" Fiore finally asked, briefly wondering if she would be allowed to ask the question at all, or if Cattleya would just keep giving all the answers.

"He knows that my first husband died in an accident that wasn't really an accident, that I left my old home because I feared for the safety of my daughter," Cattleya explained. "He took us in, married me, knowing that. It's why Veronica's first surname is Resendiz, rather than Yolotl, as is the case with you." She took a deep breath. "He knows Vero and I sometimes know things, that we're different, special, but has never asked what makes us like that. He simply doesn't care to know. He knows the King's history and his legend, of course, but like most people nowadays he doesn't see it as anything more than old history and myth, doesn't believe it to be real."

The enchantress nodded, to herself more than to the other woman, that was enough for her. It wasn't like she planned on them staying for long, there would be no need for Sergio Resendiz to find out anything.

For several minutes no one said a word, the two women just kept drinking their tea and eating their toast. Eventually it was Cattleya who broke their silence.

"My lady..." she began.

There was something in her tone of voice, and in her aura, as she addressed her, that snapped Fiore to attention instantly. She raised her head in time to see the older woman bowing her head deeply, penitently.

"I offer my deepest, sincerest apologies my lady, for failing you," she said stoically. "For not being where I was needed, not doing my duty to you... I cannot ask for forgiveness..."

"No!" the Enchantress cried out abruptly; then, when understanding how that sounded, she revised: "You need not be forgiven, and I need no apologies..." She swallowed, forcing herself to calm down, putting the full-force of her old-self into her demeanor and voice as she stated: "Never apologize for being a mother, Cattleya, for putting your daughter first. You did the right thing and need no forgiveness for that. Nothing, no duty or fate, will ever be more important than the responsibility a mother has to her daughter."

She knew, of course she knew, after all, her own love for her children was what had started the whole reincarnation-mess they'd been in for the past thousand years. And her love for Rosie... yes, she understood what it was to be a mother, and that nothing could or should ever be more important than that. She only wished there had been anything she could have done for her little girl... Who knew? Perhaps one day she might get her own little miracle...

Cattleya had just left the kitchen when the door leading to the backyard opened, allowing Draco inside. Xochitl wasn't surprised, she'd sensed him pretty much from the moment she'd opened her eyes. She didn't say anything when he went to leave his empty mug in the sink, and then went to stand against the counter, on the other side of the kitchen table from her. She said not a word, instead just finished her tea, while waiting for him to put his thoughts into order, and eventually he did.

"How long have you known?" he asked her quietly. "About you? About me? About any of it?"

"I never forget," Fiore whispered, it wasn't the first time she said it, but every time it hit her just the same. "I think it might be a consequence of the enchantment that allowed us to reincarnate. Since I was the one who cast it and... and since I was the only one still alive, aside from Tezcatlipoca, when I did."

"What...?" Draco clearly wasn't expecting that.

"He made me watch," she admitted very quietly. "He took me captive and made me watch as the Temple was invaded, as my children were killed one by one... I felt the moment you died, the shock was enough that I lost our baby almost at the same time." Her voice broke slightly, but she pushed on, needing to get it all out. "It was then that I decided to do the spell. I knew I was calling on forces that far surpassed me, but I just didn't know what else to do. You had all died! I was alone, and there was no way I could take him on my own. I… I didn't know what else to do… I couldn't go on without you…"

For a moment it looked like Draco might throw himself to her, hold her tight, do anything he could to comfort her… but he didn't. Instead he moved to press his hands against the table, looking at her straight on.

"Why didn't you tell me before?" he still didn't understand that part, and he really, really needed to. "I've been in the country for months and…"

"I didn't know, not at first." she admitted softly. "When I met you… I felt the connection to you, but I didn't understand it. I did not know anything back then, about you, or myself or…"

"I thought you said you never forgot," Draco's eyes narrowed.

"I didn't, I… it's complicated."

"I'm trying to understand you Fiore, but you need to let me in."

He was right, and she knew that; but after so many years keeping to herself, depending on no one else, it was so hard…

"I never forget," she repeated, eventually. "Every life, I know who I am. The knowledge doesn't come all at once. It's a relative thing, I always know who I've been, who I'm meant to be; the feelings and the memories come through over time, in stages, as I grow up, allowing me to adapt to the information, to take it all in without being overwhelmed. Even then, it was so shocking the first few times, I did crazy things, got myself killed before I could even find you a couple of times. But I learned from my mistakes; because I don't only remember my first life, I remember every single life. So, I learned to handle things, all the memories, the good things and the bad." She took a deep breath, before getting to what was probably the crucial part of her explanation. "That's not what happened this time. I… Something happened, when our parents got killed. So many of the bloodline had been hunted down. It was… like a survival instinct, I gained all my memories in a rush. It was… a shock. I had no idea what to do, how to handle it, it wasn't supposed to be like that! You helped some, but then you were gone, and I was alone, and I didn't know what to do! I couldn't handle it!"

Tears were falling down her cheeks, one after the other, and Draco finally understood:

"You got all your memories... when you were six," he breathed out in a mix of shock and horror.

"I was a child..." Fiore sobbed. "A child isn't supposed to know what it's like to die, a dozen times, to have seen her children murdered time and again, to have lost... everything! I couldn't do it, I wasn't strong enough... so I enchanted myself. Used a tea rose to block the memories, it was the only way I could survive!" She was practically gasping at the thought of it. "Only... I did too good a job. So good I didn't remember anything at all, didn't even believe in the legends anymore. My grandmother couldn't handle it, she had no idea how to deal with me. She never knew anything, not about my memories, or what I did to myself. She died before I got involved with anything..."

Yet another regret, the fact that she never got the chance to talk to her Nana again, to ask forgiveness for all the cruel things that had been said; to tell her that she was no longer ashamed of who she was. She had never been ashamed, not really, she'd been afraid, and hadn't known how to handle it.

Fiore was sobbing into her folded arms by that point, when suddenly she felt arms around them, tugging at her, until she was pressed against a chest, face finding a perfect nook against a collarbone. It was Draco, he was holding her, and then she was crying, like never before, all the tears she'd never gotten a chance to cry.

"I'm... a coward..." she half-sobbed into his neck.

"No, you're not." he whispered into her hair, never letting her go. "You're the strongest person I know... Sacnité..."

"Topiltzin..." the reincarnated enchantress murmured back.

The two stayed like that, in the kitchen, holding onto each other like their lives depended on it, for a long time.

The moment everyone had had breakfast Xochitl asked if they could get some help getting home. Thankful as she was for Veronica's and Cattleya's help, all she wanted in that moment was to be home, in her own bed. She wanted to be alone, where she might mourn the loss of her baby in peace...

Veronica had known the moment was coming, and had already made arrangements, some friends of her, believers, would be driving them all to their respective homes. Veronica herself insisted on being the one to drive Fiore, and Draco, when he announced he was going with her.

Perhaps the best moment of the morning though was when, just before they were all to leave, one of the cars that would take them arrived already carrying a passenger, a woman in a wide pink skirt and sand-colored long-sleeved blouse...

"Camellia?!" Xochitl couldn't quite believe what she was seeing.

The older woman just smiled at her, embracing the younger woman tightly. She didn't know everything, of course not, but she knew that her niece had been through a lot, things that would have destroyed a normal person, but not her, not Fiore.

"How is this possible?" Lily was in absolute shock. "You... I saw you and..."

The amber-eyed girl didn't dare finish the sentence. She was so overwhelmed by everything. She and Chris weren't going to their apartment but to the hospital. Her brother had been taken there earlier, while there were no serious physical injuries on him, Tezcatlipoca's magical banishment seemed to have done something to him, something none of them could really understand. It had been one of Veronica's followers that had convinced them to take the man to a hospital, and so they had. It had taken a lot to convince Lily to leave him there, and she'd only done so on the reassurance that she could go back as soon as she'd slept and eaten something. She didn't plan on leaving him again until she was sure he would be alright, that Tezcatlipoca would never be able to hurt either of them again, directly or indirectly.

"Cattleya warned her daughter of the impending attack, and Veronica had someone following us that day," Camellia explained. "He got me out after you had to run."

"I... I didn't want to go," Lily admitted, very quietly. "I didn't want to go but you told me to go and..."

"It's okay, it's okay," Camellia embraced the young priestess tightly as she dropped to her knees before the older woman. "We're all alright now, and that's all that really matters."

It wouldn't have, if things had turned out as bad as they'd feared. But they hadn't, thanks to people like Cattleya and Veronica. Camellia was alive, and the threat was finally over. They had the chance to move past all the bad things that had happened, to heal. They all deserved that chance.

The trip to the apartment did not take too long, though when Veronica parked the car Xochitl couldn't help but feel like it'd been forever... the white rose was still in her hands, still in the vase, which Cattleya had insisted she accept as a little gift. Thankfully no one had asked about her obsession with the flower, believing it had something to do with her being the Enchantress... they had no reason to suspect anything else, after all.

"Thank you, for everything," Fiore murmured a moment before she got out of the car.

"It's a pleasure to serve my lady," Veronica nodded her head somewhat deferentially.

"No, not lady, not anymore," Xochitl shook her head, bending Veronica's head with one hand to place a kiss on her brow. "Cousin..."

"Cousin," the younger girl echoed. "What happens now?"

For a moment Fiore didn't seem to know how to answer that, she looked out the open door, to the tree planted outside the entrance to the apartment building, and all the little wild flowers growing at its base. Rose had made those appear...

"The tree is so lonely mommy, he needs company... he needs friends!"

A tear fell down her face, but the enchantress managed to control herself enough not to break down all over again, she'd already done it twice in less than 24 hours; and it would probably happen again, but not just yet.

"Now... we live our lives," she said eventually. "Like we're supposed to."

It was all they could do, really.

Finally, she and Draco got out of the car, and Fiore lead him straight to her apartment. Alondra greeted her on the way, reminded her they'd be organizing some games for the children for Easter, an egg hunt, if she wanted to help them. She didn't ask after Rosie, and while Xochitl couldn't help the ache inside her at that realization, a part of her had known there would be no questions asked. Her little girl was gone, and as far as most of the world was concerned, it was as if she'd never existed. Because she hadn't belonged, not really, all of her had vanished; only three people would ever know a little girl called Rose, with eyes like the darkest night, ebony hair and the brightest smile ever had once existed.

As far as the tenants in the building knew, Fiore was a young woman who'd needed a place to move into, she might not be a parent, like the rest of them, but she was willing to help, so they'd decided to give her a chance. Also, Camellia was a friend to almost half of them, and they all trusted her when she said Fiore was a good person.

The moment they stepped into the apartment the first thing Fiore's eyes laid on was the tiny pair of pink rain-boots. The tears she'd been fighting to hold back began falling in earnest. Draco didn't ask what she was crying about, he knew, so instead he guided her to the closest sofa, helped her sit down and then gently pried the vase from her hands, placing it on the coffee table, directly in her view.

"Tell me about her?" he requested. "What was our daughter like?"

He wanted so much to know, regretted not having gotten the chance to know her when she was around. He also wanted to believe that sharing the stories would allow Fiore to share the burden. He desired nothing more than to be able to be there for her, like he hadn't been able to in so long…

"She was…" Xochitl broke off, eyes fixed on the flower as she tried to find the right words. "She was beautiful, and kind, and gentle, always smiling… she had your eyes, dark like the night, and my hair, and her skin was smooth and… perfect, she was absolutely perfect." She sobbed slightly. "Our baby was perfect."

He sat on the sofa beside her, guiding her just enough so she was half resting on the couch, half on him, curling slightly against his chest even as he held her hands in his.

"Tell me more," he whispered very softly.

Fiore pondered on it for a moment, and then began telling him about running across a park one morning to find a girl crying because she'd pricked her finger on a thorn…

They spent the rest of the afternoon like that, with story after story, making sure that whatever might come, neither of them would ever forget the perfect little girl that was their daughter.

Chapter 24
Forget-Me-Not

They heard the news sometime in mid-April. About the influx of people ending in the hospital due to poisoning in Queretaro. Soon the news grew bigger, the poison was in the water, in the river, it was believed to be arsenic, or perhaps mercury, and there was little doubt that the reason were the mines in Sierra Gorda. Mines that had been over-exploited in recent years. It was a total circus, as business groups and men were dragged over the coals, figuratively, over the whole matter. Eventually the whole thing was blamed on the chairman of the company that owned most of those mines: Marcelo Ahumada... the same lawyer who Fiore had first met in the village, after the death of her nana.

The story took a turn then, as it was revealed that Mr. Ahumada's older brother was in the hospital, where he'd ended after a terrible accident while hiking, precisely in Sierra Gorda. It was said that he'd lost much of his memory, that he was almost catatonic, and when he did speak he spouted insane things in languages no one seemed to understand. Doctors had been called from every corner of the country, and some even from other nations, none were able to find a cure for whatever ailed him. Eventually people began to believe that he'd fallen prey to the very crime he'd committed: poisoning.

"Did you plan this?" Draco asked, having gone directly to her apartment that Saturday morning, as soon as the most recent piece of news came out.

"No." Fiore saw no point in pretending she didn't know what it was he spoke of. "He's not insane, not really, it's just... What I did, when I was six, I blocked my memories, but they were still there, even if I couldn't access them. With him... I erased them, everything that connected to his having once been Tezcatlipoca, and along with that I sealed everything that made him that, that made him a mage… A child can adapt with incredible ease to the greatest traumas; an adult, not so much. He will recover, eventually his mind will adapt, and he will learn to live without those memories."

"And who or what will he be then?" he wanted to know.

"That's entirely up to him," she assured him. "As long as he never threatens me or mine again he can do of his life whatever he wishes."

Draco nodded. He was about to walk away when he noticed her picking up a piece of white cloth, and the bag by the door. He also began paying more attention to her attire: a long brown skirt and an off-white blouse, tanned-leather boots on her feet.

"Where are you going?" he asked, unable to help himself.

"To Arroyo Seco," Fiore answered somewhat grimly. "To do what I can to help."

Which explained the bags, she was carrying all kinds of herbs there, as well as seeds, in case she ran out. She was confident she could be discreet enough not to call too much attention. And really, the people so needed the help, she was quite sure that even if she was noticed, they wouldn't say a thing. Truth was, Fiore had been feeling bad about those poor people from the very start, she couldn't help but think that it was at least partly their fault that things had gotten so bad, so quickly. Granted, according to her findings those communities were always at risk of drinking poisoned water, due to the mines in the zone; some of which could be blamed on Tezcatlipoca's current incarnation and his family; but there was no doubt that their own actions that day, when they'd pulled the river out of its natural channel, couldn't have helped any. She needed to help, somehow.

"I'm coming with you," he announced.

"What?!" she wasn't expecting that.

"Let me, please, I want to help too," he insisted.

There was no way of knowing if he'd reached the same conclusion she had, or if it was for some other reason entirely. In the end she nodded, picking up her bag, she got into his car and he drove to Arroyo Seco.

It took almost seven hours, but they'd known from the start it'd be a long trip. Still, it was worth it. Draco, being a complete gentleman, turned off the car and hurried around it to open Fiore's door, offering his hand to her. The moment she stepped out, he was breathless. He'd noticed her taking the piece of white cloth with her, but it had never occurred to her what it might be, exactly... it was a veil. A beautiful, white, knitted veil. In that moment Fiore looked more like Xochiquetzal than she ever had before, even amid their confrontation with Tezcatlipoca, and Draco hadn't the slightest idea of what to say to that.

In the days following the battle he'd tried to approach the matter with her. Their shared past, his promises... but the reincarnated enchantress had first been so lost in her own grief, and later entirely focused on her studies, it had been next to impossible to get her alone to talk about anything. Draco had begun to believe that she might simply not love him anymore; perhaps he'd waited too long. And then he saw her getting off the car, wearing that veil... and as the sunlight hit the neckline of her blouse just right he noticed something else: the silver pendant of a bird with a tail longer than its own body, hanging from her neck... his gift to her, the silver quetzal, she was still wearing it! That gave him hope like nothing else could have, and he decided to wait, to give her time, they'd get their chance yet.

That was the first, but not the last weekend that Fiore and Draco spent in Sierra Gorda. They didn't always go to Arroyo Seco either, sometimes he'd drive them to a different town, but they always did the same: Fiore would carry her pack of healing herbs, using her own magic to make them work faster and better than they'd have otherwise; while Draco helped with moving people around, and when he could, he'd purify as much water as possible, so the people might have something safe to drink.

Some of the villagers knew, they knew that the girl with the white veil and the man with the beard were gifted in ways they couldn't quite comprehend. The important part though, was that they were there to help, so they made sure no one interrupted them, or asked funny questions, that the authorities and government officials that had begun taking interest in the communities wouldn't learn about them. They had no idea who the two young adults might be, they just knew they were special, and to be protected.

Soon enough it wasn't just them. Veronica was the first they saw, she'd arrived before them, with some of her own people, including her boyfriend. And while they might not have the kind of power the reincarnated king and enchantress did, they had their ways to be of help. Some were trained in first-aid, others had collected clothes, food, bottled water, medicines, anything that might be needed; and the most important part: they were all willing to do whatever might be necessary to help those in need. A week later Xochiquetzal's children were there too.

Even Steve joined them, eventually, though he hadn't felt too sure about it at first, the others managed to convince him it was alright, and being able to help undo at least a little bit of the hurt he'd been forced to cause while with Tezcatlipoca certainly helped him heal as well.

By the end of May, the country couldn't not notice all the young people, mostly from the capital, traveling to Sierra Gorda every weekend to help. And yet when someone from the media tried to find out who was responsible for it all, who'd started it, Fiore and Draco were nowhere to be found... Veronica took charge then, giving vague answers and excuses as necessary, making sure everyone would know they were there to help, without calling attention to who they were...

On July 1st, Fiore Xochitl Yolotl Nahui crossed the stage to shake hands and receive the diploma stating she'd graduated college. Minutes later, Veronica Resendiz Yolotl did the same. Among the crowd, friends and family cheered for them, and the moment before they each walked down they could have sworn they saw several ghostly figures looking at them from a distance, the family that they'd lost, even though they never truly left them...

At Lily's and Magnolia's insistence they all went to celebrate. It was also then that Fiore announced she'd been accepted into a very prestigious graduate program on a full scholarship; she was also set to begin teaching Nahuatl to those interested. Draco shared his own piece of news: he'd finished his thesis and would be defending it the following month, soon he'd officially be Dr. Draco Yao Tamay. Veronica had accepted the offer she'd received for a double degree; she'd be spending the following year in New York. The rest had their own news: they were all going back to college, or for the first time, as was Lily's case.

For the longest time they'd felt lost. Belladonna and her group in particular. After having spent three years dedicated almost completely to finding Xochiquetzal and Quetzalcoatl and aiding them in any way they might be able to that at first, they didn't seem to know what to do with themselves, once that part was over. They'd always been so focused on their duties, they never stopped to contemplate what would happen afterwards, if there would ever be an 'after', in fact.

It took them some time to get used to the fact that it was really over, that they could have their own lives, and their reincarnated leaders encouraged that wholeheartedly.

"There's… there's one thing I told Nana once." Xochitl had hesitated, but eventually managed to put her thoughts into words. "I told her we're more than just flowers. It might not have been the best thing to say that day, but that doesn't mean I don't believe in that. I do. There's nothing wrong with who we are, with our gifts, of course not; but who we might have been in the past does not define us. It doesn't mean we can be nothing else. This life is a gift, so please, live it; be everything you want, everything you can. That's all I've ever wanted for you, for all of us."

It didn't happen in a day, but eventually they all began finding their way.

Their only doubt after the battle with Tezcatlipoca had been regarding the shades. It had been particularly hard for Fiore to explain that one, not because she didn't know the answer, but because of how much the truth hurt:

"You know what's behind the shades, the chained souls," she murmured very quietly. "What I'm not sure you understand, is where those souls truly come from. When Quetzalcoatl first ascended into power he put a stop to human sacrifices. Blood sacrifices were allowed, but no death, especially not of others, he... we both saw it as tragic, even barbaric. Once he was gone, Tezcatlipoca made sure that his successor reinstated them immediately. For years those being sacrificed were all who might dare speak against the changes, might wish for Quetzalcoatl's return, those who believed in us... it was Tezcatlipoca's way to try and excise us, to make sure we would be forgotten. He failed, but that doesn't change that so many people died." A tear fell down her cheek. "The shades... they are the souls of those sacrificed, pulled out of the spirit world to serve Tezcatlipoca, made slaves. It's why I must free them, I'm the only one who can. But with him gone... that means they can never be enslaved again. They're in peace, and that's how it'll stay."

It hadn't been easy, talking about such a topic, but the knowledge that it was truly, finally over, did give them all some comfort, and while it might not be perfect, it would have to be enough.

"There's just one question I really, really need to ask."

They'd finished dinner and even a few drinks, it was late and most of them were about ready to go home, when Lily unexpectedly got very serious as she addressed Fiore.

"What is it Lils?" the Enchantress asked, purposefully using the nickname to try and put her best-friend at ease, worried by her seriousness.

"I..." Lily smiled, just a bit, though she didn't stop being serious. "Are we forbidden... from loving? From being in a relationship I mean?"

"What...?!" Fiore really, really wasn't expecting that.

"It's just..." The amber-eyed just couldn't hold herself back anymore, she began babbling. "I love Chris, I know that's obvious enough. But half the time when I kiss him I get flashes from the past, and whenever I do I cannot help but feel like there's something wrong with what we're doing. And I'd hate to think I'm breaking some ancient vow, or tradition or something, but I just cannot stop loving him and…"

Xochitl pressed a finger to Lily's lips, not knowing how else to stop her rant. She waited a few seconds, until the girl began breathing right again, then she spoke:

"Lily…" she began, smiling her most beatific smile. "There's absolutely nothing wrong with loving. It's… it's love! Nothing could ever be wrong about that!"

There was a wordless exclamation coming from someone else then, though no one focused on that, as Fiore's whole attention was still on Lily.

"I, I think I know what makes you feel like that," the enchantress admitted after a moment more. "There were never any oaths, no traditions… when you, when all of you girls came to me you were young, children really. Quetzalcoatl brought you to me, so I might help you, raise you. You became like my own daughters. When you grew up… you could have gone, could have married, had your own families, but you didn't want to. There were some nobles in Tula that wanted you as brides, but I refused to allow them to force you, it had to be your choice, and you refused. So, you stayed. You became priestesses. It was never necessary for you to be chaste, but others believing that was one more layer of protection for you all. Quetzalcoatl eventually sent four of his best warriors, his Atlantes, which is how we all came to be together in the Temple." She let out a breath. "So, you see, there's nothing wrong about you loving, and being loved, and I'm certainly very happy and supportive of you, whatever you might decide."

That was all Lily needed to hear, in the next second she'd pulled Chris to her and was kissing him deeply.

"Hey man!" Steve called laughingly several seconds later. "Keep those hands where I can see them!"

Everyone laughed at that.

Laughter that was half broken a moment later by a rather loud eep, right as Belladonna unexpectedly kissed a very flustered Eduardo. Which only prompted even more chuckles seconds later.

They were really the only couples among Xochiquetzal's children, as Julian would never see Hyacinth as anything more than a sister, same as she did him; while Magnolia and David would always be the best of friends and nothing beyond that. But that was okay, those were their choices, and that was enough.

"I didn't do it because of that, you know?" Fiore commented quietly.

The party was finally over, Draco had insisted on driving her home, and without even thinking about it they both had gone into her apartment, to share a cup of tea while they talked.

"Not for love, not really... or at least, not that kind of love," she went on. "I did it because I love them, all of them."

"They're your children," he finished for her. "Always have been, always will be."

"Exactly," she knew he understood.

For several minutes neither of them said a word, just sipping quietly at their teas. They were in no rush, though there was some tension in the room that seemed to grow as the minutes passed. Eventually there was no more tea in the cups, and the moment Draco placed his on the coffee table Xochitl promptly took both in her hands and hurried with them to the kitchen. She didn't return immediately, instead went to stand by the glass-door leading to the small balcony, watching the moon slowly rising.

"Is that it then?" Draco finally spoke after what seemed like forever.

"What...?" Fiore turned to look at him over her shoulder, as if not understanding what he meant, though they both knew she did.

"I... I cannot do this anymore," the reincarnated King finally admitted.

He seemed to almost drag himself to his feet and towards the reincarnated enchantress, until they were so close they could feel each other's body heat, their auras thrumming with power somehow leashed beneath their human skins... and yet they weren't touching, not really.

"I thought I could," he went on, turning his eyes to look beyond her, to the same night sky she'd been losing herself in.

"That I could wait for as long as needed. I've waited a thousand years, after all, what's a few more?" He scoffed to himself. "Except this wait is driving me crazy. This uncertainty... I cannot live like this, my lady, don't ask it of me."

"I wish never to ask for something that hasn't been willingly given." The words slipped from Fiore's lips before she could stop to think about them.

"I know, I just..." he broke off, unable to find the words, or perhaps unwilling to say what was in his mind, out-loud.

"I've been unfair to you, I know. In my wish to give you your freedom I've hurt you, I am sorry about that."

"I don't understand."

"Your eyes stray to the pendant, I know they do. You wonder why I'm wearing it, the reason behind it. And while it might have been easier if I'd simply stopped wearing it, I cannot bring myself to do that."

"Is that your answer then? Am I to simply walk away from you? Forsake all the promises I once made?"

"That's... that's exactly it!"

"What...?"

"I never wanted to be just a promise to you, a duty. I want more! I deserve more!"

Quetzalcoatl's reincarnation said nothing, he either didn't understand what Xochiquetzal was saying, or he couldn't quite believe it.

"I know you loved me once, the person I used to be, all those years and lifetimes ago. And I will never deny that I loved you, that I love you even now, have never stopped, and probably never will. But I'm not her, I'm not the person I was a thousand years ago, not anymore, I haven't been her for a very long time..."

Her eyes closed briefly, and when she opened them again she brought her hands to her own neck, to unclasp the necklace. Gathering it in between her slightly trembling hands. It pained her, to take it off; she hadn't taken it off for any reason since first putting on after finding it and the jewelry box in her Nana's room all those months earlier. She never imagined taking it off... and yet.

"I am not the woman you made those promises to," she added, forcing her voice to sound sure, even as her throat threatened to close, and her eyes filled with tears. "And I... much as I might love you, and even knowing I always will, I cannot tie you to me through such promises. It wouldn't be right. Because I want someone who'll love me, who'll love Fiore, love Xochitl, as much as Quetzalcoatl once loved Xochiquetzal... but more importantly, as much as Topiltzin loved Sacnité."

"Oh Fiore..." Draco breathed out, even as his hands reached out to cup her face in between.

And it was her name on his lips, her name, not that of her past life, of an enchantress and would-be-princess and pseudo-goddess long since dead and lost in the sands of time and legend... it was her name!

When Draco kissed Fiore it was a benediction, the fulfillment of every dream ever dreamt... it was consummation of a millennia old promise, and a thousand new promises all at the same time. And when he placed the silver quetzal pendant back around her neck... everything was absolutely perfect.

Epilogue

The doorbell rang, and Veronica hurried to the door, opening without looking, or even asking who it might be, she didn't need to, she could sense the aura all too clearly; though, there was something a bit off about it… or perhaps not off, exactly, just changed. She didn't stop to think too hard about it and just smiled at the person on the other side.

"Fiore," she greeted the other girl with a nod of her head, just this side of a bow.

"Veronica," the black-haired woman replied, purposefully inclining her own head.

The younger woman wasn't expecting the visit; all the same, she wasn't that surprised either. Not with what had happened in the last few days.

Two years had passed since the final confrontation with Tezcatlipoca, and all that had followed it; since Fiore's and Veronica's graduation from college and the choices each had made to further their studies; since the rest of the group had chosen to go back to colleges, to build lives for themselves beyond whose reincarnation they might be. Some had managed to finish college during that time.

Two years during which Veronica and Fiore had met as frequently as possible, at least once the former had returned from New York; for a cup of tea, or hot chocolate, or something else like that. Time they'd spent slowly building the familial relationship they'd never had a chance to have before. Still, none of that could have ever prepared Veronica for what she got in the mail just a week earlier. A check, for three million!

"What the hell?!" she cried out the moment she closed the door to the apartment, with Fiore inside. "What was that... that...?"

The older girl winced slightly at the tone.

"I'm sorry," she murmured, playing with the end of her braid a bit. "We... I meant to call you, meet with you before you got the check. But the business with the lawyers went longer than expected, and then we had to go and..." She let out a breath. "I'm sorry."

"Don't apologize, tell me what I'm supposed to do with three million pesos!" Veronica's voice went through two octaves, stressed as she was by the whole situation.

"Change the world." When Xochitl said it, she made it sound like it was the most obvious thing in the world, like the only possible answer.

"Fiore..."

"I've seen you, these last couple of years. Since Sierra Gorda, and all the good we did there. I know you've tried to do the same kind of thing again, in other places, to help other people... and it hasn't worked out, not like you wanted anyway. And it's not that you lack the hands, because your people... they follow you, and they always will, because they believe in you. But you don't really have the resources." She let out a breath and smiled. "Well, now you have them."

"But... three million?!" Veronica was really having trouble getting her head around that detail. "Where did you even get that kind of money from?!"

"Ahumada. The lawyer, he went to see me, right after Nana's death, to contest the ownership of the Temple grounds... of course we now know that it was Tezcatlipoca behind the whole thing, and that regardless of any deals, he could have never set foot in that place anyway... Then Tezcatlipoca forgot, and the lawyer cannot exactly demand I return the money, for all intents and purposes the village doesn't exist, not legally at least. It would be a nightmare of epic proportions." She shook her head, that wasn't the important part. "It never felt right, having that money. It's why I never spent it, in all the months I had it, I just left it sitting in the bank. Then other things happened, and I actually forgot about it for a while." She closed her eyes briefly. "Last year... I saw you and your people, doing all you could to help after the earthquake, and all the ways you suffered when nothing you did seemed to be enough. It was then that the plan began."

"Plan?"

"A lot of it was Draco's idea actually. The non-profit organization, it's all been arranged to make it as legal and official as can be. The papers should have been right there with the check, actually."

They had been, but Veronica hadn't read any of them, too shocked by the number of zeroes on that check.

"You'll have to fill out some of them out, of course," Fiore went on. "To take possession of it all, name the organization, and decide how you want to use the money, exactly. But, essentially, everything's in your hands now."

"Why...? I... I don't understand. Why are you doing this?"

"Tell me something cousin. You must know all the legends, about Quetzalcoatl and Xochiquetzal; probably grew up hearing them as often as I did."

"Of course." Perhaps not as much as Xochitl, not when they didn't live in the village and were technically in hiding, but still. "I always wanted to be a part of it all. To find you..."

"What did you think would happen when you found us?"

"I..." she couldn't admit it out-loud, didn't dare to, but truth was Veronica had never actually stopped to think that far.

"I know what most would have expected, what some certainly did expect. That we'd become avenging angels of some kind, destroy our enemies and reclaim our birthrights... but that just isn't possible. The Toltecs are long since gone, there's no crown, no throne for Quetzalcoatl to claim. Even with the Temple, our powers and those who are actually believers, it'd have been impossible."

She was right, of course she was; and Veronica probably wasn't the only one who'd never thought that far ahead.

"This... us reincarnating," Xochitl went on. "You know by now it was my fault. But I never did it for any throne, not even for revenge. Truth is that as much as Tezcatlipoca twisted history in an attempt to erase us;" And he'd managed to twist the memory of her enough that the Xochiquetzal history that was spoken of had nothing to do with her. "the believers did the same, only in the opposite direction. They made us into… divinities, messiahs… it's ridiculous! This was never about saving the world, or ruling it, or anything like that. All we wanted, all I ever wanted, was a chance for us to live our lives, like we deserved to, without fear… that's it." She let out a breath. "It might not be the glorious purpose some imagined, but it's more than enough for us. Just to live. Don't we deserve it?"

Veronica didn't answer, but that was alright, the question was rhetorical anyway.

"And then there's you… you do want to change the world, you want to save it. And you have people willing to follow you, to do anything and everything they must. And that's amazing. I respect that. You are what the believers of our myths were expecting, what they deserve. So yes, I'm giving you the money, and wishing you the very best in all your future endeavors. Know that if you ever need us, we're available, we'll do what we can to help you, always. All you need to do is call."

It was obvious Veronica was still having some trouble getting her head around it all, but she just nodded. She'd always imagined the legends coming true, the True King returning, all the ways he and his princess might help save the world; all the ways she wanted to help them do so. She wouldn't deny that it was a bit of a disappointment, learning they had no intention of even trying; but Xochitl was right, they deserved to make their own choices, to live their lives. That didn't mean she had to bury her own wishes, she could still do things herself, she had people willing to help her; and thanks to Fiore, she had the money as well.

"So, are you coming with us today?"

Xochitl had been on the way to the door, only to stop right before opening it to look over her shoulder.

"That's today?" the younger gal asked, half-absently.

"Yeah," the black-haired one nodded. "So…?"

"Sure, why not?"

About two hours later the last car parked by the edge of a little-used road, so small the cars barely fit on it, and the trip through it had been anything but smooth.

"So... why are we here exactly?" Steve asked in a drawl as he stepped off his bike.

It was technically his sister's bike, but as she'd offered to ride with her boyfriend, so he could ride the other one...

"I was told we were going on some kind of day-trip to Tula, not sure why, it's not like the place's anything special..." Steve went on, until being interrupted by a smack to the back of his head, given by none other than his sister. "Hey!"

"Silence," Laura, the same woman most had first known as Belladonna, snapped at him. "Show some respect."

Steve rolled his eyes visibly but said nothing else.

"Tula was once the capital of a great empire..." Eduardo stated solemnly. "Our King's great empire."

"OK... even if that's the case, you do know that the city itself is technically that way, right?" the man signaled vaguely to his left, to the way they'd come.

"A lot has changed in a thousand years, Steve." Draco finally chose to explain things a bit better. "Some cities have become bigger, others smaller. This spot right here," He pointed to stones, the remains of an archway, less than two yards away from him. "This was once the entrance to Tula."

"I see..." he didn't, but he wasn't about to admit that anyway.

Steve knew of course that there were things he'd never understand. His sister was part of something so big his mind would never be able to comprehend it. He'd been told he was a part of it too, even if he couldn't remember a thing, and he had no fancy powers, unlike the rest of the group. Aside from that thing he could do with the jaguars... though they probably would never know for sure if that was his thing, or something Tezcatlipoca did to him, especially considering the mage's connection to the beasts. Still, it was useful, he was studying to be a veterinarian and his dream was to work in a zoo, or perhaps even a wildlife reservation.

"We're here to fulfill a promise," Draco clarified, knowing his friend didn't really understand. "A thousand years ago I promised the love of my life that one day she'd enter Tula on my arm, as the queen she was in my heart. I may no longer be able to offer her an actual kingdom, but that never truly mattered to us. Still, this is only right. This is, after all, our new beginning…"

No one asked why he was calling that day their new beginning when it had been two years and several months since their final confrontation with Tezcatlipoca, and a month since their marriage. Such details seemed to be unimportant in that moment.

So, without further ado, Fiore placed her hand on Draco's bent arm and the two walked slowly the yard separating them from the fallen archway and when they did… it seemed like there might be some kind of magic left in the land after all, for the moment the two crossed it was as if a power of some kind was turning time back, as the pieces of stone flew to their spots, reforming the archway, exactly as it must have been all those centuries prior. And not only that, the dry, cracked ground beneath their feet suddenly turned lush and green, and flowers began sprouting everywhere. All kinds of wildflowers, in every color of the rainbow.

The rest of the group did not say a word, instead they rushed to the archway after their once King and Enchantress. Unconsciously taking formation in a lose half-circle behind them.

The effects of whatever magic might have been left in the land did not extend very far, but it did not need to, it was enough.

"Here we are," Draco announced, holding both of his beloved's hands in his. "At last."

"It was all worth it," Xochitl assured him with a gentle smile.

"Yes, it was," he agreed completely.

They both noticed from the corner of their eyes when Veronica stepped away from the loose formation, past them and then walked several steps among the flowers, before dropping into a crouch.

"Vero..." Fiore called, turning towards her, unsure what might be going on.

For all answer her cousin straightened up again and turned to them, before offering Xochitl the flower she'd just collected:

"I believe this is meant for you... cousin..." she whispered, her voice so very soft, as if she believed anything else might break the moment somehow.

Everyone stared at the blossom in silence, most of them not quite understanding what was so special about it. Except for the one it was meant for, she took it into her hands and cradled it against her body, just below her heart, at the same time a pair of arms wound around her waist from behind, hands settling almost protectively over her still flat belly.

The flower was a white rose...

www.ingramcontent.com/pod-product-compliance
Lightning Source LLC
Chambersburg PA
CBHW021518240626
47154CB00002B/689